CRAVING CAPTIVITY

HUMAN PETS OF TALIN
BOOK 5

Warning: Author is dyslexic as hell.

The editing and beta reading team: Martha Collins, S.F., and Lauren Meghoo

Profession Editing: Edits Amanda Brown Edits, LLC

Feel free to contact me with questions, requests, or comments:
author@rk-munin.com

And, as with many writers, your reviews on Amazon, Goodreads, and/or Kindle help immeasurably, even if it's just clicking on the stars.

Thank you to all my readers!

CONTENT WARNING

In the very first chapter there is a room where several sick individuals might already be dead. The description is brief without much detail.

One of the main characters is ill in the beginning of the book with an issue breathing without coughing.

Several chapters include descriptions of abused workers. (They're basically indentured servants.)

There is an unequal legal power dynamic throughout the book between the main male character and the female character, with the latter being owned for the former, according to Talin law.

This book contains subjects including sex, mentions of sexual violence, strong language, and violence. Mature audiences, 18+ readers only.

CHAPTER
1

The smell inside the processing facility was foul. It was filled with a combination of unwashed bodies, boiling chemicals, and rot. All of it made Tamerin cough and wish he'd packed a respirator. The stench was overwhelming. Along with a few Vicpor, mostly Porian workers bustled around the large open-floor processing plant. They were nimble with their four legs and two arms, jumping over vats sometimes instead of bothering to walk around them. But the most astounding thing to Tamerin was not a single person was wearing a mask. It was as if the smell didn't bother them at all.

As shocking as it was, it went to prove that a body could become accustomed to many horrible things.

"You there!" Oglee, the Vicpor owner and overseer of the plant shouted at a Porian carrying a heavy load on his back. "Hurry up or I'll dock you a day's worth of food. Dock you!"

The obviously fatigued worker tried to move quicker at Oglee's threat. Turning his shiny, insect-like face to Tamerin, Oglee wiggled his antennae with pleasure. "You have to remind them who controls them or they get lazy," he confided in Tamerin. It was obvious this Vicpor took great pleasure in bullying his workers, making Tamerin feel sorry for every soul laboring in the industrial building.

When Tamerin remained silent, Oglee clicked his pincers a few times in irritation. "I'm an excellent overseer. My domicont coating is highly sought after by many other factories. No one can coat metal as well as me. No one!"

"I'm sure your process is exemplary," Tamerin responded, knowing he had to play nice with this despot if he wanted to collect Lasha. Although he'd already paid for her work contract, the Vicpor could still revoke the sale until Tamerin escorted the human out of the factory. Only then would Lasha be safe from reprisal.

Although Oglee stood almost as tall as Tamerin, the Vicpor's shape was nothing like his own. His three-segment body consisted of a bulbous head carapace, round cylindrical mid carapace, and a lower carapace with two spindly legs jutting out and covered in fine black hair that looked more like spikes than anything else. The mid carapace sported two arms with three claws each sprouting from both sides, and at the shoulders each side had a pincer arm.

"Yes, exemplary," Oglee agreed, his antennae moving again. He liked the compliment. "I'm going to add that word to my factory's descriptor. Exemplary!"

"As nice as your facility is, I'm here to collect the human worker, Lasha," Tamerin reminded Oglee.

"Of course. Right this way. This way!" Oglee led him deeper into the hell-scape. Tamerin noticed Oglee was loudly clacking his mid-body and lower carapace together as he moved, making the workers flinch.

Tamerin had never been fond of Vicpors. They had a reputation for treating everyone, even their own species, poorly. But this Vicpor struck Tamerin as worse than the species' abysmal reputation.

When Tamerin had first walked in, he thought there was some kind of emergency. Oglee had been yelling and clacking his pincers threateningly while waving his other four arms in the air as some poor, emaciated, elderly Porian worker huddled against a steaming chemical vat. The blasé attitude of the other workers told Tamerin this was a common sight.

The moment Oglee noticed Tamerin and took his eyes off the Porian, the elderly male had scurried off, limping badly on his hind leg. A glance around told Tamerin that most of the workers were Porian, and the moment the elderly male was close to a younger one, he was helped to a workstation to sit down.

At least there the male had someone taking care of him, unlike the human he was here to find.

Seeing the Vicpor's treatment of the Porian and the state of all the other workers made Tamerin want to grab Oglee's spindly neck and crush it. It would be easy. He walked with it fully extended out of his top carapace, a sign of confidence and power in the Vicpor world.

Patience, Tamerin reminded himself. *You need to stay patient or you might not recover Lasha. Focus on saving the human, not killing an annoying Vicpor.*

"I don't understand why you'd want her," Oglee said as they skirted around a rusting holding tank. "She's almost dead. If you wait a day or two you can buy her by the pound. That would be less than half of buying out her work contract. By the pound is cheaper. Cheaper!"

When Tamerin didn't respond right away, Oglee came to a stop and held out a three-digit lower arm to point to a group of other workers. "They're all much healthier and know the processing better. The one you want is both unhealthy and the stupidest worker I've ever bought. Buying one of these others would be better for you in the long run. And I'll give you a good price. Good price!"

Tamerin had to grit his teeth to keep from rattling his back plates in rage. Balling his hands into fists, he worked on keeping his breathing steady and not killing the Vicpor.

After he rescued Lasha from this horrific place, he might come back and give this immoral and evil creature a taste of Talin vengeance. How dare anyone treat a creature as delicate and rare as a human this way?

"I've already agreed and paid for her contract," Tamerin gritted out between clenched teeth. If he wasn't careful, he would slash his lips on his sharp front teeth. "Take me to her right now."

"Of course, of course," the Vicpor said. He must have finally started to realize Tamerin wasn't pleased with the delay. "You must want to collect your new property and leave quickly. This way. This way."

Unlike the warmer factory floor where there was better insulation and running machinery heating the area, this room was almost as cold as the temperature outside. It was frigid enough to see his breath condense as it left his mouth.

A dozen shapes were lying out on thin bed pallets lined up in a row on the floor. All of them were bundled in blankets with only hints of skin showing. He was sure several of them were already dead, sending his anxiety into overdrive.

Rattling out a loud, buzzing sound of worry from his back plates, he rushed to the smallest figure. He didn't need the Vicpor to tell him this one was Lasha. It was the only human-sized shape in the room.

"Ah, you know what humans look like then," Oglee commented as he hurried to catch up. "I only bought her because the business that sold her contract assured me she was strong for her size. They lied, of course. But you can never really trust those work-contract brokers. They lie to everyone."

Tamerin ignored the Vicpor as he dropped to his knees, straining to hear the sound of breathing or any signs of life. He could see raven black hair peeking out from under the blankets. His hand trembled slightly as he folded the blanket down to reveal a gaunt, pale face.

By the Ancestors, she looked far too still! Was he too late?

"Wake up, human! Wake!" Oglee yelled, reaching a long, pincer appendage around Tamerin's body to nudge Lasha forcefully.

"Don't touch her," Tamerin growled out, grabbing the pincer at the base and twisting hard enough to hear the limb joint groan.

"I won't touch! Won't touch!" Oglee screeched, tugging ineffectively at his pincer. Using his hold on the pincher, Tamerin shoved the Vicpor away. Oglee yowled and tucked his head down to hide his delicate neck in his lower carapace.

"You'll regret that! Regret!" Oglee warned him, cradling his pincer against his chest and holding it with several of his arms. "No one hurts me! I'm a Vicpor of significance. Apologize to me, Talin, or I'll nullify the sale. Apologize!"

Tamerin let loose with a war rattle by slapping his back plates together with force. It sounded like hundreds of feet pounding on the ground and echoed in the cold, dim room. Oglee jumped at the sound and took a half a step back, but then he seemed to center himself and stood tall. "I want my apology or I'll have you removed without this useless worker."

"You won't nullify anything and I'll be walking out with her," he growled at the Vicpor. Getting to his feet and letting his claws slide out of his fingertips, he sounded another war rattle before speaking again. "I didn't plan on fighting today, but I will if you push me. Any excuse to separate your head from your body."

"You—you can't talk to me like that," Oglee sputtered as he backed away. "Can't!"

Tamerin took another threatening step forward. "I just did. Now get out. If I see you again, I'll rip every limb off your body one by one."

Oglee stumbled back, terrified. "I'm in charge here," he declared in a shaky voice, all his limbs tucked tightly against his body and his antennae folded down flat against his domed head. "I'm in char—"

Tamerin sounded a last war rattle that had Oglee turning tail and running. Several workers were peeking in through the open door and he ran into them, sending all of them tumbling.

Oglee screamed insults and orders at the workers as Tamerin turned his attention back to Lasha. A clattering rattle of surprise came out of him when he saw her eyes were open. Luminous, copper-colored eyes gazed up at him.

"Lasha?" he murmured gently. She kept staring but didn't respond, and her eyes didn't seem to be truly focusing on him. He started up a soothing rumble with his chestbox. Humans said it was like the purr of an Old Earth animal called a cat. All the humans he'd met liked the soothing rumble, and he hoped Lasha was the same.

"Lasha, I'm Tamerin. Zia sent me."

She blinked a few times, as if processing his words. She had to have an INT. No company would hire anyone without an Innercranial Translator. Could illness cause problems with it? He tried again, this time switching to Universal, a language few Talins ever bothered learning.

"Hello, Lasha. You're safe now. I'm Tamerin and your friend Zia sent me. I'm going to take you somewhere warm and care for you. Please don't be afraid."

A hint of a smile crossed her face as she whispered, "Zia." Then her eyes closed and her face went slack. Leaning his head close to her chest, he waited a breathless moment before he heard a slow, faint heartbeat and shallow breathing.

He wanted to talk to her first, make sure she understood what was happening before he took her away from everything familiar, but that wasn't going to happen. She couldn't stay here any longer.

He wished he could help the others in the room, at least one of which was still alive, but he had to focus on Lasha.

Tucking the meager blankets around her frail figure, he gently lifted her into his arms. She didn't wake, and he was shocked at how light she was. Humans were small to begin with, but Lasha weighed little more than a child.

Scared that even a bit of jostling might cause her to die in his arms, he moved as smoothly as he could. The moment he was outside the factory, he stopped and realized he was stuck on this forsaken planet. The ship he'd arrived on had only orbited the planet long enough to transfer passengers via shuttle. The next passenger ship wasn't due to arrive for another five rotations.

He'd never expected to find Lasha in such poor condition. Worn out, yes. On the verge of death? No!

His original plan was to buy her contract, take her out for a nourishing meal, and discuss where she'd want to stay before he booked rooms. Obviously, that was out of the question. This tiny wisp of a human could barely breathe! He needed to find them a place to stay and contact whatever passed for a healer or doctor on this planet.

Glakor was almost entirely covered in water, with only one dense city that spanned the single continent of the planet.

With so little land, every part of the place was used. To that end the port was deliberately kept small to allow for more factories. This meant large ships couldn't land; they had to ferry goods and people using shuttles. A larger floating port was under construction, but it looked only half finished.

Because the city was focused on industrial production, few rooms were for rent. Workers and owners lived at their factories. The only lodging to be found was the hotel near the port.

The small port wasn't the only thing they'd done to save space. They had no roads or streets as most cities used. This one had a rail system hung high overhead and used to haul goods and raw materials to and from the port. For the average person trying to get around, a narrow, automated cart system crisscrossed the entire city. Only a short distance from the factory was a loading zone for carts going to the port. He got lucky and found one loading as he got to the platform. Sitting down on the low, wide bench running down the center of the cart, he cradled Lasha close.

The cart moved at a fast clip and only stopped at dedicated spots. If anyone wasn't paying attention and stepped in front of it, it had no programming to allow it to slow or halt. He noticed everyone was quick to move out of the way of the carts.

Stepping off the cart at the port, he quickly found a tall building advertising rooms with modifiable atmo generators. He hadn't expected this benefit. He could make the room extra warm for Lasha. This cold planet had to be miserable for her.

Checking in was difficult because he wouldn't set her down. The kiosk froze up after he input his info incorrectly several times in a row. He cursed under his breath at the many backward civilizations that didn't use voice recognition in their tech.

Superstition kept most species from making these things voice activated. Many species considered voice-capable computers as bad omens. With such a prevalent belief, most manufacturers didn't bother developing or including the capabilities in their machines.

Frustrated, he kicked the machine. The kiosk sounded a shrill warning and flashed angrily at him, causing a Vicpor attendant to finally show up.

Instead of helping Tamerin, he regarded Lasha with distaste. "Are you going to eat that here? If you want to butcher it, you're going to have to rent the kitchen space. We don't allow that in the rooms. Or you can pay one of our cooks to do it. Pay a cook!"

Tamerin didn't rattle with outrage at the question, but he could only barely speak.

"This is my human. She is not food," he gritted out between clenched teeth. "I want a room I can make warm with a full cleansing unit. I want human-appropriate food sent up, and I want whatever passes for a healer in this backwater place."

The Vicpor's right pincer snapped in annoyance. "We are not backwater. We are the second largest manufacturing planet in this sector. Furthermore—" He stopped talking abruptly as he looked down at Lasha and then back up at Tamerin, his pincer falling down to rest at his side.

When he spoke again, his tone was cheerful. "You're Talin. Correct? Yes, yes, I can see the quills on that forearm. But the other is damaged. Isn't it? And the whole arm and shoulder. Are you in the military? Are you here to have weapons manufactured? My brother runs a fine place. Top-grade products. Top-grade. I can introduce you, no fee. No fee."

"I'm not here for that," Tamerin snapped. "I came here for her only."

The attendant inspected Lasha, tapping one of his pincers on his chest carapace as a sign of confusion. "Why would you… oh, it's human! Talins love having human pets. They're prized among your kind. Aren't they? You must think yourself lucky to have found one. If this one survives, you'll be the envy of all the Talins without a human. Envy!"

What Tamerin really wanted to do was stomp on this Vicpor until his head was nothing but an oozing pile of goo mixed with broken bits of carapace. For Lasha's sake, he held his temper back. He could hear the delight in the Vicpor's voice. They loved nothing more than being able to lord something over others. This Vicpor was patting himself on the back for "figuring out" why Tamerin would have a human if he wasn't going to eat her.

Really, this species was irredeemable.

"Room," Tamerin reminded him. "Food and a healer."

"This one is doing very poorly," the Vicpor agreed as he tapped at the kiosk display. "It's unlikely the little thing will survive. But if it survives, you'll have gotten a human cheaply and new stock to import to your homeworld. The one who bought the human's contract must not have known about their value to Talins. Otherwise they would have sold her contract to you right away."

"He certainly didn't know her value," Tamerin muttered to himself, angry all over again at Oglee.

The Vicpor didn't hear him and continued cheerfully talking. "I worked on a station that helped build the Talin repeater station on Olgosi. I saw a few humans there. Such strange little, useless creatures, but pets don't need to be useful. You must be very thrilled with your find. I bet many other Talins will be wanting to breed their humans with new stock. Much esteem could be had. Esteem!"

Finally done with the check-in process, all Tamerin had to do was shift his body so the Ident Cube hanging off his left hip could touch the funds transfer pad on the kiosk. After a ping sounded, the number and location of his suite flashed on the screen.

"I'll have food sent up and charged to your room," the Vicpor added as Tamerin turned away. "Send food!"

"And the healer," he said as he followed the signs to the west tower.

"I'll put your room in the queue for the med tech," the Vicpor called out. "Med tech queue!"

Then Tamerin maneuvered into the lift and swiftly traveled up. As the lift moved, he studied Lasha. If anything, she looked even paler than earlier. Feeling helpless, Tamerin put his mouth near her ear. He whispered encouraging words. If nothing else, at least he could keep telling her she was safe and he'd take good care of her. She'd be warm, fed, and never experience deprivation again.

Those words were for himself as much as her.

CHAPTER 2

The bed under her was much too soft, and she was warm. She hadn't felt truly warm since arriving at Glakor. Given these changes, she was afraid to open her eyes. What if this was a dream? If she opened her eyes and ended the dream, she'd be thrown right back into a frigid hell where she was too sick to work.

Workers who couldn't work didn't get to eat. She couldn't remember the last time she'd eaten. She wasn't even sure what day it was. After she'd collapsed at her workstation, Oglee had her dragged into the recovery room, which all the workers called the dying floor. It was rare for anyone to leave the room alive.

Once she was dumped in the "recovery room" Oglee only given her a single flask of water and one nutrient bar, ignoring her tears and requests for more blankets and food. Oglee was like that. If she lived, she got to go back to work. If she died, her body would be sold for food.

It had all been spelled out in the contract she couldn't read but had signed anyway. She'd known it was going to be bad, but she'd never expected it to be this horrific.

Without opening her eyes, she rubbed the blanket covering her between her fingers. She should be surrounded by the rubbery fabric of the standard-issue blankets. This one was much too soft and thick.

Had one of the overseers taken pity on her and given her a comfortable place to die? It wouldn't have been Oglee. That Vicpor made the rest of his species look kind. But Onel would occasionally give everyone extra rations, and she never hit them.

No, that couldn't be it. Onel was gone. She'd been called back to her family. To all the workers' despair, she'd even sold her share of the company to Oglee. No, there was no overseer to treat her kindly.

Another oddity was the lack of smell. She didn't have the stench of the factory in her nose. And it was quiet. So very quiet. No yelling overseers, no shouting workers, squealing equipment, burbling vats, or alarms constantly screeching for attention. All she could hear was her own breathing, which sounded abnormally loud.

That's when she realized she was breathing with ease. Her body wasn't racked by violent coughing fits. That didn't make sense. Even in a dream, she should be coughing. Right?

There was only one explanation—she was dead.

That had to be it. Being dead explained everything. The question now was what afterlife had she ended up in. She'd learned about several different traditions growing up, but no one practiced much in the way of religion on Wimol Colony.

Was she a soul waiting to be judged and sent back to live another life? Was her soul going to be put on a giant scale and weighed? Then the deities would decide which one of the many worlds of the dead she would spend eternity? Or was she in a heaven-type place where she got to sleep on clouds and slide down rainbows?

She wouldn't know until she opened her eyes. Bracing herself, she lifted her lids only to be met by darkness.

This couldn't be a good sign. Then her vision adjusted. It wasn't pitch black. A dim light illuminated enough for her to make out shapes. She was in a room with two doors. One was open, but she couldn't see beyond the outline of the entry, and the other door was closed. The doors were set in adjacent walls reminding her of rooms an individual could rent while traveling. Independent of place and species, they all tended to look the same.

Was her heaven a rented room? How odd. She would have thought it would be the fallow fields of Wimol where she and her friends cavorted as children. She never thought she'd long to be back on the struggling human colony, but life on Glakor had changed her. The community of her birth might have been poor, but they were good to each other. After her parents had died her best friend Zia's family adopted her—even though it meant another mouth to feed. Life was hard there, but at least there was love.

Maybe this was a type of waiting place where souls stayed while the gods decided what would happen to them next. She should tell them what she wanted.

"I want to go back to Wimol," she whispered into the darkness. Her voice sounded hoarse and loud in the quiet, despite how softly she'd said the words.

"Are you awake, Lasha?" A deep, unfamiliar voice asked from behind her. The INT in her head didn't bother translating the words because she'd learned Universal at a young age.

She tried to roll over but ended up curled into a ball, coughing so hard she struggled to breathe. Looked like she hadn't escaped her illness even in the afterlife. Damn, that was bad luck!

Something like a rumbling purr filled her ears with comforting vibrations.

"Easy, let me sit you up. The med tech said sitting up would make breathing easier." Strong hands pushed between her body and the bed. Then they lifted her and settled her against a mound of fluffy pillows. The moment the coughing fit was over, something smooth was pressed against her lips.

"Sip this, it will ease your throat and lungs," the voice urged. "The med tech didn't have the type of system used to give humans hydration or medication through their veins, so you need to drink."

Eyes still closed, she sucked. Her mouth was filled with a cool, refreshing liquid that tasted vaguely citrusy. It soothed the rawness in her throat and seemed to ease the pressure in her chest. She drank greedily until there was nothing but air.

"I'll get you more," the voice promised. "Let that settle first. The med tech said you need to consume many small meals and to start you off with a gentle liquid food supplements first."

Curious about her caregiver, Lasha opened her eyes. The room was still dim, but she could make out a hulking outline kneeling on the floor next to her. In typical Vicpor style, the bed was on the floor. Even though the figure was on the floor with the bed, they still towered over her.

"Light?" she asked, wincing at the sound of her hoarse, ragged voice.

"I forgot about the limits of human eyes," the caregiver said. "Room, set lights to–"

The stranger abruptly stopped talking and muttered a soft curse. "So backward and illogical," the figure muttered. "It's perfectly safe to use voice-command programs. They're not going to rise up and become sapient just because they can hear or talk."

What a strange afterlife that vexed a god!

Rising from the bed, the maybe-deity strode over to a nearby display to tap a few glowing icons. Soft light flooded the room, allowing her to see everything clearly. The stranger turned and stood there, letting her look her fill.

And look she did! Whatever this species was, she'd never encountered them before. It was hard to judge, but going by the standard height of displays on Glakor, she would guess this individual was roughly seven and a half feet tall, minimum. They also had a humanoid shape with one head, two legs, two arms, and four digits on each hand. But that was where the similarities ended.

This hulking figure was only wearing pants, allowing her to see the natural overlapping, plated armor that covered his body. The plates on his head, neck, and arms were small. They almost like scales to her, but the ones covering his broad shoulders and chest were as large as her hand. Everything was a light rust red, except his eyes, which were a deep and fascinating magenta. There was only the hint of a nose with two slits for nostrils and no outer ear she could see. Thin lips were slightly parted, showing a hint of white, pointed teeth.

The stranger's fingertips ended in short claws, which probably extended out further for fighting. They also had quills jutting out on the outside of their arm from wrist to elbow. As she watched, the long quills moved a little and then folded back to lay streamlined with the arm.

Except that wasn't quite right. Only one arm had the quills. As she ran her gaze over the left side, she saw no quills at all, and the entire arm's armor plating looked distorted and damaged. It must have been a bad incident to leave such a tough-looking hide so mutilated. Or maybe this individual was a deity for the injured and sick? Being so big and powerful, this individual had to be a god. Right?

"My name's Lasha. I've tried to be good, honest. And any time I got into trouble it was Isla or Zia's fault."

The figure's facial expression didn't change at her declaration, but the purring stopped for a second, replaced by what sounded like marbles clicking around inside a cloth bag.

"You're not dead, if that's what you're thinking. And we're not in the Domicile of the Souls." That deep voice was tinged with amusement. "My name is Tamerin. I'm a Talin male and a retired soldier. I earned a Mattil Medal during our war with the Braxin. I'm a male of worth and means."

That was a lot to take in.

She didn't know what a Mattil Medal was, but she'd heard of Talins, even if she didn't know one on sight. Their war with the Braxin had been big news for a little while. She'd arrived on Glakor just before the end of the war three years ago. Several of the factories on Glakor were built based on contracts for manufacturing weapons for the Braxin, which meant the overseers followed the progress of the war closely and were constantly talking badly about the Talins.

Until they'd won. After the Talin Empire was successful, the Vicpors had become very pro-Talin.

Now she remembered the image from a news vid she'd seen briefly. The Talin had been wearing military armor on their bodies and a helmet obscuring their head. No wonder she didn't recognize what Tamerin was. It's hard to identify a species from only their feet!

"And you know Zia?" she asked.

"Yes! Zia is an exceptional human," Tamerin responded with obvious affection.

"She is," Lasha agreed, already distracted from talk of her friend. Her neck was starting to get a crick from looking so far up. "You're really big."

To her shock, the giant sank to his knees. The sound moved with him, making her realize it was emanating from his chest. He was purring!

"I know I might seem big and intimidating to a small, soft human, but don't be concerned. I'm very aware of how delicate you are. After I retired from the military, I went to work installing security vid captures on Talin space stations. I'm skilled at handling fragile components."

A grin stretched across Lasha's face before a wave of fatigue washed over her. "I think I might be slightly more substantial than electronics," she murmured. Although maybe not by much after three years of hard work on minimal rations.

Tamerin was silent for a moment, and while his facial expression didn't change, she got the impression he was working on a diplomatic response. "There are many ways to be fragile," he finally said.

Wasn't that the truth? If this short conversation hadn't already exhausted her, she'd enjoy discussing all the intricate ways people could be strong or brittle. Asking questions and understanding different worldviews was one of her favorite things, but life on Glakor was all about work and frivolous conversation distracted workers from their tasks.

It had been forever since she'd gotten to have a conversation for fun. She never thought she'd miss hearing words, but she did. So very much!

How sad that this brief interaction had exhausted her.

She probably shouldn't trust this stranger so quickly, but it wasn't as if she had much of a choice. He might have cruel intentions, or he might be sincere in his promise to care for her. Either way, she wasn't getting up and storming out of the room anytime soon.

Especially if her afterlife theory proved correct and this Talin was a test set up by some gods. What the gods were testing she couldn't figure out, but who knew what kind of nonsense deities might get up to.

"I think I'm going to fall asleep again," she whispered, giving up on keeping her eyes open. "Please keep talking to me."

"I can do that," Tamerin agreed readily. The gentle percussion noise coming from him reminded her of the wind chimes her father had hung outside their small domicile when she was young. Then that noise was gone and the purring was back. She could almost feel it vibrating through the air and touching her skin. "What should I talk about?"

"Anything," Lasha answered, feeling sleep pulling her under.

Tamerin's low, steady voice followed her into sleep and soothed her dreams. No nightmares plagued her with this Talin's voice filling her ears while she slept.

CHAPTER 3

"Lasha? You need to wake."

She didn't want to, but Tamerin's voice was gently insistent. It helped that he made that purring sound she liked so much. He was right next to her, putting off so much heat she could feel it even though they weren't touching.

Opening her eyes revealed nothing but fuzzy shapes and colors. Blinking rapidly, relief filled her when Tamerin's face swam into focus. She was lying on her side near the edge of the bed. She must have rolled off the mound of pillows Tamerin had propped her up on earlier.

"Hi, Tamerin," she murmured. Was that her voice? It sounded as rough as an engine stymied by grit.

"I'm going to help you sit up," Tamerin warned her before his enormous, clawed hands pushed between her and the mattress to lift and place her back on the mound of pillows.

She opened her mouth to thank him but all she did was start coughing. This time the coughing hurt. When it stopped, her throat felt sore and her head throbbed. The familiar ache she'd lived with since she got sick was back, and her joints felt swollen and stiff.

Maybe she wasn't dead. Damn, she'd been looking forward to no longer being in pain.

Focusing on breathing, she tried to keep her tears at bay. She was so tired of suffering.

"Drink," Tamerin demanded, holding a disposable canister of the same liquid as the last time. She swallowed greedily. The citrusy liquid soothed her throat, making her unwilling to stop. Tamerin only pulled the canister away once it was empty.

"The med tech is coming to check on you," he explained. "By the sound of your cough, the strong medications she gave you yesterday have worn off. She wouldn't leave me with additional doses. We'll have to call her every time, but I'll make sure she comes earlier for your next appointment."

"Med tech? Drugs?" she wheezed out. It felt hard to breathe or even think. She had vague memories of talking to Tamerin before but couldn't remember much.

"While you were unconscious yesterday, I had a med tech treat you," Tamerin explained. "Your lungs are scarred from breathing in harsh chemicals for so long. The scarring inhibits your ability to breathe and causes the coughing. The med tech is sure she can reverse the damage, but it will take a few days. In the meantime, we can only soothe the cough. We can't eliminate it completely."

Lasha's pulse had spiked at the scarred lungs part of Tamerin's explanation, but knowing she could be healed calmed her. As long as she was getting better, she could put up with the cough for now.

"I'm sure the med tech is doing what's best," Lasha croaked.

Tamerin's purr stopped, and her ears were filled with the sounds of a swarm of angry wasps. She knew that couldn't be possible. There weren't any insects on Glakor. The sound was all coming from the Talin. How fascinating!

"I'm sure if we had access to Talin healers the cough would already be gone," Tamerin said with heavy contempt, telling her the angry-wasp sound was disdain or annoyance. "As soon as we can travel, I'm taking you to see a Talin healer.

They're far more skilled with human anatomy than any of these Vicpors. Or probably any other species."

His statement raised more questions, but she didn't have the breath to ask them. A chime at the door announced the med tech, and Tamerin hurried over to usher her in.

"She's coughing and can't breathe," Tamerin said as he dragged the Vicpor across the small room.

The Vicpor calmly pulled her pincer out of his grip and folded long, triple-jointed legs to settle next to the bed.

"Open your mouth, human," she demanded.

Before Lasha could comply, Tamerin made a sound like a weapon rapidly firing hard projectiles. It made both her and the med tech jump.

"Don't talk to her like that," Tamerin growled. "Her name is Lasha. You will treat her with respect."

The med tech wobbled her head a little to show deference. She didn't withdraw her pincer arms, but tucked her four arms with claws close to her body, intimidated.

"Apologies, warrior. I'll use her proper name." The med tech turned her attention back to Lasha. "Hello, Lasha, my name is Ilee. I'm here to treat you. If you would please open your mouth, I'm going to pour in a small vial of medication. It will ease the congestion in your lungs. I'll also pour in one that will help with the pain. Hold both of them in your mouth. When they stop fizzing, you can spit or swallow."

Eager for relief, Lasha opened her mouth. Ilee poured in one vial and then a second in rapid succession. It was hard to fight the urge to swallow, especially with the strange sensation of something bubbling up to fill her mouth. She was sure it was about to dribble out between her lips when the fizzing reaction finally stopped.

"That was weird," she muttered after swallowing a few times to clear her mouth.

"You did well," Ilee praised with a quick sidelong glance at Tamerin. The Talin had remained standing perfectly still and silent, staring at everything the med tech did with intense focus.

"Now I'm going to run a few tests. You won't feel anything. If you could limit your movement for a few minutes, that would help me," Ilee requested.

"Sure, no problem," Lasha murmured, relieved to find her raw throat and inflamed lungs were already feeling better.

Tamerin stepped over to the opposite side of the bed from the med tech and sank to his knees.

"If you grow fearful or anxious, you can cling to me," he offered.

"Cling?" she questioned as the drugs went to work, making her feel floaty and pain free. Ah, there was the nice, content calmness from before. She liked drugs. Drugs were her friends.

"Cling," he repeated, as if she should know the word. He opened his arms up as if accepting a hug. "Humans like to wrap their arms around each other. You can do the same with Talins. I welcome you to cling or clutch at my neck. I can nestle you against my chest and sound a soothing rumble." The purring sound started up again as he dropped his arms back down to his side.

"Rumble?" she murmured. Had she slurred that word? Didn't matter, the sound of the word felt good on her tongue, so she repeated it. "Rrrrrrumble. Rumble. Rum-rum-rumble."

"Lasha?" Tamerin questioned. The pitch and rhythm of his rumbly sound changed. Now it was like a distant thumping bass drum. That must be the sound he made when concerned. "Are you well? You're speaking oddly."

Lasha wanted to explain that her brain was a cloud floating in the wind, but when she opened her mouth to talk, only an rrrr sound came out. Which made her chortle. "Arrrrrrrrgggg!" she whispered, rolling her R. "Pirrrrate."

"What's wrong with her?" Tamerin hissed at the med tech.

"Remain calm, warrior. It's the medication," Ilee explained. "She wasn't awake last time for you to witness the full effects. Talking in a nonsensical way is a common side effect."

"Will she remember this?" Tamerin asked, going back to his purring sound.

"Nothing I've given her will cause amnesia. She'll sleep soon, and when she wakes, you must make her drink. These bottles need to be consumed." Now Ilee sounded slightly aggravated.

Lasha lolled her head to the side to watch the med tech testing each bottle on the squat table next to the bed, finding most of them full. "I told you last time I was here, these all needed to be drunk. All of them." Even if she hadn't been clacking one of her pincers in irritation, Lasha would've heard it in her voice.

"She was sleeping," Tamerin protested. "You said to let her sleep."

"I meant you shouldn't keep her awake. I didn't mean for you to starve her," Ilee answered, her four clawed-arms clasped tightly in front of her in a sign of annoyance while she snapped one of her pincers-arms to emphasize her words. "These contain medication boosters. This is why she had the coughing fit earlier."

When Tamerin spoke next, he sounded contrite. "I didn't realize. How badly have I set back her progress?"

Ilee stopped and released two out of four of her clawed arms. "I'm not sure, probably not by much." Her tone was less severe, but still authoritative. "But you can't dismiss my orders."

A boisterous laugh bubbled out of her throat. "Tam-tam messed up!" she sang. "Bad Tam-tam the tall Talin!"

Both Tamerin and the med tech focused their gazes on her. She bounced her eyes between the two of them. "Rrrrrr!"

Then she dissolved into another fit of laughter.

"I can see why some like humans," the med tech murmured as she let out a hissing Vicpor laugh. "They can be rather adorable."

"I'm not adorable," Lasha explained. "I'm trrrrrrouble."

"I don't think those two descriptions are mutually exclusive," Tamerin murmured. At the same time he talked, his rumble changed from the bass sound to a much faster and higher-pitched one. It was the glass-marbles-in-a-bag-clinking-together sound. That had to be a laugh!

She smiled up at the big, intimidating Talin. "You make so many pretty sounds. I wanna hear all your sounds." At her words, the clinking-marbles disappeared, replaced with the purr. Gosh, she loved that purr. "I think this one is my favorite."

"I'll sound a soothing rumble for you any time you want," Tamerin promised before speaking to the med tech again. "What about food?"

"Only the bottles of nutrients for now. As I explained before, no meals. Once I'm sure her system will handle solid food without trying to void her stomach, you can feed her small amounts often," Ilee explained. She began packing all the instruments she'd pulled out to scan over Lasha, test her breathing, and sample her skin.

She wanted to ask about the ones she didn't recognize, but her tongue was feeling thick in her mouth. Hmm, was her tongue a balloon now?

"Ballooooon," she trilled.

"Balloon?" Tamerin repeated. "I wish I could be in your brain to know how you got to that word."

Oh, she could explain that. "My tongue."

After a beat of silence Tamerin's clinking-marbles rumble came out much louder than last time.

The Vicpor was hissing in amusement as she rose to her feet. "I'll come back at the same time tomorrow," she said.

"I need you back here sooner," Tamerin argued. "She was in a lot of pain before you got there. I don't want her to wait as long next time."

"It's dangerous to give her medication any sooner than I have her scheduled," the med tech explained and Lasha was surprised to hear real sympathy in Ilee's voice. This species wasn't known for either empathy or sympathy. What a sweet Vicpor she was! "But if you have her drink the canisters at regular intervals, it will help the pain medication stay effective longer along with all the other medication in her system."

"Whatever is best for Lasha," Tamerin agreed. Wow, a lot of unhappy was packed into that single sentence!

"If you notice any serious issues sooner than tomorrow's appointment, you can contact me. If I'm not with a patient, I'll prioritize coming here," Ilee offered.

"That's acceptable," Tamerin agreed.

"Sweetie med-techie!" Lasha cooed at the Vicpor. "Tam-tam tell the med-techie how great she is." Those words sounded so fun she sang them. "Med-techie to the rrrrrrescue!"

Clicking-marbles again. "Yes, Lasha," Tamerin said. "Thank you for your gift of time and skill, Med Tech Ilee. You've been most helpful."

"Sweeetie!" Lasha reminded him.

"Uh, yes, thank you, sweetie Med Tech Ilee," Tamerin dutifully said. The med tech's hissing laughter was louder now.

"You're most welcome, Tamerin," Ilee replied.

"Good Tam-tam. Nice Ilee. Happy Lasha," she praised all three of them. She tried to look up, but now that Ilee was standing, it was much too far to bother focusing. Easier to close her eyes.

Yes, closed eyes were the best. Who needed to see? She could hear the two moving across the room to the door. Then she heard Tamerin walk back to the bed and drop to the floor. She was seeing with her ears instead of her eyes!

She had super powers!

"Tell Zia I can hear," she whispered before letting sleep take her.

"I'll tell Zia you can hear," Tamerin agreed, even though he was sure the little human was asleep again. He'd thought her small and cute before. Then she'd started burbling nonsense under the influence of the med tech's drugs, and she'd turned endearing.

"I'll make sure you drink this time," he assured her. "You don't have to fear. I'll work very hard to keep you comfortable and help you heal quickly."

His only regret was that she hadn't been interested in clutching or clinging to him. It was hard, but he had to accept that she might be one of the rare humans who weren't interested in being touched.

"You don't have to do anything you don't want to," he explained to her sleeping form. "I'm not that kind of Talin. I'm enlightened. I know humans can be just as smart as Talins."

The idea that she'd never want to touch him broke his heart, but there was no question he'd still care for her.

Lasha turned on her side and mumbled one word. "Zia."

"Yes, I'll make sure Zia knows you can hear," Tamerin repeated although he was sure Lasha was in some dream world now. How odd was it that humans made up stories in their heads while they slept? It was another example of how different Talins and humans were.

But her mention of Zia was a good reminder. He needed to contact both Zia and Palforma. They'd want to know he'd found Lasha alive, if not well. The last communication he'd gotten from them indicated they were moving to a Talin colony planet named Sorana. The entire planet was owned by one of the potential heirs to the Talin throne, Prime Son Searin, and they were in the first wave of settlers there.

He'd need to send his message using the planet's powerful long-distance comms system. To do that, he'd have to leave Lasha alone. He didn't like the idea of leaving her alone, even for a few marks.

"I wish I could've come for you sooner," Tamerin told her. Her relaxed face didn't move or twitch. Was she still dreaming or was there a state of sleep too deep to dream?

Leaning closer, he listened to her even breathing and steady, strong heartbeat. Both were a balm to his nerves. Before the med tech had gotten to the room the first time, he'd worried every raspy breath might be her last. The thought of losing her so soon after finding her made his chest feel tight and a mournful rumble pressed against his chestbox, demanding release.

But the med tech had been confident she'd live, and now she looked so much better. Her color had gone from sallow to a rich tawny brown. Her narrow face didn't look so drawn and her beautiful copper-colored eyes had sparkled earlier when she'd been giggling. With regular food he was sure her face would fill out, but she'd still have those high cheekbones and cute, pointed chin.

Reaching out, he rubbed some of her black hair between his fingers. It was thick and luxurious. Right now it was only a finger-length long, probably kept short because of factory rules. He could picture it grown out. It would flow down her back in a heavy, straight mass and gleam in the sun.

Taking her hand in his, he petted the back of it and her lower arm as he talked. This was a good time to practice his speech to her. He needed to get the wording correct or risk scaring her.

"My kind keeps your species as pets," he explained. "Hundreds of years ago, a warrior named Bazium came across a bunch of humans stranded on a mining facility. He and his crew adopted them and got permission to bring them back to Talarian. Those were the first humans. They were so affectionate and entertaining that every Talin they met was charmed. Some Talins went out looking for more humans to bring back. We provide food, shelter, and safety, and you give us your human-style companionship."

Did that sound like he thought she was inferior?

"It's not that I think humans are dumb—far from it. I know your kind can be quite clever. Your friend, Zia, is an excellent example. She's not only smart but very brave."

There, that sounded better!

"But you must admit, humans need help." Yes, that was a good way to phrase it. Lasha didn't need him to remind her the human homeworld was uninhabitable. She knew that. She'd lived that reality every day while growing up.

After Old Earth couldn't support life anymore, humans were forced to accept jobs any place that would take them. With no cohesive government to back them, humans were easily exploited and most human communities barely made ends meet. Some of the lucky groups were able to set up colonies on planets owned by other species.

Lasha's position on Glakor was a perfect example of dire consequences that could befall humans. Desperate to find a job, Lasha signed a work contract that basically turned her into a slave. It would have been her death if he hadn't shown up.

"I'm going to take you away from this place," he told her. "You'll never be cold or hungry again. No more worrying about food or shelter. I'll provide you with soft bedding for your nest and all the things a human needs to be comfortable and happy. You'll never be exploited again."

Not that he'd hold that over her. He wanted her genuine affection, not the false warmth he'd seen a human display once. It had left him feeling sick and heartily glad when he heard the human had been taken away from the Talin family by the Committee for Pet Welfare and reallocated to another clan that would treat him well.

That's something he should explain early, how well humans were protected!

"It's rare for human pets to be mistreated. If the authorities discover abuse or poor conditions, they will act swiftly. An entire branch of government is dedicated to safeguarding humans, the Committee for Pet Welfare. We even have strict laws about bonded pairs being kept together. Human offspring have to reach a minimum age and be willing to separate from their parents before they can be moved or sold."

This was good. He was hitting all the important points. Except, perhaps he needed to make sure she understood his stance on human pets.

"Some Talins see possessing a human as a way to gain prestige. They don't care enough about the life they're responsible for and only want the status of owning something rare and valuable. Those Talins aren't common. Most of us know how a human can change a Talin."

Tamerin paused, the scent glands in his cheeks were starting to ache. He fought to keep from rubbing his bonding oil on Lasha. He refused to scent mark her while she was unconscious.

"Talins can scent-bond to a human. I know we can, even though most Talins think it's impossible. Your kind calls it love. It's something humans offer freely to each other, but we Talins have lost that kind of bonding in our pursuit of empire and aggressive expansion. We might be a strong and wealthy species, but a sickness is growing among us."

Was this speech too soon to explain to her about the Fading disease? Maybe, but he should test the words now, even if he didn't speak them until later.

"It's the worst-kept secret among Talins," he explained, his words coming out slowly. It was hard to talk about such a taboo subject, even when no one could hear. "Human love can cure or prevent Fading. No one admits it. No healers research it. But everyone knows; Talins who own humans almost never suffer from the deadly Fading. I—"

Words failed him. He didn't want to admit the truth out loud.

No, he was stronger than this!

"I've developed the Fading. Just before Palforma and Zia came onboard the space station I was working at, I'd lost my appetite. That's always the first sign. You have to force yourself to eat. First food loses its flavor. Then you stop seeing color. As the disease progresses, you lose interest in everything. Eventually, you lie down and can't get back up. You die staring at a colorless world through sightless eyes." He whispered that last part, as if saying it out loud might advance his condition irrevocably.

Dying of the Fading was so shameful that most Talins suffering from it would sequester themselves. They'd die alone in remote or hidden places. Their bodies would be discovered by family, friends, or coworkers rotations later. It was never pretty.

He pulled a deep breath into his lungs, letting Lasha's unique human scent fill his nostrils. What would she smell like when his bonding oil was rubbed into her skin?

The ache in his scent glands grew more intense. They were overfull and might even leak soon. Letting go of her hand, he forced himself to move away from the bed. Giving himself a little space from the temping human helped.

A soft, loving rumble sounded from his chestbox. "I don't know if you're my cure. Even if you aren't, I promise to care for you until I'm gone. We'll be going from here to Sorana. Palforma and Zia are there. Even if I die, you'll be among friends. I'll go to the Domicile of Souls knowing I was a good Talin to you."

It was hard for anyone to be content with dying, but at that moment he was the closest to being at peace as he'd ever been. He whispered the words to her sleeping form he'd never have the courage to say otherwise.

"My life is literally in your tiny hands, sweet little Lasha. Please don't cast my scarred body aside."

CHAPTER 4

Tamerin was reluctant to leave Lasha alone in the room, but if the comms office wasn't too busy, he'd be able to get a message out, pick up a few things, and be back before Lasha woke up. He wished he had an information square to leave her with a message in the unlikely chance she woke up while he was gone.

Looking around the room, he realized he didn't have a single way to leave her any kind of message she'd be able to read from the bed. He would buy her an information square while he was out, and some gentle cleanser for her skin and hair.

Determined to be quick, he hurried out of the room. It didn't take long to get to the comms office, but the place was busy. He bribed a few Vicpors into letting him cut in line and was soon closing himself into the small booth.

He was quick to enter the coordinate data and then tapped record. "I've found Lasha. She's ill but recovering. We'll make our way to Sorana when possible."

That worked. Quick and informative, as the military had taught him to be. Tapping his Ident Cube to the pay register, he watched the transaction complete and the message enter the queue. By the queue number his message was assigned, it wouldn't be sent until tomorrow. Good enough for now.

Leaving the comms office, he went to one of the few mercantiles on the planet. As was common with industrial places like this, the selection was poor. He was forced to get substandard items for Lasha, including the low capacity information square. The only thing that made him feel better was the knowledge he'd be replacing everything with better products soon.

As he was making his way to the payment station, he noticed some outfits. They weren't the wrap-dress style garment the human pets normally wore. It was a tunic-style dress that would probably drag the floor, but he could easily cut a few finger-lengths off the hem for her. What attracted him were the bright colors. Humans liked colors and his Lasha should have things that would make her happy.

Reaching out, he touched the fabric and found it tolerably soft. At a minimum it would be an improvement over the badly worn uniform she currently had on. He'd wanted to take it off of her when he'd first put her in the bedroom but didn't want her to wake up naked. Humans rarely liked to go unclothed, even in warm, sheltered places. It made them feel vulnerable. If he bought this, he could coax her into changing.

A flash of gold caught his attention. Turning, he examined a display of belts. Most were practical, but plain. As he examined the display, he found several made of intricate overlapping gold plates. He picked the one with purple stones set in the gold plates. The stones matched the tunic.

Proud of himself for finding his human a pretty gift among all the bland offerings, he rushed to purchase his items.

The need to pee forced Lasha out of her dreams. She was still lying propped up and could clearly see the room was empty.

"Tamerin?" she called out weakly. It wasn't a shock when no one answered or appeared. He'd probably decided to go out for a meal or stretch his legs while she was sleeping. She couldn't blame him. Who wanted to sit around and watch someone snore?

"Crap," she muttered, gazing through the open door to the cleansing room. The floating feeling from before was still there, making the room move a little even when she kept her head still. Walking was out of the question, but crawling might work. No one was around, and she'd be way more embarrassed if Tamerin came back to find she'd wet the bed than discovering her walking on all fours to the cleansing room.

Moving slowly, she rolled onto her side. The mound of pillows acted like a gentle slope, guiding her over and off the bed. At least the bed was so low she only fell about a foot to the hard floor, landing on her side with a little huffing laugh.

"That probably could have been more graceful," she muttered to herself with a grimace. "But we'll take the win."

She started shivering even before she made it to her hands and knees. Why was the floor so cold?

She was still wearing her grungy and worn uniform. The fabric was old, but it should have insulated her better than this. She could tell by the color bar of the door display that the room's temperature was set as high as it could go on Glakor. Still chilly by her standards but not cold. She'd dealt with way worse temperatures, so why did this feel so horrible?

Then her teeth started chattering, and she felt sweat break out over her body. What was going on? Fear made her heart pound. Dizziness forced her to lie down on the hard floor. The room was tilting around her and even the floor was moving. Closing her eyes, she focused on pulling air into her lungs and telling her senses they were being lied to.

"You dumbass," she grumbled. "You're high on drugs and you're sick. That's why you're cold and sweating at the same time."

The urge to urinate was rapidly becoming painful. She needed to move through the vertigo. When she opened her eyes again, the room was steadier, but the moment she got back on all fours, everything tilted and wobbled again. She moved despite the way the room kept shifting, and nausea churned in her stomach.

At least the violent shivering and sweat dripping down her face distracted her from the urge to vomit.

"You're crossing a room, not a continent," she reminded herself. She'd learned pep talks were invaluable when you were the only human and everyone treated you like an idiot. Glakor had taught her to be her own cheer squad. "This is doable. And you're tough. Remember back on Wimol when you walked all the way home with a sprained ankle? It took a while, but you made it. This is the same thing."

As usual, talking like this helped. She was halfway across the room before she was forced to stop and rest. "See, look how much closer you are!" she congratulated herself.

Too bad the remaining distance seemed insurmountable. Lying there waiting for the world to stop listing, she thought about crawling on her belly but then dismissed it. That would put too much pressure on her already aching bladder.

"One more crawling sprint and I'll be there. Two max," she announced to the room with more determination than she felt. "You've got this. Don't forget, we carried durion sheeting from one end of the factory to the other when the sled broke. This is nothing compared to that."

Except that had been early in her time on Glakor, and she hadn't been sick.

The next crawl got her into the doorway of the cleansing unit, but she was hit by a wave of agony. Her bladder felt like it was going to explode, forcing her to curl up on her side, moaning.

"We're almost there," she panted. "Can't you wait a little longer?"

Her plea didn't help. Tears sprang to her eyes and humiliation washed over her as her bladder released. Warm urine soaked her clothes and pooled around her hip.

She should make a quip. Crack a joke. Make fun of herself or the situation. Point out to herself that at least she wasn't shivering anymore.

But nothing came to her. She couldn't think of anything but how mortified she was.

She'd had a few close calls, but no matter how bad it had been, she'd never soiled herself. To compound the issue, these were her only clothes, and now they were beyond filthy. She'd made a mess on the floor and couldn't even clean it or herself up.

There was only one thing to do now—sob.

Giving up on being brave, she let the tears loose and cried. It wasn't as if she could make herself look any more unappealing by having a good old-fashioned emotional meltdown.

She was so busy weeping she didn't hear the room door slide open. As if summoned by magic, Tamerin was suddenly kneeling at her side, purring and talking with frantic speed.

"Did you fall? Where does it hurt? Did anything break? I'll call the med tech. Don't die!"

Either he hadn't noticed the puddle she'd made or he didn't care because the left knee of his pants was close to getting sullied.

"Going to get dirty," she gasped, trying hard to get her crying under control. She didn't want to draw his attention to what she'd done, but he didn't deserve to kneel in the puddle she'd created while trying to help her!

Would this be the point where he decided she was too much work? Was this when he threw up his hands in disgust and declared her useless and revolting?

More tears flowed and she couldn't get any words past her sobs. Then she started coughing. Now she was sob-coughing. This gave new meaning to ugly crying.

She needed to get herself under control. If she could stop crying, the coughing would probably subside.

"I have to go to the door display to contact the med tech," he explained. "I'll still be in the room. I'm not leaving you. I promise."

The threat of having another person here to witness her shameful state finally got words out of her mouth between coughs. "No, don't. Please."

"I'll only leave your side for a submark," he assured her.

"No med tech," she corrected, forcing her sobs back and grabbing one of his clawed hands. That stilled him, and their eyes met. His entire focus was on her. His gaze was intense and the purring loud. "I didn't fall. I needed…I was trying to…"

The strange coldness and sweating intensified. She was shivering violently again but with sweat dripping down her face. It looked like emotional pain made being sick worse. That wasn't a discovery she wanted to make!

Letting go of him with one hand, she pointed to the elimination unit and then the wet area of her clothes. His gaze filtered from the elimination unit to the mess she'd made, and a slow irregular rumble came from his chest, a sound like a faulty engine running poorly.

"How did you get wet? Did you try to bathe yourself? Is that why your face is wet? But—" The sharp clatter of many metal items falling into a jumble on the floor came from him, interrupting both his words and the irregular rumble sound. "You soiled yourself!"

Ah, so that sound was surprise. Would the next sound be one of disgust?

Pulling her hands back, she pressed the heel of her palms to her eyes. She pressed hard, as if she could hold back the tears and humiliation with her hands. "Sorry."

Tamerin's next words shocked her into dropping her hands away from her face to stare up at him. She must have heard him wrong.

"What did you say?" she croaked.

"This is my fault," he repeated and started purring loudly again. "I've been making you drink and didn't think about the natural consequences. Will you ever forgive me for being so careless?"

"Careless?" she echoed. Was this Tamerin, or were the drugs making her hallucinate? She couldn't imagine anyone, except a few humans on Wimol, who wouldn't be at least annoyed with her right now if not completely grossed out.

He bowed his head. "If you'll let me, I'll care for you. Trust me one more time, little Lasha," he entreated.

His words finally made it through her emotional maelstrom. "I'm not angry at you. I'm crying because I'm embarrassed."

Those two simple sentences had a profound effect on Tamerin. He straightened up and reached a hand out to her, stopping short of touching her.

"You have no reason to be embarrassed. This was out of your control, and I should've been a far better caregiver. If you'll allow it, I'll carry you into the cleansing chamber and bathe you."

His acceptance of blame and eagerness to make her comfortable was a balm to her nerves. Sniffing, she grasped his powerful clawed hand in one of hers.

"Yes, please," she agreed. "I trust you."

CHAPTER 5

She was still shivering and sweating when Tamerin lowered her into the Vicpor-style cleansing unit. Vicpors needed to soak in water if they were trying to shed a piece of their carapace. The cleansing unit was roughly three feet deep and five feet long—massive by human standards but average-sized for a Vicpor.

Tamerin had filled the tub before carrying her to it. Looking down at the steaming water, she smiled despite the tears still trickling down her face. Having a bath was a luxury she hadn't experienced since before she signed her work contract.

She hissed as the water hit her skin. It felt both too hot and perfect at the same time. Tamerin froze with her half lowered in the water.

"Does this hurt?" Tamerin asked with a sharp clatter of sound. Worry, maybe? When she was feeling better, she really needed to see how he was making all those sounds.

"Feels good," she insisted. At her words, he resumed settling her into the water. Like most civilizations, the cleansing water was treated with microbes and nanos that started cleaning her skin. Vicpor nanos were programmed to be aggressive cleaners, so she couldn't stay in the bath for long or her skin would get nano-burns. But a short bath and slight discomfort of the aggressive nanos was a small price to be clean.

And she felt warm. So perfectly warm. This was even better than the bed.

Leaning over, Tamerin examined her wrist and hand where they were submerged under the water. "This isn't right," Tamerin muttered.

She followed his gaze and saw the nanos were ripping open an old scab. Hastily, she pulled her arm out of the water. "Drat, I forgot that happens."

"Why would—" he started to ask and then muttered a curse. "Damn Vicpors!"

Rising to his feet, Tamerin stabbed viciously at the controls on the cleansing unit display with his finger. The water drained so quickly it made her dizzy.

"No, it was so warm!" she wailed, her teeth already chattering again and her body shivering

"Let me change the setting and refill," he responded as he focused on the display. Soon, fresh hot water poured rapidly into the unit and she could uncurl and relax again.

"Why'd you do that?" Her question came out sullen. She'd been comfortable for the first time since waking and he'd ripped it away from her.

"Nanos," he explained. "I'd forgotten species like the Vicpor set their washing nanos close to maximum. That's much too harsh for human skin."

She watched him take his belt off and set it with everything hanging from it down on the floor, but he kept his pants on. Then he knelt next to her in the tub, uncaring about getting his pants wet. They were probably made of expensive nano-infused, hydrophobic fabric. It must be nice to have such wealth!

"That's the way it is in a lot of places," she murmured, looking down to find the scab on her arm wasn't being attacked like before. Then she realized what he'd done. "You filled the tub with drinking water!" she gasped. "That's going to be so expensive."

Ignoring her comment, Tamerin lifted her arm to examine the old healing wound. "I'm going to have the med tech look at this. I think she should use a flesh knitter."

"Good luck with that one," she muttered, letting her head fall back to thunk against the side of the cleansing unit. The warm water made her think this was what being in a cocoon must be like. "I don't think I've ever been in so much water before."

The thumping bass rumble sounded again. "Don't you like this? Would you rather take a sand bath?"

Ignoring the question, she opened her eyes and fixed her gaze on him. "What do all the sounds you're making mean? And how are you making them?"

A sharp clatter of sound came out of him for a few seconds before he went back to purring. "We Talins have a chestbox." He tapped his sternum. "We make different kinds of rumbles from there, like the sound I'm making now. We call this a soothing rumble."

"And the clattering sound from a little while ago?" she pushed.

Carefully, he turned around to present her with his back. Overlapping plates ran down his spine. As she watched, the ones from the base of his neck down to his lower back all lifted and came down in a wave, sounding like a box of tools being upended to clatter on the floor.

"That is the sound for surprise," he explained. All the plates started vibrating up and down so fast she couldn't track their movement, making a buzzing sound like a swarm of large, angry insects. "That's a rattle of annoyance or frustration. I don't want to sound a rattle of aggression or a war rattle. Those are too loud for this enclosed space. But those are the basic rattles all Talins have. Some of us can move our back plates in ways others can't and make unique sounds. The current Prime Family, our royal family, are famous for being able to make a war rattle so loud it's deafening."

Lasha was fascinated. "Can I touch them?"

"Of course." Moving carefully, he scooted closer. "Don't touch the bottom edge, they're sharp. The skin under the backplates is highly sensitive."

Running her fingers up one plate, she noticed they were a slightly darker color than the rest of him. At her touch, he opened his plates up, exposing the vulnerable skin underneath. Her hand was small enough to slip between the plates, allowing her to stroke his skin. It turned out a Talin's hard plating protected unbelievably soft flesh.

Tamerin shivered, his rumble changing from the purr to something with a slower, deeper, thrumming beat. Afraid she'd hurt him, she jerked her hand away. "I'm sorry!"

Going slow to keep from disturbing the water, Tamerin turned to face her. "It didn't hurt. It felt good."

"Good?" she asked. "So that rumble wasn't a pain reaction?"

"The rattle from pain is usually the same rattle as surprise," he answered. "But enough about rattles and rumbles. We need to finish cleaning you and get you back in bed. I'm determined the med tech will see you again today."

"Yes, sir!" she responded with a little dramatic splash.

The marbles rolling around in a bag came out of Tamerin. She'd made him laugh! She was really coming to like the way the Talins showed emotion. His facial expression might never change, but the sounds created a rich way to communicate.

"If you grew up with Zia, I know you aren't as obedient as that sounded," Tamerin retorted, tugging at the ragged bottom of her sleeve. "How do we get this uniform off you? I bought you an outfit you can wear until we can get you better clothes."

"You're spending too much money on me." She sighed, even as she lifted her arm up and pointed at a spot on the underside of the cuff. "It's got an interlock panel that goes all the way down both sides. But…"

Her words were cut off when Tamerin ran his claw down the interlock panel, separating the right side of her uniform from top to bottom. All business now, he urged her left hand up and did the same to that side, not stopping until his clawed finger finished the interlock panel at her ankle. With both sides unlocked, the fabric automatically released the interlock panels on the insides of her legs and at her shoulders.

Now it was two separate pieces of fabric. The back half stayed pinned under her, but the front floated free.

That's when she remembered she was completely naked underneath!

With one arm across her chest and the other angled over her stomach and crotch, she held the worn garment to her body.

"Um, no!" she squeaked.

"No?" Tamerin asked, pulling his hands away as if he was afraid of hurting her. "Has some of the fabric adhered to a wound? If we continue to soak your body in the water, it should loosen on its own. Or I could get my knife and cut around the spot."

Tamerin was only wearing pants, no shirt, no shoes, and no other covering. His kind probably weren't bashful, but Lasha was. She'd always been reluctant to disrobe in front of others, far more than any of her peers.

Feeling stupid but still determined to maintain her modesty, she held on to the uniform.

"I don't have any undergarments on." Her voice was tight and small. She felt like a teenager again, in trouble with her parents.

"Of course you don't have undergarments on," Tamerin said, sounding the slow, irregular rumble of confusion.

"If I take the uniform off, I'll be naked," she explained.

"How else would I bathe you?" Tamerin asked, still sounding the puzzled rumble.

"I can't, um, I don't like..." Her voice trailed off.

The confused rumble stopped, replaced by the purr. "You're shy!" he declared. "I've heard some humans are. You don't want to be naked while being bathed. Let me think."

"I can get myself clean," she offered.

"Helping you bathe is a good way for me to look for injuries or problems," he responded even as he looked around the room as if searching for a solution. "I need to look after every aspect of your health and wellbeing."

Wow, he was taking his responsibility really seriously. How long had he and Zia hung out together? A spike of jealousy hit her. Had they been lovers? Or was he trying to win Zia's affection by helping Lasha? It wouldn't be the first time someone had used Lasha to get to know the beautiful and vivacious Zia.

Still, he was literally the reason she wasn't dead right now, so she needed to be grateful no matter what his motivations were.

"That's nice and everything, but maybe this time I'll do it," she offered.

His gaze swung back to her. "Do you feel you need cloth to cover you, or would an opaque layer of water be acceptable?"

What a strange question. "As long as you can't see my, um, private areas."

"Then I have a possible solution." Uncaring about the water he was dripping all over the floor, he got out of the unit and left the small room, returning in seconds with a small, bulging bag. Dumping a pile of colorful items out on a shelf, he pulled out a bottle of something.

"This is a gentle cleanser that will turn the water a chalky white," he explained, tugging off the top of the bottle and upending the entire thing into the unit. Leaning over, he swished a hand around to disperse the additive. True to his word, it suddenly looked like she was bathing in milk.

And bonus, the cleanser had a soft floral scent. "Ah, this is nice."

Still wearing his pants and carrying several items, he got back into the unit. Reaching into the water with one hand, he found the front of her uniform and tugged. Reluctantly, she let go, and he tossed the front half of her uniform into a far corner.

"I'm going to start with your feet," he explained. "I've read that some humans have a reflexive response to having the soles of their feet touched. Are you sensitive there?"

It took her several blinks before she understood what he was asking. "I'm not ticklish."

"Good, that will make this easier." She recognized the cleansing cloth he had in his hand. It was one of the more expensive ones available on Glakor. When he dipped it into the water and started rubbing it over the skin of her feet, it felt luxurious.

Between the drugs still in her system, the hot water, the soft floral scent, and Tamerin's gentle touches, she couldn't keep her eyes open. Letting her body relax, she gave herself permission to enjoy Tamerin's efforts. Despite his size and those intimidating claws and quills, his touch was nothing but gentle.

And thorough. He took the time to clean between each toe!

When he was finished with the foot, he made his way to her ankle and then calf. Once he got to her hip bone, he started on the foot of her other leg and repeated the process. He was careful not to touch too close to her sex, and she found herself half hoping he pushed her boundaries.

She'd said not to look. She'd hadn't mentioned anything about touching. And it had been a long time since she'd been touched.

The few times she'd felt energetic enough to have a lover in the past, it had always been a quick exchange of pleasure. They'd had no time to spend on drawn-out foreplay or holding each other after coupling. It was hard, if not impossible, to find time for tenderness when each day was a fight for survival.

But look at her now. Sitting in a lavish bathing unit being washed like she was some kind of royalty and he was a servant attending to her needs. The whole situation pushed her to act uncharacteristically bold.

With a wantonness she'd never displayed before, she spread her legs, inviting him to wash her more intimately. He accepted the invitation and ran the cleaning cloth over her sex before moving on.

Wait, that was it? He wasn't going to linger or sneak a feel?

Oh, that's right. This was about impressing Zia. The last thing he'd want was Lasha whining to Zia about him taking advantage of the situation.

Feeling a little deflated, she hummed a familiar lullaby to distract herself.

Tamerin paused, his hand on her belly, his purring going silent. "What's that sound you're making?"

"You mean my humming?" she asked.

The rumble that came out of him could only be described as stockinged feet running on a hard floor. "Yes, that. Do it again. It's a pleasant sound."

She made a mental note of this rumble being one of agreement and started humming again. The acoustics of the cleansing room were nice, so she opened her mouth and sang the lullaby at a low volume.

Tamerin didn't move the entire time she sang. Had she hurt his ears, or was he trying to interpret the lullaby? It was in an Old Earth language that only a few on Wimol still spoke and she only knew enough to sing a few songs. His Innercranial Translator wouldn't have the language because there wasn't even a download available for it.

"It's a song meant to help babies go to sleep," she explained before he could ask. "The words roughly translate to telling the child to close their eyes and invite sleep to come to them."

The next thing Tamerin said shocked her to the core.

"We don't have songs or singing among Talins," he noted, going back to cleaning her. "I do like the sounds you make. If you enjoy voicing them, please continue."

Lifting her head, she stared at him, agog. "You're joking with me. Right?"

His melodious purring was interrupted by the irregular "confused" rumble. "Joking?"

"You don't have music in your culture at all?" she questioned.

"We don't," he affirmed, going back to purring. "And I was unaware that humans had developed such talents. But it's been my misfortune to have spent little time in the company of humans."

"Oh, yeah, that makes sense," she agreed. What would it be like to have no music? She couldn't imagine, but if you never had something, you couldn't miss it.

She relaxed back and started singing. By the time she'd gone through half her repertoire, Tamerin had finished going over her body and was focused on her hair.

"I wish I had the nicer products for your mane," he murmured, working his clawed fingers through the short but tangled strands. Not only did he tame her tangles with no painful tugs, but he gently ran the tips of the claws over her scalp in a way that sent pleasant tingles all over.

Someone moaned.

It was her!

A rumble of amusement danced in her ears. "Enjoying this. Aren't you?"

"Feels so good," she agreed. Had she slurred her words? Her body felt loose and her brain was calm and quiet. She was going to fall asleep and drown if she wasn't careful. "Don't stop."

Purring, he kept running his claws through her hair, making her moan again. Forget having sex. She wanted him to do this to her forever!

She might have fallen asleep because the next thing she knew he'd wrapped a sheet around her. With the cleansing gel so thick in the water there was no need to rinse off, but now there was a soaked sheet. She appreciated his dedication to her modesty, but this seemed excessive.

"Sorry about the sheet. If you put me on the floor next to the bed, I can dry myself and then roll over onto the mattress," she offered.

Slitting her eyes open, she saw the room moving as Tamerin carried her. Even that brief glimpse was enough to cause severe vertigo, forcing her to clamp her eyes shut again.

"It's fine. I requested extra pillows and sheets so I could build you a proper nest after you didn't need to lie propped up anymore," he explained. "I have a plan so you can remain covered while I tend to you."

He set her down next to the bed and then draped a dry sheet over her. Reaching under the dry sheet, he pulled the wet one away and then dried her off. He did it while she sat in her own little sheet-tent, hidden away from sight.

The only problem was she kept listing to the side as he worked. Her muscles had lost all rigidity and didn't want to hold her up. She heard his rumble of amusement interrupt his purr a few times as he was forced to straighten her back up.

It was difficult, but he got a tunic dress under the sheet and over her head. She tried to lift her arms to help, but neither of them wanted to cooperate. Dressing her like a child and using only his sense of touch as a guide, he got her arms poked through the correct holes and pulled the overlong tunic down to her hips.

"Peek-a-boo," she whispered when he pulled the sheet off her head and let it pool in her lap to preserve her modesty.

"Is that a human phrase?" he asked, lifting her and the sheet in her lap onto the bed.

"Yup," she hummed, slumping back onto the mound of pillows. "Ah, nice."

Tamerin tucked the sheets and blanket around her and then reached under the blanket to retrieve the sheet used to tent her. Now she was dry except for her hair. It felt good to be clean, warm, and nestled in bed.

After coaxing her to drink some more, he finally let her close her eyes.

"You can sleep," he offered. "Until the med tech gets here."

"Don't go," she whispered.

"I won't leave you again," he promised. She felt the bed dip a little and then his warm body stretching out next to her. Rolling her head to the side, she pressed her face to the hard, smooth surface of his side.

She was out before she could tell him that he smelled like cardamom. She loved cardamom—a smell that meant home.

CHAPTER
6

Lasha woke up with a scream on her lips. With the remnants of the nightmare clinging to her and the unfamiliar surroundings, she fought the urge to scream again. It didn't help that pain was shooting through her head, making her eyes water.

A door to her left slid open and a massive individual rushed into the room, making a deafening sound that could have been the pounding of thousands of feet. With claws bared and quills up, he looked ready to do battle.

"Where's the threat?" he growled out, surveying the room. It was empty except for the two of them.

Hazy memories of the last few days came flooding back. Tamerin caring for her. Visits from the med tech. Tamerin bathing her and then tucking her in. Waking her to hold bottles to her mouth and encouraging her to drink. Tamerin feeding her meals by hand until she was steady enough to feed herself. Carrying her to the cleansing room and back whenever she needed.

She couldn't picture a single moment without him in it.

"I think I was having a nightmare," she admitted, feeling both shaky and embarrassed. The poor guy was simply trying to use the cleansing room, and she freaked out.

At her words, his loud rattling cut off, and he straightened up. The quills of his right arm folded back to rest flush and his claws retracted. "A nightmare? Is that a type of pain?"

Talins didn't have nightmares? Lucky bastards. "I guess you could call it that. It's when you're asleep and you imagine something scary and it seems real to you."

Striding over to the bed, he started up a loud purring. "Nothing is here but you and I", he assured her. "If anyone was foolish enough to try to hurt you, I'd rip them apart. Despite my imperfect form, I'm still an effective warrior."

"I'm not worried," she promised, grabbing his left hand the moment he was close enough. He knelt on the bed next to her and let her drag his scarred hand against her body so she could hug his arm to her chest. Her memories might be clouded from the drugs Ilee had administered, but she remembered his warmth with perfect clarity.

Tamerin's purr got louder for a moment before squeezing her hand gently. "I'm not surprised you were scared when you woke up. This place isn't fit for a human. Soon we'll leave this ugly, nasty planet."

She smiled up at him. Neither of them would be sad to see the last of the island city. "I'm sorry I screamed. Was that a war rattle? It was earsplitting!"

"It was, but mine wasn't even the loudest in my class," Tamerin admitted.

"All of you doing that together could make an enemy go deaf," she admired.

He sounded a rumble of amusement. "Not deaf, but it can be disorienting."

She thought about the one image of a Talin she'd seen in a newsreel and tried to imagine dozens or hundreds of them all lined up with full armor making that war rattle. They'd be both magnificent and terrifying. No wonder others whispered about the Talins like they were the boogeyman.

Thinking of a deafening sound made Zia's face appear in her mind's eye.

How had Zia even met Tamerin? At the time Lasha had signed the work contract and been shipped off to Glakor, Zia had a job working on a salvage trawler far from Braxin space. She made enough that it was unlikely she'd have changed jobs. It must have been a strange set of circumstances to have brought Tamerin and Zia together.

And if they were a couple, why wasn't she here with him? Why had she sent Tamerin on his own?

Lasha wanted to ask, but at the same time, she was scared of what Tamerin might tell her. What if the answer was that she was back home at their domicile somewhere raising their children waiting for him to return?

A heartfelt homecoming scene popped into her head. Zia throwing herself into Tamerin's arms. He would hold her tightly but with care, and rumble out that purr.

Or maybe he had a special sound only for her.

Feeling a little ill, she pushed those uncomfortable thoughts out of her head. Tamerin and Zia had saved her life. She owned them a lot.

"Has the head pain come back?" Tamerin asked. "Your brow is scrunched up like humans do sometimes when they're uncomfortable."

"My headache isn't any worse than normal. I was just having some heavy thoughts," she answered.

Tamerin's purring went silent. "Thoughts can be heavy?"

Laughing, Lasha shook her head. "It's an expression. It means the thought was serious."

The purring started up again. She wished she could drag him down to snuggle her on the bed, but that would probably be intrusive presumptuous.

"How long have we been in this room?" she asked, realizing she didn't know how much time had passed.

"This is the sixth rotation," he answered. Vicpors used the term rotation instead of day, so she knew what he meant right away.

"Six?" she exclaimed. At most, she would have said two days.

"You were weak and heavily sedated at first," he explained. "You'd swim in and out of consciousness."

Lasha grimaced. "I'm so sorry for anything insulting, off-putting, or just plain weird, I might have said over the last few days."

He sounded a rumble of amusement. "You've said nothing unkind to me," he assured her. "The worst was when you were in pain, and I couldn't get the med tech to give you more analgesics."

"I honestly don't remember much," she admitted. Then a vivid bit of memory hit her. "Oh no. No, no, no! Tell me I didn't pee on the floor."

Tamerin started purring loudly. "That was entirely my fault."

Another memory filtered past her humiliation. "And you had to bathe me. You were so nice and I was such a weirdo about being naked."

She heard a fast-buzzing sound, like a swarm of angry wasps. Oh, she'd annoyed him.

"It's my honor to see to all your needs. You were in distress, not a *weirdo*." He managed to pronounce the foreign, human word although it was heavily accented.

Looking down at herself, she let go of his hand and tugged the sheet off her. She was wearing a bright purple, nicely made tunic dress. Not only had he cared for her, spent outrageous sums of wealth on a med tech, but he'd also bought her an expensive garment.

"Nice is too mild a term for you," she murmured to Tamerin. "I'm going to get better and figure out some way to repay you. And Zia."

"You owe me nothing," he insisted. "And all Zia wants is for you to be safe and happy."

She smiled up at him. "That's already happened. For the first time in a long time, I feel both those things."

Tamerin shook his head slightly and gestured to the surrounding room. "This is the bare minimum I plan to provide for you." Getting up, he crossed the room to a pile of items and a large sack. After rummaging around, he pulled out a fancy information square. "This came with my last order from the mercantile."

Stepping back to the bed, he settled down again while handing her the square. Forcing a smile on her face, she took it. The thing was large for a square, but light, telling her it was one of the more expensive models available on Glakor.

She tried to hand it back. "That's a nice one."

He didn't take it. "It's for you," he explained. "Humans need enrichment in their living spaces. I got one already set up to access the Unibase here on Glakor and it has a Universal translation program. We can download any books or articles you're interested in."

Grabbing his Ident Cube, he worked the old but expensive piece of tech until it dinged and her square lit up. "I've sent you the official Talin guide we send to species we're first meeting. It's a good introduction to our government, culture, and clan system. I've also put your paid and nullified work contract on there so you can show it to anyone here who asks. Not that it should happen."

"Thanks," she answered weakly. Giving up on him taking it back, she set it on her lap and activated the screen. The thing came to life, giving her options with icons next to them. The words in Universal danced around and wouldn't still into any kind of readable order, but she recognized most of the icons.

Tapping one she thought was safe, she found herself confronted by a menu she couldn't make heads or tails out of. Biting her lip, she picked a line at random.

"Oh, that's a fascinating historical account of Emperor Mulium." Tamerin settled down next to her and stretched his legs out on the bed. "The historian did an excellent job of being factual but still drawing the reader into Mulium's life story."

Lasha worked hard on keeping her expression neutral as she stared at the square filled with dense, small Universal script. Using a tactic that worked well in the past, she handed the square to Tamerin.

"Would you read out loud to me?" she requested. "I like the sound of your voice."

"If that would make you happy," Tamerin agreed, sounding pleased. Purring, he took the square back and started reading. Snuggling against his side, she closed her eyes and focused on the deep timbre of his voice. She was surprised at how quickly she fell into the story of Monarch Mulium. She'd risen to power early in the Talin unification process over five thousand years ago. It had been a turbulent and often violent era, but she'd been a strong and fair leader.

Tamerin was describing a particularly tense interaction when the door display chimed, interrupting the story before she found out what happened to Mulium's husband during the battle with the Illorian Clan!

"Ignore that," Lasha demanded. "Keep reading."

Turning off the square, Tamerin set it aside and got up. "That will be the med tech."

"No!" Lasha wailed. "You can't leave me with a cliffhanger like that! Does her husband survive?"

"You'll have to wait to find out," Tamerin responded with an amused rumble. He tapped the display, letting the med tech in.

Lasha pouted. "Mean Tamerin," she accused as Ilee stepped into the room.

"You sound much more coherent today," the med tech declared, tapping her pincer against her side in a display of happiness.

"I'm feeling much better," Lasha agreed.

"Yes, very good," Ilee responded, stepping closer to the bed. "This is excellent. Let's test your balance and motor skills today."

What followed was an hour of movement others wouldn't have had issues with but made Lasha look like a drunk toddler. By the time Ilee let her collapse back into the bed, she was sweating and out of breath from doing nothing more than walking in a straight line, trying to stand on one foot, and jogging in place.

The jogging in place lasted all of two seconds before she was out of breath and coughing again.

"Was that all necessary?" Tamerin growled as he cracked open a canister of water. He'd stayed close to her for the entire process. Any time she even remotely looked like she was going to lose her balance, he'd grabbed her and ruined whatever test Ilee was trying to run. It annoyed the med tech and drew everything out, but Lasha didn't mind. His care made her heart do all kinds of flip-flops in her chest.

"Her recovery is on schedule," Ilee announced after tapping on her information square. Then she pulled a vial from her bag and handed it to Tamerin. "This is the last dose she needs. I'd suggest having her checked again in about ten rotations."

"I will," Tamerin agreed quickly. Although Ilee had been professional and proficient, Tamerin still considered her substandard to a Talin healer. Lasha tried to tell him this med tech was the kindest Vicpor she'd ever dealt with, but Tamerin wouldn't be swayed. Ilee was only *acceptable at the moment*.

"And she needs to walk every day now," Ilee insisted. "You can't carry her everywhere. She'll never fully recover if she doesn't move on her own."

A displeased rattle of agitated hornets sounded from Tamerin. "She tires quickly."

"Then she gets tired and sleeps after she walks," Ilee responded, meeting Tamerin's intense stare without flinching.

"What if she falls?" Tamerin challenged.

"Then you catch her," Ilee retorted.

They went back to glaring at each other.

"I think I can figure out my own limitations," Lasha announced to the room, drawing them out of their staring contest.

Ilee looked down at Lasha and tapped her pincer against her side again. "Make sure you tell him that repeatedly," the med tech grumbled. "He seems to be slow to understand."

Lasha stifled a laugh. "I will. Thank you for treating me."

"I've been paid well," Ilee pointed out and then cast a sidelong glance at Tamerin. "But perhaps not enough."

This time Lasha couldn't hold back her chuckle. "He's just overprotective."

"I'm standing right here," Tamerin groused. "And I'm going to take all necessary precautions."

"And for that you have my eternal gratitude," Lasha offered with a big smile.

"That's a good place to start," Tamerin muttered so quietly she wasn't sure she'd heard him correctly. Then the med tech was standing up and speaking.

"My office is not far from here and on the ground floor," Ilee told Lasha. "Once you're able to walk all the way there on your own, you're healthy enough to travel."

She could tell by Tamerin's rattle that he didn't like that pronouncement. "I can carry her onto a ship," he argued. "We don't need to delay our departure."

"If her lungs aren't ready, the artificial atmo on the average commercial ship might cause her pain," Ilee answered. "But if you want to cause her more discomfort, I won't stand in your way."

Tamerin's annoyance vanished along with his rattling. "I hadn't thought of that."

Ilee snapped her pincer in the air. "That's why you hire professionals."

Lasha hid her grin at Ilee's sassy response.

"After we're able to visit your office, we'll be leaving." Tamerin's words were a declaration of intent. She couldn't blame him. Glakor wasn't a pleasant place to be for anyone. Not even the overseers who owned or partially owned businesses here liked the planet.

"I look forward to seeing you there," Ilee said to Lasha before leaving.

"Are you hungry? I could order a meal for you," Tamerin offered once the door closed on the med tech.

"I don't need food. I need to know what happened next!" Lasha demanded, patting the bed next to her. "Hurry up!"

Tamerin rumbled out a purr as he settled into the bed next to her and picked the square up. He found his place and started reading. Lasha didn't hesitate to snuggle up against him and close her eyes.

She focused on memorizing every aspect of this moment because it was perfect.

CHAPTER 7

Tamerin was thrilled.

Not only was Lasha's health progressing well, but she was still showing affection toward him even after the mind-altering medication was out of her system.

And she liked the sound of his voice!

The first time she'd requested he read to her had come as a surprise. He'd worried she was doing it to placate him. But then she'd put her body close to his and was genuinely upset when the reading was interrupted. He'd been told it could take many rotations and perhaps even solars to earn the trust of a human, especially one who wasn't raised among Talins.

Not his Lasha. She was growing fond of him and didn't even seem to care about his deformed arm and shoulder. He'd never thought of his arm with the missing quills, scalded off armor plates, and exposed scarred skin as an advantage, but Lasha loved cuddling that arm to her chest. She often fell asleep curled around his arm with her face pressed to his shoulder. She'd said his scarred flesh felt soft under her fingers.

And what those little fingers did to him! He had to fight hard to keep his shaft from engorging and pulling free of his flesh pouch. But some days were a struggle when Lasha insisted on caressing his arm with her fingers and even going as far as rubbing her face on his scarred flesh.

With her increased vitality, each day became a challenge to fight his instincts to rub his bonding oil into her hair and on her skin. His scent glands were constantly full and aching. He rubbed a special salve on his cheeks to keep the glands from leaking bonding oil down his face, but he was rapidly running out.

He didn't want to rub bonding oil on her without consent, but what if he explained it to her and she looked at him with disgust?

Fear also kept him from voicing the speech he'd practiced so many times in his head. What if she was horrified at the idea of being a human pet, even if only in name? Could he avoid telling her any of it? If they didn't go to his homeworld or any of the stations, only went to Sorana, he wouldn't have to explain that under Talin law, he owned her. But how would they get there without traveling on a Talin ship or stopping at a Talin station?

He still wanted her evaluated by a Talin healer, but to do that she'd need to wear a collar and be registered.

It was all a mess, and he couldn't figure out where to start with his explanation so he didn't.

"You've gone quiet," Lasha noted, her musical voice drawing him out of his thoughts. "Do you need a break from reading?"

"I thought you were asleep," he admitted. She often dozed off when he was reading. He'd note the spot in the reading when she'd fallen asleep so he could start again when she woke up.

Letting go of his arm, she sat up and stretched. "I'm not sleepy. In fact, I want to walk all the way to the med tech's office today."

As Ilee had instructed, Lasha worked on lengthening their walks each day. Yesterday she'd successfully made it down the hall to the lift and then through the lobby area. They'd stopped at the outside doors because it was much too cold for her to risk going outside without more layers.

But she'd also been swaying badly by the time they made it back up to their floor in the lift. He'd carried her down the hall and into their room, worried she would stumble and fall.

It made him reluctant to push past the front door of the building yet.

"Let's order you a heavier garment today and take the walk outside tomorrow," he countered. Using the city interface, he pulled up the mercantile stock list on the information square he'd been reading from. Then he handed her the square.

"Choose any of these. They're all ugly, but they should fit."

Hesitantly, Lasha took the square. She only glanced at the list and then tried to hand it back to him. "You pick for me."

He wouldn't take it. "I've selected everything so far. You should get the one that appeals to you. I worry you don't believe me when I say I can easily afford all this and more."

"I'm going to pay you back," she insisted. "I'm not sure how, but I'll do it. Besides, I don't need anything fancy. Pick the cheapest coat. Then let's do my daily walk. I want to check out the food kiosk in the corner of the lobby this time."

"We can take the walk after you order the coat of your choice," he insisted, pushing the hand holding the information square back toward her.

She looked at the square again running her eyes down the list of items. "These are all coats on here?"

Why did she look so apprehensive? He thought her anxiety over picking things for him to buy her was because of guilt over money, but he was growing suspicious something more was going on.

"Yes, they're all coats," he answered.

"Um, can you make it display the images of the garments?" she requested.

He had to hold back a surprised rattle. Had she never dealt with a standard online ordering system? "You only need to tap the index and select the image catalog. It's right there at the top."

She bit her lip and stared hard at the screen. Reaching out a finger, she tapped the negotiation page instead of the index.

When the screen changed to display the few items the mercantile was willing to trade or barter for, she shook her head.

Her body was tense, and she refused to look up. "That wasn't right. Was it?"

"I set everything to Universal, but I can download and set up a different translation program if that would help," he offered. Maybe that was why she was constantly trying to hand the information square back to him? She might never have learned to read Universal. It was rare, but it did happen. "What language would you like?"

Dropping the square into her lap, she covered her face with her hands.

"You're not going to let this go. Are you?" Her words were muffled, but he could hear the frustration in her voice.

Fear built in him. Why was she distressed at something as simple as ordering a coat? What wasn't he understanding about this situation?

"You don't have to do anything," he assured her, plucking the information square from her lap. He found the correct page and picked the most insulated coat on the list. It took him a little while to get through the verification process, but finally a message flashed. The coat would be delivered to their room early the next day.

"There, it's done," he declared, setting the square aside. "You don't have to be upset."

When she moved her hands from her face, he was relieved to note her eyes were dry. She was biting her lip and the skin between her brows was furrowed. Running her fingers through her short hair, she sighed out an aggravated sound.

"I hate telling people about this, but I'm, uh, flawed," she stated.

He couldn't help the confused rumble that interrupted his purring for a submark before he got himself back under control.

"I know, but we're fixing you," he reminded her. "Soon you'll see a Talin healer and they'll make sure your lungs work perfectly so you won't have problems breathing again."

Her mouth curved up in an adorable human smile so wide it showed her flat, white teeth. "I mean my brain is flawed. I was born mis-wired."

"Mis-wired?" he questioned. "I don't understand. Was your INT installed incorrectly?"

"No, my INT works fine." She pointed to the square with one hand and her head with the other. "I can't read that."

"Let me download some translator programs. You can have it in something besides Universal. I think we even have one Old Earth written language translator program for information squares. That will have to wait until I can get access to it."

"That won't help, I can't read anything," she confessed.

This time the surprised rumble made it through. "No one ever taught you? How abominable!"

"They tried," she corrected him, her expression turning sad. "Trust me. Everyone tried. But I was born with this thing where the words or symbols want to jumble on me. The harder I stare, the more confused they all get." She took a deep breath and then continued.

"That's why I'm here working on Glakor. If I could've worked the machinery on Wimol, I would've had a job that was safer and been able to stay with my community. You have to read to program the planters and harvesters, and you have to read to communicate with the landowners."

"Why didn't they just install speaking programs?" Tamerin asked and then realized the answer to his own question. "Because most species don't like speaking programs."

"Yeah, exactly," Lasha sighed. "Everyone on Wimol tried really hard to get me work, but no one wanted to hire me once they found out. It was a nightmare."

"I can't believe they sent you away," Tamerin growled. How uncaring of her fellow humans!

Lasha looked aghast. "No, never! But I had to leave. I was nothing but a burden to my community. I couldn't live like that."

"And this job didn't require you to read?" he pushed.

"I used a labor broker." Lasha looked like she might be about to cry. "I didn't realize until later how manipulative those brokers are. They were always visiting the poorer areas on

Wimol trying to find workers. When I showed interest, they put me in a small room and pressured me to sign."

"They forced you?" Tamerin asked, working hard to keep his rattle of anger at bay.

"Not forced," Lasha answered slowly. "But they told me there wasn't time to let anyone else from the colony read the contract. I had to decide right then. If I left the room we were in, I couldn't change my mind later and say yes." She heaved out a deep sigh. "I had a lot of time to think about their tactics and realized what they did."

"I'm surprised no one in your colony protested and tried to talk you out of it," Tamerin commented, angry at her community for letting her leave.

"They tried," she confessed. "I was too excited to listen. Part of why I did it was to be like Zia. Every couple of months she sent a series of vids stitched together of all the places she'd been and the stuff she'd seen. I envied her and wanted to be like her. I had visions of getting to live a life like hers. I should've known better. She's a skilled worker, and I'm nothing but dumb labor."

"Not dumb," Tamerin argued.

"But not capable either," Lasha countered and then continued talking before he could press the issue further. "Anyway, once I signed, the brokers only gave me enough time to grab some of my stuff and say goodbye before their ship left. It wasn't long enough for anyone to do more than hug me." She gave him a rueful smile. "Not that they could have talked me out of it."

Tamerin had heard of work brokers but didn't know much about them. "Were you the only one on the ship?"

"No, the ship was full of contract workers from other places, I was the last one they needed to have a full docket to sell on Glakor. Looking back, I had a great time on the ship. They fed us well. We had access to a game room. It was the last bit of fun and food before we landed on Glakor. We were all unloaded there and I never saw them again."

"And then you went work for Oglee," Tamerin concluded.

"Yup, and he was pissed when he found out I couldn't read," Lasha agreed. She tilted her head and looked at him with mild confusion. "You're awfully accepting that I'm flawed."

"Don't ever call yourself flawed again," Tamerin growled. She flinched at his harsh voice, so he focused on lightening his tone and keeping up his soothing rumble. "Zia is deaf. Would you call her flawed?"

"She isn't flawed, she's amazing," Lasha argued vehemently. "She's probably the smartest person I know."

"Her lack of hearing says nothing about her intelligence, just as your inability to read isn't indicative of your mental acuity," he proclaimed. "But more than anything, I'm in awe of your willpower. I've never seen your match."

The tension was slowly leaving her body as they spoke, giving him hope she was truly taking in what he was telling her.

"What do you mean? What willpower?" she asked.

"You survived," he stated simply. "Every single shift you got up and toiled for marks on end with no hope of relief in sight. Despite cold, fatigue, hunger, and pain, you kept going. You didn't give up. Not until your body literally started shutting down. Until then, you marched on. That's the kind of fortitude a warrior is made of."

"I never thought about it like that," she murmured.

"And I'm sure you had to constantly improvise," he continued. "This place would be horrific for any species, but you're small by Vicpor standards. Nothing here would have been made for you to handle, yet you did. That tells me you must have figured out ways to get your job done despite your smaller size and lesser physical strength. I'm sure you're as smart and clever as Zia."

"Probably not as smart as Zia, but I did a few things." She hummed a little as she thought. "After I rigged a simple rail system for the carts in my section, they made it permanent and added it to all the rooms. I didn't consider it until now because all I cared about was that it made my life easier, but I inadvertently made everyone's life easier."

"Exactly," he responded with an approving rumble. "Let me tell you about Palforma. He suffered a terrible head injury that ended his military career and almost took his life. Although he can think and reason just fine, he had trouble speaking. He stuttered badly and often couldn't make the words come out of his mouth."

Lasha's expression turned sympathetic. "Poor guy!"

"Most thought so, yes," Tamerin agreed. "Even I felt pity for him when I should have been more supportive. It shames me now, but at the time I avoided Palforma because I didn't know what to say to him or how to interact."

"If you explained that to him, I'm sure he'd understand," she was quick to say.

"Even if he does, I'm not sure I'm ready to forgive myself," Tamerin admitted. "But that's not the point of this story. When he met Zia everything changed. She got the silent tapping language of the Norka installed in his INT. She gave him back the ability to communicate clearly. Nothing was wrong with him. He just needed the right tools to make everything work. Now they are building an entire colony together, and my worthy cousin is more content than I ever thought possible."

Lasha blinked up at him. "Hold up. Palforma is with Zia too? Are you guys in some kind of threesome?"

"What's a threesome?"

His question made her snort out a laugh. "It's when three people are in a relationship together."

Understanding dawned. "Oh, that's right. I remember now that humans aren't limited to pair bonding. Your kind likes to form all kinds of romantic bonds independent of gender or number of participants."

"Yup, we're an adventuresome bunch!" she agreed with a chuckle. Then her expression turned inquisitive. "Wait, does that mean you aren't with Zia?"

Tamerin sounded a brief negative rattle, the sharp sound bouncing off the walls of the room. "Zia isn't my human. She and Palforma are bonded."

"Bonded?" she questioned.

He forced himself to explain, despite how uncomfortable it made him. "Talins can scent-bond with humans. We have glands in our cheeks that produce an oil. When we put that oil on humans, the smell changes and we get addicted to the scent.

Humans do a type of scent-bonding back, but nothing as intense as we Talins."

Her mouth formed a little O of surprise. "Zia is with Palforma, not you," she repeated. "And they're basically the Talin version of married?"

"We have a formal marriage in our culture, but scent-bonding is like a marriage without the ceremony or official recognition."

"So you're single?" she asked.

"I'm not married," he agreed.

"And you're not scent-bonded to any other Talin or human?" she pressed.

Feeling like she was picking on his lack of companionship, his answer was short and sharp. "No bonds."

A huge smile broke across her face. "Perfect!" she cried before launching herself at him. He was quick to catch her and settled her comfortably in his lap.

"What–" he started to ask, but she interrupted him.

"I've been wanting to do this for days!"

Then she pressed her lips to his, and the world disappeared.

CHAPTER 8

Despite working hard to avoid it, Lasha had still fallen for Tamerin. Every time he'd cared for her, snuggled with her, or read to her, her feelings for him got stronger. She constantly reminded herself not to kiss him. He wasn't hers. He belonged to Zia, and friends didn't poach.

She'd resigned herself to unrequited love, but now she found out he was single. Joy made her act without thought, jumping into his lap and pressing her lips to his.

Then his arms tightened around her, and he opened his mouth to kiss her back. His kiss was like his touches, gentle and lingering. The slight scent of cardamom always perfumed the air when he was near, but now it filled her nose as his tongue invaded her mouth. She'd never had a smell turn her on so much.

But it wasn't just the smell or taste of him. His rumbles had gone from the faster purring beat to a slower, longer thrumming. This rumble brushed across her skin and made heat pool in her belly. Who knew a sound could tug at your libido?

When he pulled away she couldn't help but whimper as her eyes fluttered open to find his face still close to hers. He was breathing hard and his eyes were intensely focused on her. Both sides of his face were shiny, as if oil had been dripped down his cheeks.

"I need…" He stopped talking and swallowed convulsively a few times. "Please. Need you!"

Even though he didn't explain what he needed, she wasn't going to deny him. "Yes," she whispered. She thought she was agreeing to intercourse, but he didn't move to strip either of them.

With her legs on either side of his thick, muscled thighs, it was easy for him to draw her against his chest and rub his cheek against the top of her head. The cardamom smell grew stronger and she felt some kind of liquid soak into her hair and scalp.

When he stopped and tilted his head to push the other side of his face against her, she reached up to run her hands through her short locks. Her hair was coated in some kind of light oil.

Tamerin froze while he examined the oil coating her fingers. The feel of it reminded her of the expensive hair or skin products humans on Wimol would occasionally splurge on. Bringing it to her nose she realized this was the source of the Tamerin's cardamom smell.

She loved it so much she wanted to rub it all over her body but contented herself by brushing her fingers over her lips. The oil made her skin tingle a little as it soaked in. When she met Tamerin's gaze again, she smiled.

"This is nice," she whispered. "You smell so good."

Her words made Tamerin's slow rhythm rumble get loud for a few seconds. "Bonding oil," he murmured. "Need to put it on you."

He might be struggling with speaking, but his touch stayed gentle as he cupped the back of her head with his big, scarred hand. He took his time, rubbing his scent glands all over her head and neck. Her skin started tingling everywhere he touched, making it hard to remain still.

"I need you to touch me more," she moaned.

"Yes," he growled out. His arms wrapped around her body, holding her firmly against his chest and then he was standing. She flailed a little as he stood her on her feet next to the bed. He made sure she was steady and then gripped the front of the tunic dress and ripped it down the center. She gasped and reached up to help but he was already drawing it off her.

"Tamerin!" she protested as he lifted her in his arms so he could place her back on the bed.

"I needed to be expedient," he said, kneeling on the bed next to her.

With access to her entire body, he started rubbing his face against her neck and working his way down to her shoulders and clavicle. The tingling became more intense, making her wiggle under him. The sensation was both wonderful and horrible all at the same time. God this was the best kind of torture.

"I need more," she begged.

"More," he agreed and then put his mouth to her neck and sucked. His touch over skin already made sensitive by his oil was like a jolt of electricity through her. It shot down her spine, beaded her nipples, and made her pussy weep with need. Desperate for relief, she reached between her legs as he nipped at the skin he'd just sucked. His bite was light, mostly teeth scraping across skin, but it was such a different feel than his warm mouth pulling at her that she gasped and jerked before moaning.

She'd never been so turned on in her life. Simply running her finger over her clit made a shiver run up her body.

Rearing up, Tamerin looked down at her body. "What are you doing?" Before she could answer, his nostrils flared. "You're touching yourself," he surmised and pushed Lasha's legs apart.

"Wha—" she didn't even get the full word out before he pressed his face into her sex. She thought he'd start using his mouth, but instead he tilted his head to get his scent glands against her clit. His armored face felt hard but smooth against her delicate skin.

The oil spread quickly, making the sensitive flesh throb with need. Once her sex was coated in a thick layer of his bonding oil, he pulled back.

"No," she protested and tried to push him back down with one hand while pointing to her clit with the other. "Put your mouth here. Suck right here."

"I will," he promised, but then he moved back to rubbing, sucking, and nibbling on her shoulder.

"Tamerin!" she wailed. "Please!" She undulated her hips, trying to entice him back. The tingling was getting worse, bordering on pain.

"Not yet," he murmured.

"Right now!" she insisted, frustrated enough to shout the words. Taking a breath, she tried again in a more reasonable tone. "I promise to return the favor, but I need to come. Please Tamerin!"

"Not yet," he repeated.

"Fuck," she grumbled. Fine, if he wasn't going to give her relief, she'd do it herself.

She moved the heel of her hand to rub against her aching clit and dip the fingers of her other hand inside her pussy. Without pause he caught both her wrists in one hand and easily pinned them over her head. His touch was gentle but strong. She wasn't getting loose until he released her.

"Waiting makes everything better," he purred in her ear.

"Or kills me!" she panted, struggling against his hold. With the number of sensations rioting through her, she couldn't remain still.

"I know it won't kill you," he answered with one of those amused clinking-marbles rumbles.

"It might," she insisted. "Frustrated humans expire all the time."

That made him pause for a second and she thought her ruse might have worked before the clinking-marbles filled the air again.

"Naughty human," he whispered. "Fibbing to get your way. You might need to wait even longer."

As he spoke his warm breath ghosted over the skin he'd been licking moments before. Gooseflesh broke out on her neck and shoulders. Suddenly her skin felt too tight, making her moan.

Yup, this was torture!

"You taste so good," Tamerin breathed against the skin of her chest. His mouth was at the slope of her breast.

Arching her back, she moved her nipple closer to his mouth. "More."

"Here?" he asked, his breath warm against her beaded nipple.

She whimpered instead of speaking, and then she cried out when his mouth closed around the turgid peak. Each gentle suckle caused her hips to jerk. Desperate to come she pressed her thighs together and rubbed. It didn't help, but Tamerin noticed and was quick to force her legs apart and settle between her knees.

Cool air flowed across her heated sex making her shudder. As if her clit wasn't dying of need, he focused back on her breasts. Taking up where he'd left off, he ran his cheek across every bit of plump tissue and followed his bonding oil with his lips, tongue, and a little bit of teeth. Every place he touched felt sensitive nearly to the point of pain.

Then the evil male blew a soft breath across where he'd been rubbing on bonding oil, licking, and nibbling. She wasn't sure there was a word to describe the sensation this caused. It was like being frozen and burned at the same time in one little patch of skin.

Then he did it again to a different spot.

"No more," she sobbed.

"Yes more," he insisted as he moved to worship the skin on her sternum. Looking down at the line of his body, she saw his pants bulging in the front. He was turned on but refused to even remove his only garment. Was this a Talin thing or a Tamerin thing?

"Pants," she gasped. She didn't expect him to understand, but when he rolled his eyes up to meet her while licking a trail of fire down to her belly button, she knew he understood. His answer told her how cruel a Talin could be.

"No." That one word was forceful and final. His right hand was still holding both her wrists pinned above her head, but he was so much bigger he could still reach most of her body with his mouth.

When his trailing kisses got close to her sex, she writhed under him desperate to get his mouth between her legs.

Heck, she probably wouldn't need his whole mouth. She'd be happy with only his lips. Or even the tip of his tongue.

"Tamerin, please!" she begged. "Please touch me there. Just the tip!"

"Here?" he asked, his thrumming rumble getting louder as he placed a single fingertip on her clit.

She gasped, jerking her hips up but he was quick to remove his finger before she got any really good pressure. Screaming in frustration, she tugged at her hands.

"Tamerin, I'm gonna kill you!" she threatened.

A brief amused rumble interrupted his thrumming. Then he leaned forward and licked down her sex, all the way from her clit to her puckered hole. Before she'd even finished gasping, he turned his head and rubbed his scent gland into the flesh of her sex, mixing more of his bonding oil and her slick together. The incredible tingling started up right away, but more intense now that she was so frustrated. It was as if her flesh was inflamed and desperate for touch.

Once he'd slathered his oil all over her, he fit his mouth to her clit and sucked.

After all the teasing and tormenting, this move was unexpected and forced a scream out of her. Bowing her back, she sucked in air as the most powerful orgasm she'd ever experienced rolled through her. Fire washed across her skin, stealing her breath and turning her muscles rigid.

Tamerin kept sucking on her, drawing out her pleasure. It didn't matter that he still had her hands trapped, she couldn't have moved even if she wanted to. Her joints felt locked in place. Was this what it was like for other women? She'd been missing out her entire life!

"No, no more!" she begged when her muscles finally released and she collapsed. Her clit was so sensitive his touch bordered on painful. Letting go of her wrists, he sat back on his heels and surveyed her body. She remained wantonly spread out before him; she didn't bother trying to move.

"Your turn?" she questioned, bending her knees as an invitation.

"I want to," he admitted, breathing hard as if he'd sprinted a long distance. His eyes kept roving over her body, even as his thrumming rumble speeded up into a purr. "But we're breeding compatible and I don't have any seed blockers with me."

She didn't know what a seed blocker was, but the context told her everything she needed to know.

"Don't worry about it," she was quick to assure him. She swiped a lazy hand in the air as if sweeping away his concerns. "Part of the contract was to allow a med tech to implant a birth limiter. Until it's removed, I can't get pregnant."

Tamerin jerked and sounded a brief rattle of angry wasps. "Wasn't that painful?"

She grinned up at him. "It wasn't pleasant, but once they're in you don't feel it at all."

Still, Tamerin didn't move. "I don't want to hurt you."

"Then don't," she answered simply. "You lie down here and let me take your spot. I'll be as gentle with you as you were with me."

A rumble of amusement burst out of him. "That is definitely a threat, my sweet songbird."

"Payback is a bitch," she agreed and then patted the bed next to her. "Now take off those pants and lie down. It's your turn."

CHAPTER 9

Tamerin hadn't expected this. He'd started their interaction fully intending to give Lasha all the pleasure he could before tucking her small body against his so she could fall into a satiated sleep.

But now she was staring at him expectantly.

"I said pants off," she reminded him.

He wanted to. Every part of him wanted to shed the too-tight garment and present his mating shaft to her. But what if she was intimidated by his size or didn't like how he differed from human males?

At least he didn't have to worry about her seeing his scarred flesh pouch. That had long since retracted under his aching seed sac and was safely hidden from view.

"Come on," she pushed. "I want to see. It's my turn to play."

"Let me," he hesitated, glancing over at the open door to the cleansing unit. When he'd been a youth just finished with his final growth shift, he remembered taking himself in hand many times to alleviate the constant need to mate. If he was careful he could keep his mating shaft and seed sac from folding back into his flesh pouch. Lasha could explore his body and he wouldn't have to worry about giving in to his raging lust.

If he was honest with himself, he'd never felt so close to being out of control in his life.

"Tamerin?"

While he'd been distracted, Lasha had gotten to her knees on the bed and crawled over to him. With him sitting back on his heels and her kneeling up, they were almost eye to eye.

"Hey," she whispered, cupping his cheeks with her hands. Her palms felt so unbelievably soft, and when she glided her fingers over his scent glands, shocks of pleasure shot down his spine. "I like you. No matter what's in those pants, I'm not going to go running. We might have to get creative if you've got bone spurs or hooks, but I'm sure we can figure it out."

"No spurs or hooks," he promised.

"Then we're good," she said with a grin. "Even if you're too super-sized to fit, we can have some fun. Do you trust me?"

"More than I've ever trusted anyone," he answered honestly. She didn't know it, but she held his life in her hands now. The moment he'd started rubbing his bonding oil on her, he'd felt the shift inside his chest, something dormant being triggered. If he wasn't fully scent-bonded to her now, he would be very soon.

Leaning forward she brushed her lips against his. "I won't let you down."

When she pulled away and sat back, he rose from the bed to tug off his pants. The expensive, well-made garment fell to the floor, pooling at his feet. Keeping his eyes downcast, he stepped out of them and stood, letting her take in his naked form.

"Oh, you're perfect."

Her breathy words made his eyes fly up to meet hers. She was smiling as she stared at his fully erect mating shaft.

"Can I touch you?" she asked, without looking up.

"Of course," he grunted, bracing himself for her gentle caresses.

This was going to be torture.

She was hesitant at first, running her fingers under his rock-hard shaft, rubbing across the tip and then down the top.

"You're big," she murmured, leaning in close to examine him. "But not scary-big. A nice-big."

He couldn't respond. He was too busy focusing on remaining still. When she brought her mouth close to the head of his shaft and flicked her tongue across it, he nearly came right there.

"Oh, you taste like cardamom here too," she announced with a pleased expression. Then she licked him again, as if he was a piece of candy she wanted to savor. "Mmmm, I want to taste your cum. I bet it's going to be amazing."

If she wasn't careful she'd find out what he tasted like sooner rather than later. Clenching his fingers into a tight fist, he dug the tips of his claws into his palms, fighting for control.

Leaning her head to the side, she examined the length of his shaft. "You have ridges. Humans don't have these ridges."

"Many Talins don't have them either," he explained, managing to get the words out despite how tight his jaw muscles felt. "I'm considered a throwback because of the ridges. They get larger as I—oh!"

As he spoke she put her face right against his shaft and ran her tongue up the length. Then she pulled the tip into her mouth and sucked. The intense pleasure made his head go back and his mouth open in a soundless cry. His aroused rumble was loud enough to echo in the room as her hot, wet mouth worked on the tip of his mating shaft.

Her hand reached up to cup his seed sack, another difference between him and human males. Not that he felt the need to explain that to her. She didn't seem to care about the difference, and forming words while her lips were wrapped around his shaft wasn't going to happen.

He whimpered when she pulled away. Looking down, their eyes met. Her lips were red, wet, and swollen as she grinned broadly. "Your ridges got bigger. I think I could tease them into swelling even more."

Those words set off some primal part of him. With a roar, he grabbed her up and thumped her onto the bed. She gasped from surprise but didn't fight him.

Grabbing her ankles, he pulled her legs apart. She was still wet from his mouth, bonding oil, and her own slick from earlier. Their combined scents made him moan. From now on he was going to make sure she was always covered in his scent, especially the soft, dark skin of her sex.

Fitting the tip of his shaft against her, he pushed in, eager to feel her hot warmth surrounding him. Her shocked gasp and sudden tensing made him freeze, his rumble of arousal giving way to worry.

What was he doing? He could be hurting her!

"My sweet songbird," he whispered brokenly and began to pull back. "I'm so very sorry!" But Lasha wrapped her legs around him and held him in place.

"No, it's good!" she cried. "So good! I promise. Fuck, please don't stop!"

Relief made him feel giddy. He started the slow, thrumming rumble and pushed in, easing his shaft into her soft sheath. The feeling was beyond pleasure. Her body squeezed him as if trying to draw him in deeper.

"Yes!" she breathed, clutching at him tighter with her legs. Her arms were out to the sides, gripping the bedding. When he'd started moving again, her eyes had closed. Now they fluttered up and met his. "More. I'm so close. It won't take much."

He refused to rush. It wasn't about trying to tease her. He was fearful of losing control and hurting her, but she wouldn't be denied. Even after he'd seated himself inside her, his shaft pulsing with the sensation of being surrounded by her hot, tight flesh, she wasn't appeased.

"Tamerin!" she shouted. "Move damn it!"

Still trying to maintain control, he eased out and was going to slowly push back in when she locked her ankles around his waist. In a show of strength he didn't expect of her, she used that grip to slam her pelvis against his, making them both moan.

"Like that," she demanded. Panting and at the end of her strength, she let go with her legs to flop back on the bed. His shaft was pulled from her body and he gazed down at her open, waiting sex with a hunger he'd never known before.

Now that he had both permission and proof she could take him, he grabbed her hips, fitted himself at her opening, and thrust home. He set up a punishing pace that left them both gasping as the sound of flesh slapping flesh filled the room.

She was groaning and begging while he moved against her. She went rigid under him, her eyes shut and her head back. Then he felt it. Crying out, she convulsed under him. Her sex tightening around his shaft and ushering in his own climax. Sounding a rattle of triumph, he filled Lasha with his seed.

They hung there, both of them frozen in a moment of pure ecstasy. Time stilled. He felt both at peace and energized all at once. Opening her eyes, she met his gaze and the words from a traditional marriage ceremony flowed out of him.

"My body will act as a shield between you and all others. My strength and my loyalty are yours to command. I'll guard you 'til my dying day. If any other thinks to do you harm, I'll meet them on the challenge field. We are as one, and I will promise to always act accordingly."

Her expression turned gentle and happy. "I love you too, big guy," she whispered back.

CHAPTER 10

"Are you sure you want to walk outside?" Tamerin asked, sounding a soft buzzing-wasps rattle of anxiety. "We were very energetic last night. Perhaps you should spend today resting."

Ignoring Tamerin's worry, Lasha threw off the covers and swung her legs to the floor. Pushing off the low bed with her hand, she rose to her feet. Ah, it was nice to stand up and not feel any dizziness at all.

"I promise I'm fine," she assured for the fourth time in the last ten minutes. "And after this walk we can fool around again."

"If you have enough energy," Tamerin said, making a rattle that was reminiscent of a hatch whooshing open and closed rapidly. That had to be his worried sound. Bouncing from worry to anxiety couldn't be good for him.

"Last night was fun, but I think I've recovered by now," she teased with a grin. He didn't sound any humorous rumble, which told her he was too tense to respond to her banter.

"We were very active last night and then early this morning," he reminded her. "Too much physical activity could inhibit recovery."

"I'm feeling great," Lasha argued. "And I think the sex helped me feel even better. Besides, you did most of the work. Remember? And I'm looking forward to letting you do more work later. It's something else fun we get to do while I recover besides you reading to me or sleeping."

"Does my sexual skill set rank higher or lower than sleeping?" Tamerin asked with a sexy, throbbing rumble.

"Let's see how you do tonight," she teased and then realized they had a minor problem. She was naked. The remnants of the tunic she'd been wearing were still on the floor at her feet. "Did you say you bought several of those tunics?"

Striding over to the room's only table, he pulled a bright blue item out of a pile and showed it to her. "Do you like this?"

"Perfect," she agreed, holding out a hand. Instead of tossing or handing it to her, he bundled it up as he came to stand in front of her.

"Arms up," he instructed. Obediently she raised her arms, and he lowered the tunic over her head. He was careful and even dropped to his knees to work the tunic down over her hips, tugging on the hem to make sure it wasn't bunched anywhere. She felt both silly and special to have Tamerin dressing her like this. But mostly she felt loved.

Everything about their interactions screamed love to her, even if he never said the words. And now that she knew he wasn't involved with Zia, she could look back at everything he'd done for her through the lens of affection instead of obligation.

"There," he said once she was dressed. "But it's not complete yet."

Standing up, he returned to the pile and rummaged around again until he found the item he was looking for. This time he pulled out a finely crafted, jeweled belt that made her gasp.

"Tamerin, that's too nice for me," she protested even as she remained still so he could wrap it around her waist. He sank to his knees again to secure the belt and then sat back on his heels to admire the fit.

"This is only barely good enough for you," he argued. "I plan to buy you many fine things."

"I'm not sure I've done anything to deserve your gifts yet," she countered, running her fingers over the belt. This was by far the nicest piece of clothing she'd ever had.

"You survived," he answered simply. "Despite your disadvantages and the pain you've suffered, you endured and persisted. In this world with the odds you faced, that is enough to warrant everything I plan to give you and more."

Looking up, she smiled at him. "Don't go crazy, okay? This is wonderful. Perfect. Amazing. But I don't need a lot of stuff. I just,…" She blinked because tears were suddenly burning in her eyes. "I just want you. I don't want you to suddenly get frustrated with me and leave. I know I can be hard to teach, but I'll always try my best and—"

Pulling her down onto his lap, Tamerin cut off her words with a kiss. As she melted into his embrace, the smell of cardamom filled her nose and calm washed over her. By the time he pulled back, her tears were gone.

"I'm your Talin," he whispered. "I'd never willingly leave you."

"If you're my Talin, I'm your human," she murmured back, smiling. "I'm sorry, I get worked up sometimes."

"We all have scars," he noted. "Some of us have them on the outside and some of us carry them around on the inside."

"Yeah, that's a good way of putting it," she agreed. "Thanks. Maybe you can buy me an information square with voice capabilities?"

"The moment I can find them, we're buying three," Tamerin agreed, setting her on her feet.

"Three might be overkill," she responded with a laugh.

"Three is a minimum," he argued. "One small one you can carry on your person at all times. One regular-sized one to keep in our domicile and another regular-sized one to travel with when we go places."

"But isn't the small one for traveling?" she asked, confused.

"The small one is for going from one domicile to the next. The bigger one would be for traveling long distances. I don't want you struggling to interface with a small information square when I could provide you with a larger one at your request."

She chewed on that a moment before shrugging her shoulders. "I still vote for one or two, but I'm sure we can find uses for more. It's not like others can't use them too."

"If necessary, they can be lent out to others," Tamerin agreed, but she got the distinct impression he didn't like that idea. It was cute that he was possessive of her toys for her. Toys she didn't even have yet!

Getting to his feet, he picked up the thick utilitarian coat he'd bought her. "I'll carry this for now so you won't be burdened by its weight before you get cold."

She knew better than to argue. Sliding her feet into her slippers, she held out her hand for his. "I'm ready. Let's go. I'm ready to see things other than these four walls."

"Go slowly," Tamerin cautioned as he led her out the room door and down the hall. He kept his strides short and slow, allowing her to match his pace with ease.

No one was in the hall or the lift, which made the journey down into the lobby quiet except for Tamerin's purring. When the lift doors opened, the lobby was almost entirely empty. Only two Vicpors were standing near a food kiosk. One was a female who worked for the hotel and the other was a guest gesturing at the flashing kiosk display.

Both looked up as they walked through the lobby but immediately went back to their conversation.

Lasha focused on the lobby doors. "I want to see if I can walk all the way to Ilee's office."

Tamerin stopped walking and sounded his whooshing-hatch rattle of worry. "That's farther than you've gone before."

"That's the point," she argued. "Remember what Ilee said? I shouldn't leave until I can walk all the way to her office. Well, let's see if today is the day we can finally make plans to get out of here."

Tamerin sounded his purring rumble. "You must be eager to leave Glakor."

"Aren't you?" she challenged. "It's not like anyone here likes this place. Its only redeeming quality is how close it is to a major shipping lane and the abundance of water. Otherwise I'm not sure Vicpors would have bothered colonizing Glakor. They'd have sold it off to someone else instead."

"All true," Tamerin conceded as he lifted the ugly coat and held it out for her. "But I'm unwilling to do anything that might compromise your fragile health. Let's step out of the lobby first."

"Sure," Lasha agreed, confident she'd be able to walk the short distance to Ilee's office. She worked her arms into the coat and let Tamerin secure the front closures. It hung nearly to her ankles and was so thick it was stiff and mildly uncomfortable. Wrapping both her arms around Tamerin's left arm, she smiled up at him. "Ready."

They walked to the lobby doors. As usual the sun was shining brightly outside, but the moment they passed the air barrier around the door, the cold hit her hard.

Clenching her jaw to keep her teeth from chattering, she pointed to a kiosk one building down. Tamerin, who was still only wearing his pants and belt, began walking her to it. At least the wind wasn't blowing. Most days were calm, despite the city being surrounded by a vast planet-wide ocean. Occasionally, a freezing wind would whip through the city. It could be deadly if you were caught out in it, but today there wasn't even a breeze.

"I think that's a food kiosk," he told her as they drew closer. "Are you hungry? When we get back to the room, I can order more food to be delivered on top of the regular meals."

"More curious," she said, proud that she got the words out. Then she couldn't take it any longer. "Aren't you cold?"

"The temperature is low, but within my tolerances," he answered, and envy spiked through her.

"Must be nice," she mumbled.

"It is," he agreed, oblivious to her sarcasm. His response made her laugh. Laughing in the cold made her lungs hurt a little, but the happy mood was worth it.

By the time they got to the kiosk, she remembered why she'd rarely left the factory. Her lips were numb, her eyes were watering, and she was pretty sure her feet were frozen blocks of ice. At least having her hands wrapped around Tamerin's arm was keeping her fingers warm.

"Hmm, it's Vicpor food," Tamerin said as he peered at the kiosk's display. "What is an egg agent?"

"Vicpors lay eggs," Lasha explained. "Egg agents supposedly promote females to lay large clutches of eggs, but it's all snake oil."

"What's snake oil?" Tamerin asked as they turned away from the kiosk.

Lasha laughed. "You know, I'm not sure. It was something my grandmother used to say. It means it's not real. It doesn't work."

"A lot of those kinds of products are out there," Tamerin commented as he turned them around. She didn't protest when he guided her back to the hotel, only pausing to let a public transport cart flash by.

Once the path was clear, Lasha focused her eyes on the hotel doors. She was determined not to complain or shiver too badly. By tomorrow, she was sure she'd make it to Ilee's office. Then she was off Glakor forever!

That raised a question for her. "We haven't talked about where we're going after we leave here."

"I thought we'd go to Sorana," Tamerin answered.

"That's where Zia and Palforma are. Right?" Lasha clarified.

"Yes, exactly," Tamerin agreed.

"We're not going somewhere closer first?" she asked.

Tamerin sounded the slow, irregular rumble of confusion. "Don't you want to see Zia?"

"I do, but when do I meet your family?" Lasha asked. She didn't want him to think his family didn't matter. When he hesitated, she got a bad feeling. "Um, does your family not like humans? Or is it that I'm not Talin?"

"They adore humans," he assured her quickly, with a soothing purr. "But they're all the way on Talarian. That's at the heart of the Talin empire. Sorana is on the outskirts. It's easier to go there first."

Tamerin wasn't lying. He'd never lie to her, but she could tell he wasn't being entirely honest. When she spoke, she chose her words carefully.

"You can tell me. If anything is wrong or if you're in any kind of legal trouble, it won't matter to me," she assured him. "I'm your human. Remember? And you're my Talin."

The doors to the lobby slid open and Tamerin urged her to step a little quicker into the sheltered warmth. Even as he did that, his purring got loud for a moment in reaction to her words.

"I'll never forget that," he promised. "I have no legal issues with the Talin Empire or any other civilization."

She opened her mouth to ask him when they'd visit his family. He distracted her by picking her up and cradling her to his chest, sounding his purr the entire time. "Now, you must be cold from our short walk outside. How should we warm you up? A bath?"

"Or you could use your tongue," she offered.

"Why would I—" he cut off his words with a sexy, thrumming rumble. "Oh, yes. Let's do it that way. I think you've had enough exercise for the day. Brace yourself."

The next thing she knew, he was jogging to the lift. Laughing, she wrapped her arms around his neck and held on. "This time I'm going to use my tongue on you," she whispered in his ear hole as the lift doors opened. "All over you. Just like you did to me!"

That he stumbled a bit when he stepped forward filled her with all kinds of satisfaction.

CHAPTER 11

Tamerin's Ident Cube pinged, drawing his attention down to where it was attached to his belt and resting on his leg. The side facing up was blinking slowly, demanding attention. He tapped it a few times and then grunted along with a sharp rattle of surprise.

"Interesting. The message I sent has a return message."

Lasha frowned slightly, unhappy with the interruption of their cuddle and reading time. "So soon? That's not possible."

"If all the stations were aligned and the queues short, it could happen this quickly," Tamerin pointed out.

"What did Zia say? Or is it from Palforma?"

"I don't know," he said with a buzzing rattle of annoyance. "The comm station is requesting I pay an extra fee. And they won't release it to my Ident. I have to appear at the comms office. How unnecessarily complicated."

Lasha got a bad feeling. "That doesn't sound like something a Vicpor would do," she warned him. "The extra fee, yes. But making you physically go across the city is unusual if you've already sent one message and input all your Ident codes at the comm station. There's no reason to make you do it again."

"I'm sure it's nothing," Tamerin answered. He looked down at where their hands were joined. "I'm afraid you're going to need to release me or we'll never find out what's in the message."

His tone was humorous, but it didn't lessen Lasha's anxiety. "Let me go with you," she requested. "I've spent the last four years working for the Vicpors. I'm good at reading their tone and body language."

"You already did your walk for the day," he argued. "And we're going to try walking all the way to Ilee's office tomorrow. If we make it, a ship is arriving later that day. We can book passage on it."

"I can do all of it," she countered. "You can carry me to the comms station. And tomorrow I'll walk to Ilee and we'll leave. There's no reason to leave me behind today."

"It's not only the exercise. It's exposure to the cold. Don't be stubborn about your health," he responded. "Be patient and have some faith in me. Watch the next Ugarian soap opera, and I'll be back before they've finished warbling the last lines."

She wasn't ready to give up yet. "Do you have any weapons?"

"I have my military dagger and a single-use projectile weapon," he told her. "Will it make you feel better if I take one of them with me?"

"Yes," she agreed quickly. "Take both of them, but keep them hidden if you can."

Without another word, he reached over and picked up his bag. It didn't take much rummaging before he pulled out the small, single-use projectile weapon and tucked it into the pouch on his belt. Then he pulled out the dagger.

She'd expected something smallish and sleek. The thing Tamerin presented was the length of her arm with an ornate handle. When he pulled it out of the sheath, she was dazzled by the iridescent blue shine of the blade. It looked deadly sharp and highly intimidating.

"That's not a dagger!" she exclaimed. "That's a damn sword!"

The sound of marbles-clacking hit her ears. She'd made him laugh.

"This is the weapon all Talins receive when they complete their military training. We get to keep them if we retire as honorable soldiers. Many will wear them as civilians to remind others of their role in maintaining the prestige of the Talin Empire. It's the only weapon that doesn't require special permission to carry on our homeworld, Talarian."

As he talked, he sheathed the dagger and secured it to his belt. With the hidden gun and a big-ass knife openly displayed, Lasha was feeling much better about Tamerin leaving.

"Hurry back, okay? And if anything doesn't seem right, leave."

"Of course," Tamerin assured her. Getting up, he made sure several nutrient packs and canisters of drinking water were within easy reach. "And I can pick you up several more tunic dresses while I'm out."

"No, don't bother," she responded. "Just come straight back."

His purring got loud. "I'll be quick. I won't leave you alone for too long. I promise."

And then he was out the door, and she was left to wait with anxiety as her only companion.

No way would she be able to sleep, so she did as he'd suggested. It took a moment to uncover the information square from the nest of pillows they called a bed, but soon she was embroiled in a Ugarian soap opera.

A conversation between a sibling pod was getting heated, and she was worried for the smallest sibling. She was so tense the door chime made her gasp and fumble the information square off its perch on her knees.

After she stopped the episode and set the square aside, she eyed the door. Why would anyone be chiming this room?

With careful movements she got up and walked to the door display. A few taps on familiar icons brought up an image of three unfamiliar Vicpors standing on the other side of the door.

The bad feeling from earlier returned even stronger. Clearing her throat she pressed the speech button on the display and used her best Vicpor voice.

"Who are you and what do you want?"

All three of the Vicpors jumped a little at her strong tone and forceful words. It made her smirk.

The one in the middle spoke. "We're here looking for a small human named Lasha Chandra. We have a work contract termination she needs to sign."

That was bullshit. Tamerin had bought and nullified her work contract. She couldn't read it, but he'd tried to show it to her back before he found out she couldn't read.

Anger at these Vicpor and worry for Tamerin caused her skin to flush and made it easy to hiss out the harsh Vicpor syllables. "I don't know who you're talking about. I'm here nesting and waiting for my contract mate. Go away."

Vicpors didn't do marriages. They would sign contracts, meet in a neutral location, and then breed until one of them got pregnant. Vicpors always laid multiple eggs, so after laying the clutch, the couple would divide up the eggs and separate.

That was the only reason this hotel stayed in business.

"We're sorry for the intrusion," the one in the middle said as all three of them backed away slowly. A Vicpor waiting to be bred wasn't someone to mess with. When hormones were high, Vicpors were just as likely to get into a fight as to have sex with each other.

She watched until the three of them disappeared from sight, all of them talking at once. She couldn't catch much, but she thought they were angry that the person they'd bribed gave them the wrong room.

No doubt they'd be back, and she needed to get out before that happened.

Moving quickly, she dressed. First she pulled on all three of the tunic dresses Tamerin had purchased. She probably looked silly, but the easiest way to pack them was to wear them, and they'd provide a little extra warmth.

She only had the pair of flimsy, hard-soled slippers Tamerin had bought her for the short walks outside. He'd long since thrown away her old work uniform and ratty boots. Her feet were going to get cold quickly, but it couldn't be helped. She was thankful for the heavy-duty coat Tamerin had bought for walking outside. It was bulky, but it was one of the best available on Glakor.

Once dressed she packed everything up in Tamerin's bag. Between the two of them they didn't have much, but she also packed all the nutrient bars and water canisters she could fit. By the time she was done, the bag was overfull, and she almost didn't get the closures to catch.

Hefting the bag onto her shoulder was another matter. She nearly toppled over, but on the second try, she got it on a shoulder and staggered out of the room. To her relief the hallway was clear, and she made it to the lift, which was also empty.

Her heart was beating hard when the lift let her off in the center of the lobby. She'd pulled the hood of her coat over her head, but her small stature was a dead giveaway that she was human. Or at least wasn't a Vicpor or related species.

Thankfully the lobby was far busier than normal.

Conversation buzzed and foot traffic flowed around her as she made her way through the crowded area. Even though individuals in her path moved out of the way after some verbal urging, it was still slow going. The heavy bag impeded her pace as much as the crowd. Maybe she shouldn't have been so greedy and packed less. But memories of going thirsty and hungry were too fresh for her to leave anything behind.

The trip through the lobby was nerve racking. She wanted to look everywhere, but she didn't want to draw attention to herself.

She thought she'd made it when she stepped outside but was faced with another issue. An unbelievably harsh, freezing wind slapped her in the face the moment she passed the air barrier around the outside door. She gasped and fought back a coughing fit. Her skin was immediately chilled despite the layers of tunic dresses and heavy coat. Her toes started to tingle right away, telling her she didn't have much time before they went numb and made walking even more difficult.

About once a year Glakor experienced what everyone referred to as a "cold day." Cold days happened when a howling wind came off the southern ocean and swept across the entire city. Sometimes it was bad enough to halt production at some of the poorly constructed and insulated factories. She'd seen city carriers frozen in place by the frigid wind. And it was always bad enough to drive everyone indoors to seek shelter.

Of course today would be a cold day! Wasn't that just her luck?

Shivering violently, she ducked her head and started toward the med tech's office. She could make it. The wind hadn't really gotten started yet, so it was probably only about twenty below. Soon it would be closer to ninety below and could go even lower depending on how long the wind lasted.

She was sure she could convince Ilee to let her hide there until Tamerin got back. And she could promise payment from Tamerin for letting Lasha occupy a chair. No Vicpor would refuse that deal.

But first she had to get there. The wind was against her and pushed violently as she leaned into it. It ripped the hood off her head, tried to tear the clothes from her body, and pulled hard at the heavy bag. She'd only made it a few dozen feet when she had to take shelter in an alcove. The cold was irritating her lungs. Despite her best efforts, she was coughing hard enough to see stars behind her closed eyelids.

"I think this is her!"

Before she could even raise her head to look up, a pincer grabbed her. She lashed out but her blows were ineffective against the Vicpor's hard carapace. She was quickly out of breath. Narrowing her eyes against the low temperature, she stared at the male holding her. She didn't recognize the Vicpor or the other two rushing to his side. "This is the runaway."

If there was a runaway bounty on her, it couldn't have been filed by Tamerin. If Oglee was trying to claim her, he was in for all kinds of legal trouble!

"I'm not a runaway!" she gasped out, her voice weak from the coughing. "I'm out with permission. A male of wealth named Tamerin owns me. If you take me, it'll be stealing. You're going to get fined!"

Money was the quickest way to get them to release her. The threat of a fine didn't make them let go, but they did hesitate.

"Could Oglee be mistaken?" the one holding her asked. "What if the contract was legally transferred and she isn't a runaway?"

"We should take her to him anyway," another responded. "It's too cold to be out here arguing. We take her to him and still get our money. Any fine will have to be paid by Oglee, not us."

No, this was bad.

"My true owner will pay you more to get me back," she promised them between coughing fits.

"Ba, who would pay extra for a worker so small and weak?" the one holding her mocked.

"A Talin bought me, not a Vicpor," she explained. She didn't expect that one sentence to be so effective.

All three of them hissed in shock and the one holding her loosened his grip. "A Talin? Here on Glakor?"

"Yes! He's a Talin and decorated soldier! He'll be very angry if I'm not allowed to continue on my way," she said, trying to sound confident even though one of her lungs was trying to cough its way out of her chest.

"Our governor wouldn't let him do anything to us," one of them said, but he didn't sound confident.

"He might not be able to stop him," the one holding her commented, sounding scared.

"Then he'd be executed himself," the third declared. "Wouldn't he? Any violence against one of us is an automatic death sentence for outsiders."

"Not if the trade treaty with the Talin military has gone through," the one holding her reminded them. "That treaty gives diplomatic immunity to their military and political leaders when visiting."

"He must be here negotiating," the second one decided. "Let her go on her way. I've heard stories about their warriors using any reason to fight, even with each other. We don't want to upset him."

"That's true! He's a violent one, even for a Talin," Lasha lied. "And he hasn't gotten to kill anyone in weeks." She gave them her most sincere expression. "Just this morning he was tempted to use his claws on me because he claimed to be bored."

The one holding her let go as if she was contagious. "Get away from us."

All three of them backed away, and if Lasha wasn't coughing, she'd probably be laughing. Stepping out of the alcove, she watched them all move away while keeping a wary eye out for her murderous Talin. Grinning between coughing fits, she crossed the empty street to the med tech's office.

The cold had forced everyone to take shelter, and it got even more intense as she stepped inside the med tech's building. The door wobbled on its track as the wind put increasing pressure on it as it tried to close. Relief filled her once the door was safely shut and she was fully sheltered.

Still, she was forced to stand in the foyer of the building and cough. Her lungs didn't give her a break, and she started getting dizzy. Unfortunately she'd stumbled into the center of the foyer without even a wall close by to lean against.

There was no help for it. She was going to have to sit on the floor. And that's where Oglee found her when he forced his way past the reluctant door and into the building.

"Lasha! Oh, the Great Makbee has seen fit to bless me," Oglee intoned, clacking both his pincers and waving all four of his arms with excitement.

Those words and the look on his shiny, black insect-like face made it clear that she wasn't going to be able to talk herself out of this situation. Oglee hadn't sent those other three Vicpors after her because of a work contract issue. He'd done it out of pure spite.

"You're going to regret this," she wheezed out.

"I can promise you I won't," he hissed.

Another seven Vicpors piled into the room as Oglee closed a pincer around her arm. Shit, this was going to be bad.

CHAPTER 12

Tamerin cursed himself for a fool as he stared at the empty rented room. Lasha's suspicions had been correct. He'd gotten to the comms office only to find no waiting message or any record of him being summoned. When he took a closer look at the notice he'd received, it was easy to spot a few small details that revealed it came from a fake account made to look official.

He'd rushed back only to be confronted with a missing Lasha.

He saw no signs of a struggle, but that might mean they took her by surprise. And his little human was still recovering. She wouldn't be able to put up much of a fight against anyone, even another human.

"I'll always listen to you from now on," he promised the empty room. Then he noticed his bag was missing. Looking around he realized all the items he'd accumulated were gone also. Had his little Lasha decided to flee the room before any threat arrived?

And if so, where would she go?

Turning on his heels he hurried back down to the lobby. It was crowded and busy. No one wanted to brave the sudden freezing wind that had begun as he'd traveled back across town. He rushed to a Vicpor he recognized. She was in charge of keeping the lobby kiosks running.

"Have you seen my human?" he asked, sounding a single sharp, demanding rattle Lasha had described as a metal weapon being struck hard against a shield. She was fanciful with her descriptions of his rumbles and rattles.

"Human? Is that the little soft creature you take for walks?" the Vicpor asked.

"Yes, that's Lasha," Tamerin agreed. "Have you seen her?"

"Has she run away?" the Vicpor asked. "We didn't know we were to keep her confined, or we could have put a limiting collar on her so she couldn't leave the building without you."

He growled, making the Vicpor take a step back. "Did you see her?"

"Yes, not long ago." The Vicpor pointed to the front door of the lobby. "She was wearing a heavy coat and had a large bag full of items. If she's stolen from you, we can't be blamed. Unless you—"

Tamerin stepped close to the Vicpor, looming over her. "Which direction did she walk?"

"East," the Vicpor answered and then backed away from him. "I'm needed in the office."

Knowing that was all he would get from her, he left. At least he knew Lasha had been alone. She was running instead of being kidnapped, which was a good sign.

Turning east once he passed the lobby's air shield, he realized immediately where she had gone. The med tech's office would have been an ideal location to hide and a close place to take shelter.

Battling the wind that had gained strength in the brief time he'd been inside, he ran the short distance to Ilee's building. Talins could handle a wide range of temperatures, but this freezing wind was at the limit he could stand without any protective covering. If Lasha got caught out in this, she'd already be dead. He had to believe she'd left soon after him and was safely waiting in Ilee's office.

The wind was so fierce he was forced to help the door slide open when it got stuck halfway. Grunting with the effort, he heaved and the door shuddered. It took a lot of muscle, but he got the doors open far enough to slip inside. The air barrier triggered, breaking up the current of the howling wind enough for the door's mechanism to slam them back closed once he wasn't holding open it anymore.

Now that he was inside the small foyer, he looked around to find it crowded by Vicpors. That wasn't a surprise. Everyone on the street would've needed to take shelter somewhere. But these individuals were all huddled around something. At first, he assumed this was a work group who'd taken shelter in the building, but then he saw a hint of familiar spiky, black hair.

"Lasha!" he shouted, grabbing the closest Vicpor and hurling him away.

All the Vicpors turned to face him, allowing him a clear view of Lasha's face. She was being held in the pincer of her former overseer, Oglee. She didn't look scared and wasn't crying, but when their eyes met he saw relief.

"You're okay!" Lasha cried out. "I was so worried about you!"

"About me?" he answered with a surprised rattle. "You're the one in danger."

"I am now," she agreed with amazing calmness. "But I wasn't earlier and I didn't know if you'd been hurt or something."

He didn't like the sound of her voice. She was hoarse as if she'd been coughing again. He needed to assess her health. "How much do your lungs hurt?"

"I'm fine," she insisted, even as she stifled a cough.

The Vicpors, including Oglee, were a silent audience to their conversation. Their gazes bounced back and forth as they talked.

"I'll get you warm and demand more medication from Ilee," he assured her. "All of this could've been avoided. I'm sorry I didn't listen. You were right. No message was waiting for me."

"Told you!" she crowed and then winced as her triumph caused her to cough again. When she spoke, her voice was a little wheezy. "It wasn't a trap. Was it? You didn't have to fight your way out. Did you?"

"No," Tamerin assured her. "It looks like you were the only target. And I see you were trying to get away, but they found you."

"I got lucky with the first bunch of idiots Oglee sent," she explained. "But then—"

"Enough of this!" Oglee roared. "I'm in charge here."

"You wish," Lasha muttered loudly enough for everyone to hear. Several of the Vicpors hissed with amusement.

Oglee wasn't pleased.

Raising the pincer gripping Lasha's arm, he lifted her off her feet and made her cry out in pain as he stared at Tamerin.

"You came into my facility and humiliated me over this creature. I don't run away from anyone! At first I didn't care because you'd paid a lot for a dying worker. But then I heard she recovered and can work again."

"Let her go before I rip the pincers from your body," Tamerin threatened.

Undaunted, Oglee shook her. "I sold you her contract at the standard rate because you two fooled me. You owe me more money!"

"He paid as much as you asked," Lasha said, tugging at his pincer with her free hand.

"I should have gotten more! I've found out that Talins coll—"

Tamerin didn't let Oglee finish that sentence. In one fluid motion, he pulled his dagger from its sheath and sent it flying. It impaled the thick part of Oglee's pincer. Dark brown goo oozed out and the pincer went limp, dropping Lasha to the floor.

Oglee cried out in pain and clutched his useless pincer.

"Serves you right," Lasha taunted. "Tamerin paid for my work contract fair and square!"

"Let Lasha walk to me and I won't hurt anyone else," Tamerin offered the group. He was fearful of Lasha getting injured by the other Vicpors around her. He didn't like backing down from a fight, even when he was so outnumbered, but Lasha's safety came first.

She tried to move, but Oglee stepped in front of her, waving his ruined pincer in the air. "How dare you!" he cried out.

"Uncle?" one of the other Vicpors said. "What should we do?"

"Kill him," Oglee instructed as he cradled his pincer with the dagger still run through it. "We'll dissolve the body at the factory. He can simply disappear."

"And we share his wealth, right?" another one asked.

"I won't even take a cut," Oglee agreed.

"Tamerin, run!" Lasha shouted. She'd ducked out from behind Oglee but was blocked by a wall of Vicpors.

"Guard yourself," Tamerin ordered her as he pulled his single-shot projectile weapon and tossed it to her. He was proud of the deft way she plucked it out of the air.

But then she did the unexpected.

"The first one of you who touches Tamerin dies!" she shouted, holding the weapon up to show everyone she could fulfill her threat. One of the Vicpors reached for the weapon, but Lasha nimbly avoided his grip. Her small stature was an advantage in the tight, crowded space. Even though she kept coughing, she was still quick to move.

"I mean it!" she shouted between coughs. "I'll put a hole through anyone who hurts Tamerin!"

Both frustration and adoration filled him. Despite his instructions, it was obvious she wouldn't fire the weapon unless he was in danger. It wouldn't be long before one of the Vicpors cornered her and took the weapon away. He needed to get himself between her and the rest of the Vicpors.

"What's going on here?" a new voice shouted, making them all look at the open door of one of the suites. It was Ilee, her pincer clacking open and shut in agitation.

The distraction was just enough for Lasha to slip through the crowd of Vicpors and slide past the med tech into the suite. "Lasha? What—"

"No!" Oglee raged. "That human belongs to me!"

The Vicpors in the foyer tried to rush the door, but the med tech was quick to step back and shut it. Several bodies bounced off it, but the sturdy door didn't move.

Lasha was safe. Relief filled Tamerin. By the time Oglee turned his attention back to him, the warrior was ready.

"Get him!" Oglee shouted. "Extra money to whoever ends his life!"

Growling, Tamerin faced the Vicpors, delighted at this change of circumstances. Now he was free to do some damage. It'd been a long time since he'd gotten to fight, and this was going to be fun!

Quills up, claws out, and sounding a war rattle, he roared and jumped at the closest Vicpor.

CHAPTER 13

Lasha could hear the sound of fighting in the foyer. "Open the door," she demanded. "I need to get back out there and help Tamerin!"

"Help him how?" Ilee shot back, blocking the door.

"With this," Lasha declared, holding up the weapon. The med tech waggled her mandible, the Vicpor version of a derisive snort.

"Do you even know how to fire that?" she asked.

Unfortunately Ilee made a good point. Lasha examined the weapon and found a spot near her thumb that was probably the trigger. "Uh, I press here?"

Ilee sounded an exasperated sigh. "That's the release so you can fire it." With the tip of a pincer she pointed to a spot on the grip. "You have to press here at the same time. That's how this one works. And this type of weapon only fires once. I'm sure you don't even know how to aim it."

"I don't need to aim if I get close enough," Lasha answered defensively. "Now that I know how it works, let me out."

A loud bang from the foyer made them both jump, and Lasha's anxiety spiked. "Please! He could be hurt!"

"Let's look first," Ilee suggested. Turning to the display next to the door, she tapped until it showed an image of the foyer. Lasha crowded in next to Ilee to see. The angle of the image was wide from the height of the display on the wall on the other side of the door. The image wasn't great, but it was good enough to tell her exactly how Tamerin was doing.

"Oh!" she breathed with surprise. Her Talin was a badass!

Three Vicpor were lying on the floor. Two weren't moving, and the third was clutching a pincer to his chest and crying.

As she watched, Tamerin tossed another Vicpor into two others, sending all three tumbling. One jumped on his back, but the massive weight of the Vicpor didn't make Tamerin buckle. The warrior staggered for a step and then reached back and grabbed the Vicpor by the head. Ducking down, he pulled so the Vicpor flipped forward onto the ground with a hard thump.

Still holding the head, Tamerin raised a clawed foot and stomped down on the Vicpor's carapace, hitting the spot where the mid-body and lower segments met. The resulting crack was so loud Lasha thought she could hear it through the door.

"He's dead," Ilee noted grimly.

Lasha blinked up at her as the consequences of this fight hit her. "We're going to need to get off Glakor today."

The med tech twitched all four of her arms. Vicpor for *duh*. "That would be wise. Tamerin paid me good money to get you healthy, so I'd hate to see it all go to waste because you two got executed."

"But how?" Lasha asked. Mentally she cataloged the spots they could hide until the next ship came, but all of them would be inhospitable due to the cold wind.

Ilee grabbed a nearby information square and started tapping. "One of the emergency molting chambers at the port is open. You could hide there. I'll reserve it for you so no one can claim it."

"You're the kindest Vicpor I've ever met," Lasha confided in her.

"Don't tell anyone," Ilee said quickly. "Otherwise I'll get harassed!"

"No, never!" Lasha promised. "If anyone ever asks I'll say Ilee, the med tech on Glakor, was a mean bitch."

"Yes, that," the med tech agreed.

Another crack had them both looking back at the display. Tamerin was holding the heads of two Vicpors, their bodies dangling limply from his hands. Judging by the Vicpors' dazed expressions, he'd smashed their heads together with enough force to put them both in a stupor. When Tamerin let go of them, the two dropped to the floor in a heap of shiny carapace.

Out of all the Vicpors, only two were left standing along with Oglee, who was still cradling his claw with the dagger in it.

"In my back sack!" Oglee screamed his instruction to one of the remaining two. "Get it, and use it on him!"

One of them hurried forward and put a pincer into the natural pocket formed by the back of a Vicpors bulbous mid-body carapace. When he pulled out a weapon Lasha gasped.

"No," she whispered. She had Tamerin's weapon! She needed to get out there and help him.

"Don't," Ilee ordered sharply, moving to block the door again. "If you go out there, all you'll do is get him killed. Look at your warrior. He's not concerned."

Lasha's eyes focused on the display. Tamerin stood undaunted by the Vicpor with the weapon. Ilee was right. He didn't look intimidated at all. The war rattle Tamerin had been sounding off and on all throughout the fight went silent.

"Put down the weapon, and I'll let you leave," Tamerin's voice sounded unnaturally loud in the sudden quiet. "If you fire it at me, you will die."

"You're not faster than a projectile," the Vicpor said. His voice sounded confident, but Lasha could see the way his lower arms were moving restlessly and his neck was tucked tight into his midsection. Signs of fear.

"I don't need to be faster," Tamerin said confidently. "I can disarm you from here."

"Stop talking and shoot him," Oglee ordered.

"Uncle, I don't know about this," the Vicpor answered. "I've never killed anyone."

"Look at what he did to me!" Oglee shouted, waving his wounded pincer.

"I—"

The next series of movements happened so fast Lasha didn't understand what occurred until it was all over.

Tamerin threw something long and thin. The Vicpor with the gun screamed and the gun fired, but the round burned a hole in the wall nowhere near Tamerin. Something was sticking out of the Vicpor's pincer. The way it was buried had pinned the pincer shut. Oglee's nephew couldn't release the weapon's trigger, therefore he couldn't reset it and fire again.

It took some staring, but Lasha figured out the object Tamerin had thrown was one of his own quills! He'd broken it off and thrown it like a weapon.

By the time the Vicpor realized both his pincer and weapon were useless, Tamerin had crossed the room and grabbed him. In a blur of speed Tamerin disarmed the Vicpor by breaking the whole pincer off.

Lasha gasped. She didn't even know that could be done.

The Vicpor screamed as he passed out from pain. He was going to die. No Vicpor could survive a wound that grievous. She almost felt sorry for him.

Tamerin turned on Oglee. "You have something of mine."

The Vicpor was trying to get away, but Tamerin grabbed hold of his dagger and used it to force Oglee to the ground. Crying in distress, Oglee went still. "Please don't kill me."

"Why shouldn't I kill you?" Tamerin asked the sobbing Oglee. Then he ripped the dagger out of Oglee's pincer. The Vicpor howled and curled up on his side, cradling his wounded limb.

The last Vicpor standing made it to the foyer door and was about to slide out when Tamerin pinned him with his intense gaze. "I'm letting you live with only a cracked leg carapace, but only if you don't speak about what happened here. Don't force me to hunt you down and finish what I started."

The Vicpor whimpered from fear. "I wasn't here."

Then he was gone and Tamerin turned his attention back to Oglee. The overseer had slid away from Tamerin until his back hit the wall.

"Please," Oglee begged.

"My little human was sick and what did you do? You dumped her in a room with no medication or food. You left her to die, and then you were going to sell her as meat? Why should I grant you mercy when you've never shown it to anyone else."

Lasha never thought of herself as particularly blood thirsty, but at that moment she didn't have a morsel of pity in her soul.

"I lost count of how many workers died over the years," she whispered. "No one escapes this place, not even in death. Bodies were never sent back to families. They were always sold."

"The entire city was built on suffering," Ilee responded. "Vicpors here are being worked to death, not just foreign labor brought in. This is a city fueled by misery."

Now Lasha understood why a skilled and compassionate med tech was working on a third-rate planet like Glakor.

"Who do you need to save?" Lasha asked without hesitation.

For the first time in their short acquaintance, she caught Ilee by surprise. "What?"

"Someone you care about is being worked to death here," Lasha stated. "Who is it?"

"My youngest sibling," the med tech said, her voice hard. "My mother sold her and the contract stipulated she couldn't be resold. It's because she wouldn't do as Mother commanded. Easier to get rid of her and birth another clutch."

Lasha knew where this was going. You didn't spend a couple of years working for Vicpors and not figure out how their society worked.

"She must have been the last one to crack from her shell," Lasha guessed. The youngest sibling cares for the parent when they get old. That child must be perfectly obedient and do everything the parent demands. Lasha had been told stories of Vicpors going through several clutches of offspring until they got a child they deemed perfectly obedient.

Ilee made a sound of agreement. "Just so. Relee wanted to train with me to be a med tech. Out of the ten of us in this clutch, she is the sweetest and most giving. Mother never should have done this to her. Relee could have had a career and then come back to care for Mother when she was needed. There was no reason to punish her like this except hubris."

It was her nature to make rash promises and today was no different. "We're going to help you."

When she looked back, she found Tamerin had dispatched Oglee and was wiping his blade off on the overseer's uniform. As happy as she was to see the Vicpor dead and Tamerin unhurt, she was already preoccupied with figuring out how to get them all off Glakor: her, Tamerin, Ilee, and Relee.

Tamerin was re-sheathing his blade when Lasha rushed out of the med tech's suite. He was quick to cross the body-littered floor. The last thing he wanted was for her get hurt by stumbling over one of the Vicpors.

Sweeping her up in his arms, he held her gently against his chest. He purred as she wrapped her arms around his neck and nestled her face against his throat.

"You were amazing," she breathed.

"I'm Talin," he stated.

She pulled back a little to meet his gaze. "That's it? You just took on a room full of Vicpors, and one had a weapon! You could have been hurt or killed. And all you've got to say is 'I'm Talin.'" She lowered her voice trying to imitate him.

He couldn't stop the amused rumble that came out of him. "Are you injured?"

"Me? All I did was hide in the med suite with Ilee," she countered. "Are you injured? Did any of the—"

Body-racking coughs interrupted her questions. Worried, Tamerin carried her back inside the suite and confronted the med tech. "She's going to hurt herself with the coughing. Do something."

"Have her hold this in her mouth as long as she can," the med tech instructed, thrusting a vial at him. "I have to do something with all those bodies in the foyer."

Then she was gone. A glance at the display next to the door confirmed the med tech's intentions. Ilee opened a hatch in the floor. With efficiency, she went about dragging the bodies to the hatch and dropping them in.

"That's convenient," he murmured as the Vicpor made quick work of cleaning up the worst of the mess. If she got all the bodies out of the way, the cleaning bots could come in and remove the gore.

In his arms Lasha finally stopped coughing long enough for him to pour the contents of the vial into her mouth. She clamped her mouth shut and held back her coughs long enough for the medication to start working.

"Ah, that's better," she sighed after she was able to swallow.

"The cold triggered your cough and might have done damage to your lungs," Tamerin noted. "I can't wait to get away from here. I promise we'll never visit a cold planet again."

"Fine by me," she agreed, relaxing against him. Rocking back and forth in place as he'd seen human parents do with their young, he purred out a soothing rumble and rubbed his scent gland on her hair. The smell of his bonding oil filled the room. His oil combined with her skin, hair, and scalp. The resulting scent was as familiar as it was comforting.

"I love that smell so much," she whispered to him.

"That makes me happy to hear," he murmured. "Because I love that smell on you."

It was imperative they get moving. Even with Ilee's help, the bodies would be discovered eventually. They needed to be off planet before that happened.

But he hesitated. Standing here with Lasha in his arms he felt peace. He'd gotten to prove his worthiness by taking on the Vicpors. This felt like his reward. His human clinging to him and telling him how much she loved the scent of his bonding oil.

Few moments in his life could he claim were close to perfect. This was one of them.

"That's done," Ilee announced as she came back into the suite. "Let me pack my essentials, and then we can get my sister."

Tamerin stopped moving as the Vicpor bustled off into another room of the suite.

"Sister?" he asked. He knew he wasn't going to like the answer.

"Yeah, we're going to rescue Ilee's sister, Relee. Or I guess it'd be more accurate to say we're going to steal her. I hope that's okay," Lasha said without once raising her head from his neck.

It only took him a split second to come to a decision. Honestly, with her hair saturated in his bonding oil and her body snuggled against him, he could only respond one way.

"If that's what you want, that's what we'll do," he agreed.

CHAPTER 14

To Tamerin's complete shock, it was easy to collect Relee once the wind had died down and temperatures returned to normal. Overseers weren't concerned about individuals leaving the factories. Where would they go? The planet only had one port, and it was set up to keep workers from fleeing. That along with few places a runaway worker could hide made it nearly impossible for workers to successfully find freedom even with help.

Before she'd left to fetch her sister, Ilee explained to him that when Relee didn't return, the overseer's would check Ilee's business and home first. When they didn't find her there, they'd assume Relee had decided to jump into the icy Glakor ocean to escape her pain.

Lasha had confirmed it wasn't an uncommon thing for the workers to do. It made Tamerin want to hug Lasha close and thank the ancestors for giving her the strength to stay alive until he got there.

Now they were all gathered in Ilee's suite, sipping the bitter tea Vicpors preferred. Except for Relee who was sucking down the nutrient drinks Ilee had given her.

Ilee and Relee were perched on the squat, square stools Vicpors favored and Tamerin sat on the floor with his back against a door. Lasha was happily cuddled in his lap, and for her comfort, Ilee had turned the heat up as high as it would go.

There was a chance he might never let go of her again. Even with her hair soaked in his boding oil, the image of Oglee holding her arm with his pincer kept coming back to him. What if he hadn't found them when he did? What if his aim hadn't been good enough and his dagger missed Oglee's pincer?

What if she'd been killed before he'd arrived?

Those thoughts caused panic to flare, chasing off all the calm hormones the smell of his bonding oil on her had released. The only way to keep the panic at bay for the moment was having his arms wrapped around her.

Hopefully his feelings of impending panic would subside, but for right now he needed her small body held close to his. Her head resting on his shoulder and her warm breath ghosting across the small strip of exposed skin at the base of his neck all helped to keep his impulses under control.

"I want to help," Tamerin said to the room even as he kept his soothing rumble up for Lasha. "But I'm worried about the punishments we might face if we're discovered. It would be easy enough for Lasha and me to leave. Trying to get Relee off planet would increase the danger of discovery ten-fold."

"It's a real concern," Ilee confirmed. "If we're caught, Relee faces harsh punishment from the overseer who owns her work contract. I'll be forced to choose between death or a lifelong work contract. And because we're sisters, my contract will be sold to a different planet. But the two of you face the worst punishment. Especially if the bodies are found. There's no way the authorities won't tie the wounds on those dead Vicpors to a Talin. The punctures from your claws and quills are much too distinct."

Tamerin buzzed out a frustrated rattle. "I'd still do the same thing again."

Sitting up, Lasha smiled at him. "You were amazing! I was so scared for you, but you mowed down an entire room full of Vicpors like you were cutting through some bushes."

"None of them were an issue once you were safe," he assured her. "I'd willingly challenge a hundred Vicpors at once if that's what it took to keep you safe."

Lasha grinned up at him. "Aww, that's so romantic."

A sharp clattering rattle of surprise escaped him. "It is?"

"You're willing to maim and murder for me? Hell yes, that's romantic. It's like something a morally gray hero out of one of Isla's Old Earth novels would do."

Tamerin wasn't sure he liked being referred to as morally gray, but if Lasha approved, he wouldn't object. "I believe I'm very morally gray when it comes to you."

"Same," Lasha declared before settling her head back down on his shoulder. "I'm definitely willing to be morally gray for you too. Maybe even a little blood thirsty."

Ilee clicked her pincer a few times to get his attention, hissing a little in amusement. "Back to the matter at hand. It's best we all get off the planet as soon as possible."

"It all comes down to figuring out how to get Relee on board the next shuttle," Tamerin murmured without moving. "We've got a short window to get off planet and a lot of things that could go wrong before then, including someone deciding to check the basement of Ilee's building."

Lasha gave a little shudder. "Yeah, lots of bodies down there."

"The good news is once we're on a transport we're safe," Tamerin said as he thought about the ship he'd taken to get to Glakor. He'd noted the crew didn't like stopping at the remote planet and had barely allotted enough time for the shuttle to land and return.

Relee spoke for the first time. "We are? What if the ship finds out they have criminals and a runaway worker onboard?"

"We're only criminals as long as we're on this planet," Tamerin explained. "Do you know about the trade crimes agreement Glakor has? No crimes off world are acknowledged here, but it also works in reverse."

Lasha looked confused. "What?" she asked.

Ilee spoke up. "Yes, Tamerin's right. It's because Glakor is willing to produce goods that are illegal in a lot of places. The middle men for these sales are often criminals, warlords, pirates, or raiders. To make these types feel safe to come here, Glakor has a special policy in place: Outside authorities have no jurisdiction here. But that works to our favor because it also means criminals from here can't be pursued off-planet. That's one of the reasons they focus on security at the port."

"Once we leave Glakor atmosphere, we'll be secure," Tamerin elaborated.

Everyone was looking pleased with themselves until his next words caused them to tense up again.

"But that still leads us back to our biggest problem—how to get Relee through the port and aboard a shuttle? As it's been explained to me, the port is set up to keep workers from escaping. How do we get around that?"

"Could we steal someone's identity?" Lasha asked.

"I don't think that would work," Ilee answered, her four clawed arms clasped tightly in front of her as she spoke. A clear sign of frustration. "They do a bio check at the port. If your biosignature doesn't match the information in the system, the authorities are called to straighten it out."

"And it would probably take too long to pay someone to have a false identity attached to Relee's biosignature," Lasha guessed.

"I don't want my freedom if there's a chance you'll end up as slave labor," Relee objected, casting a fearful look at her sister.

Tamerin's gaze focused on Relee. Her carapace was much too pale and looked soft, probably due to malnutrition. Her gait had been slow as they'd walked back to Ilee's office, and she didn't perform the many little movements most Vicpors did out of habit as they talked. It was all testament to how depleted she was.

No worker on Glakor died of old age.

"This place needs to be sunk into the sea," Tamerin muttered.

Without lifting her head, Lasha reached up and petted his chest as if to soothe him. "I agree. Places like this shouldn't exist."

He was so distracted by Lasha's fingers running along the edges of his chest plates, he spoke without thinking. "Maybe someday the Talin empire will take this land and release the workers."

"Talins do that?" Lasha asked, surprised.

"We abhor slavery," Tamerin explained, purring as he tightened his arms around her. "It's an archaic and unnecessary way to find labor. As we conquer territory, we end all slavery, even if it's under the guise of contract work. Those freed are allowed to stay and continue to work for a negotiated wage, or they can return home."

All three of them were staring at Tamerin, Lasha with wide surprised eyes and the two Vicpors with open mandibles.

"Do the Talins need med techs?" Ilee asked. "I want to live among a civilization where I can't be sold."

Ilee's question caught Tamerin by surprise. "You could probably get hired on one of the worlds or colonies we control but don't inhabit. However, you'd be looked at as an outsider your entire life, and you run the risk of a bounty hunter finding you. I have a better suggestion. You should relocate to Delorta-controlled space. They tend to colonize ice planets, they don't allow slavery, and will often employ those outside their species. Some of their colonies are the most diverse I've ever seen, and they don't allow bounty hunters or collectors."

"A Delorta-controlled planet then," Ilee announced with a definitive clack of her pincer. "I don't care where we settle as long as Mother can't come after us."

"It'd be unlikely she'd find you there," Tamerin assured her.

"There's still the issue of getting off Glakor," Relee reminded them. "Where we go from here doesn't matter if we can't get off the planet."

"I have a really stupid idea." Lasha paused after speaking, as if to give everyone a moment to dismiss her.

"I doubt it's stupid," Tamerin countered. "Please share."

"Zia and her sister lived on a space station for the first ten years of their lives," Lasha began. "The two of them would make extra money by performing for visitors to the station."

"What does that have to do with this situation?" Relee asked. Tamerin sounded an annoyed rattle and she hastily added.

"I'm not being dismissive, just confused. Are you going to preform and distract the port agent?"

Lasha laughed. "In a manner of speaking, yes. When performing wasn't working to bring in money, the two of them would pickpocket or run scams."

Tamerin was intrigued. "Scams? Do you mean they cheated people out of money?"

"All the time," Lasha answered with a wide grin. "But they were careful to keep the betting low so it wasn't likely the authorities would be called."

"What scam could two ten-year-old humans perform that could possibly be applicable here?" Tamerin asked.

"The three cups," Lasha answered excitedly. "Although we're going to do it with only two cups."

"Could you explain," Ilee asked before Tamerin could.

"You set three upside-down cups on a table with a ball under one of them. Then you shift them around a bunch and ask the person to pick the cup where the ball is."

Ilee clicked a pincer with mild annoyance. "That sounds like it would be easy to keep track of the location of the ball."

"Not at all," Lasha argued. "Because the ball isn't in any of the cups. Even before Zia started moving the cups around, the ball was hidden in her hand."

"And now I understand why it's a scam," Tamerin commented and then pointed at Relee. "But how do we make an entire Vicpor disappear?"

"With two cups and a distraction," Lasha said. "We're going to need two identical travel cases." She looked to Relee. "You're going to have to be squished in one of them for a while. Can you handle that?"

"Without question," Relee responded. "If you have to break my legs to make me fit, do it. I'll endure."

Tamerin sounded a rattle of alarm. "I'm sure we can get a travel case big enough for you to fit. No limbs need to be broken."

"Tamerin's right. We don't need to do anything extreme," Lasha agreed.

"You said two travel cases," Ilee commented. "What will be in the second one?"

"Here is where the cup game comes in. I need you to figure out what you can put in the second case that looks like it should trip the port scanners but wouldn't actually make them go off."

"That doesn't make any sense," Relee argued. "How does packing something that won't activate the scanners help sneak me through?"

"That's where the distraction part of the cups game comes into play," Lasha said with what Tamerin decided was a ruthless grin. "I'll explain as we get ready. Along with the cases and the decoy contraband, I need two hover carts. Both of them need to look the same and they should look old but work well."

"I have two travel cases here that should work," Ilee volunteered.

Even though the cold wind had died down, Tamerin wasn't letting Lasha leave the clinic except to go to the port. "I'll fetch two hover-carts and bring them back here," he offered.

Standing up with Lasha in his arms, he set her on her feet. "You stay here. Don't open the door to anyone but me."

"Wouldn't dream of it," she agreed.

CHAPTER 15

Tamerin was so proud of his little human he had to fight to keep from rattling with pride. He'd done it once already and Lasha had laughed and told him that the rattle sounded like an audience clapping with appreciation.

It was a fitting description, he wanted to applaud Lasha's cunning.

Not only had she come up with an excellent strategy, but she'd even thought of several details that hadn't occurred to him. The most important being making sure the hover-carts looked exactly the same by scuffing the corners and obscuring the large serial numbers on the side.

The part he didn't like was the uniform she'd made him buy. It was the same kind as the one she'd been wearing when he'd rescued her. He'd hoped to never see her in one of those horrible garments again, but she insisted.

The other thing he didn't like was that she'd started acting meek and subservient when they got to the port. The moment they'd exited the public carrier, she'd put herself behind him, making a show of guiding the hover-cart and apologizing for every little thing.

He wanted to step around the hover-cart and snatch her off her feet to hug her to his chest and sound a soothing rumble. Most of all he wanted the haunted look off her face. She was trying to be convincing, but it broke him every time he glanced over to see her looking so fearful.

Only one person was ahead of them in line. They'd deliberately arrived almost too late to catch the shuttle. This was to give the gate attendant as little time as possible to ask them questions.

Ahead of them and just past the gate, Ilee paused with her hover-cart, acting like the thing was giving her problems. She even kicked the side of it and cursed softly.

The single Vicpor at the gate didn't spare her a glance.

"Ident and load declaration," he demanded as Lasha pressed their hover-cart's remote control and brought it even with the agent.

Before Tamerin could say anything, Lasha spoke. "This is General Tamerin with the Talin Board of Military Supplies."

As she talked she rolled her eyes toward him as if she was afraid to turn her head to look at him. She kept her shoulders hunched and her head bowed as she spoke.

He couldn't help the buzzing rattle of annoyance that came out of him. Hate for this subterfuge made him lose control of his backplates.

Lasha turned and bowed deeply to him. "Please don't be upset, sir. We'll be boarding soon."

"Are you leaving with him?" the Vicpor asked.

"He bought my work contract from Oglee," she confirmed. "I work for General Tamerin now." Leaning in close she whispered to the agent. "Please hurry so we can board before he loses his temper."

The agent glanced at Tamerin. To fulfill the role Lasha had assigned him, Tamerin sounded a loud, buzzy rattle of annoyance and took a menacing step forward. "What's taking so long? Stop cavorting with the Vicpor. I'm tired of this cold planet. I should've been back on Talarian ten rotations ago."

"I'm sorry, sir!" Lasha squeaked and cowered slightly. It took all of Tamerin's willpower to stop himself from snatching her up and holding her tightly against this chest while purring.

The gate agent blinked and tucked his long neck into this middle carapace—a clear sign Tamerin had succeeded in intimidating him. He glanced down at his information square, tapped it a few times, and then waved them through the scan-gate behind him with two arms and a pincer.

"If you'd please move the hover-cart through the scan-gate," he invited.

Tamerin almost forgot his cue, but Lasha looked over her shoulder at him and motioned at the hover-cart with her eyes.

"You heard what he said," he roared at Lasha. "Move!"

Because everyone jumped at his high volume, no one was surprised that Lasha cried out with fear and mashed the hover-cart remote with her hand. The hover-cart jetted off through the scan-gate, setting off loud alarms.

"Bring that back!" The gate agent yelled as he jumped over the small barrier between him and the rest of the room and jogged after Lasha and the hover-cart.

But neither of them stopped.

"It's not working!" Lasha cried out as she made a production of trying to smash the safety-stop button on the remote while chasing after it.

The hover-cart kept going until it barreled into Ilee's parked hover-cart, sending both of them skittering off into opposite directions.

"What have you done?" Ilee screeched, waving her arms and pincers in the air. "That case has my eggs in it!"

"I'm so—uff!" Lasha appeared to trip over her own feet and come up hard against Ilee. To help add to the confusion, Tamerin let loose with a war rattle that filled the room with the sound of pounding feet.

"Let go of my property!" he roared and rushed up to the females to grab Lasha and pull her away from Ilee. Both controls dropped to the ground, allowing Ilee to pick up the control to their hover-cart instead of hers.

"Your property ran into me!" Ilee retorted, clacking her pincers aggressively. "Twice! Once with your hover-cart and again with her body. How dare you let her touch me! I'm a respected med tech, not some lowly contract worker."

"And I'm a Talin general!" Tamerin answered, keeping up both his war rattle and his loud voice. "You will not speak to me like that!"

The sound of the shuttle warning klaxon filled the room. "All of you will miss the last shuttle to the waiting ship if you don't calm down," the frantic gate agent called out.

"If I miss my shuttle I'll rip this place apart," Tamerin threatened as he turned to face the gate agent. "Starting with you!"

"I have eggs to get home," Ilee cried out. "I can't miss this ship!" She rushed up to one of the hover-carts and worked the remote in her hand. The cart was quick to obey her commands and started up the ramp ahead of her. To Tamerin's relief he saw it was the hover-cart he and Lasha had brought through. The one carrying the crate Relee was hiding in.

The gate agent didn't give Ilee a second look as she and the hover-cart disappeared up the ramp. As they'd planned, his entire focus was on Tamerin.

"Terribly sorry!" Lasha said as she darted out from behind him and snatched up the second remote from the floor. She started steering the remaining hover-cart toward the ramp but the gate agent was quick to step between her and the ramp.

"You set off the sensor. I can't let you through," he stated grimly. Glancing down at his scanner, he read something there before looking back up. "It looks like your box might contain something illegal, such as a worker trying to flee or a biological entity not sufficiently packaged for safe travel."

"Didn't you hear what I said?" Tamerin asked. "I want to leave now."

"General, please," Lasha begged meekly. "I can open the case and he can see there's nothing there. It will be quicker than arguing."

"Very well," Tamerin said and then muttered about backwater planets loudly enough for the gate agent to hear. Lasha had told him to be insulting, and he hoped he wasn't overplaying his role. "Make it quick."

Lasha rushed to unlock the case and throw it open for the agent to inspect. The moment he looked inside, the Vicpor started clacking his claws with agitation.

"Are these contagion tubes?" he asked.

"Why would you ask me such an obvious question?" Tamerin shot back. "It's perfectly clear that they are. Those are samples of a new programmable virus. My superiors want to test it for effectiveness before agreeing to a contract."

"Sir, uh, General, you can't transport contagion tubes in this kind of case," the gate agent explained. "It's too dangerous. They need to be in a specially made and sealable case with the appropriate warning labels. I can't let you get on the shuttle with these. If the ship finds out we let you on with unsecured contagion tubes like this, they won't stop here any longer."

"This is unacceptable," Tamerin argued, making sure to loom over the gate agent. The poor Vicpor was intimidated enough to pull his neck in so deep his head was nestled against the top of his mid carapace.

"Please don't make me call the security agents," the Vicpor begged. "I can get a suitable case to house the tubes and all the proper labels if you'll only be a little patient."

The last warning to board the shuttle sounded. "Sir?" Lasha said, touching his damaged left arm. "There isn't another ship for ten rotations if we miss this one."

"I want to go home more than I want those samples," Tamerin announced with a last roaring war rattle. "Keep the travel case. I'll report back to my government that Glakor isn't worth the trouble of a contract."

With that, he grabbed Lasha and made a show of tossing her roughly over his shoulder and stomping up the ramp. The gate agent didn't call after them, probably relieved that Tamerin wasn't his problem any longer. Eventually gate security would figure out that the contagion tubes were empty, but only after they secured them in a safe place for inspection. By then they'd be aboard the ship and long gone.

Halfway up the ramp and out of sight of the gate agent, Tamerin set Lasha back down on her feet and ran his hands over her to check for injuries. He'd tried to be gentle but worried he might have gotten carried away.

"Are you okay, songbird?" he whispered.

"I'm great," she enthused, grabbing his right hand in both of hers. "And you were brilliant!"

He had no time to return the compliment for concocting such an exceptional plan. They heard the crew shouting from the shuttle, making both of them hurry up the rest of the ramp.

Ilee was standing at the open door of the shuttle, her entire body vibrating with tension. The moment she saw the two of them, she breathed out a loud sound of relief.

"Praise be!" she hissed out, her body deflating a little as the tension left her. "We all made it."

Before Lasha could agree, Ilee rushed back into the shuttle to stand next to the travel case holding Relee. They couldn't let her out yet, but Ilee had a small information square she could use to communicate with Relee. Sitting on the floor next to the hover-cart, she started tapping the square.

Tamerin found an empty seat on the shuttle and pulled Lasha into his lap. He held her tightly as the shuttle doors closed and the launch procedure began. Then the entire ship shook. They'd launched.

"Goodbye and good riddance," Lasha muttered as she snuggled into him.

Rumbling out a purr, he brought his head down to rub his scent glands over the top of Lasha's head. They were mostly shielded from the view of others by a support strut. Even if they weren't, they'd left the port and no other Talins were on board. He was free to show affection.

Maybe now was a good time to start preparing her for their trip to Sorana.

"I should tell you some things about Talin culture and laws you won't like," he whispered to her.

"That you guys are pushy?" she quipped. "And seem to be taking over the universe?"

"We are pushy, but you knew that already," he replied with an amused rumble. He kept rubbing until both his scent glands were empty and Lasha's hair was soaked in his bonding oil. She breathed in deeply and let out a soft sigh.

"That's the best smell," she murmured.

"You're the best smell," he responded, pulling their combined scents into his lungs. It settled him deep inside, making it easier to talk. "This might not be the best time, but just in case Talins are on board this transport, you need to know Talins don't scent-bond."

"I'm sorry, what?" she asked, pulling back a little so she could meet his eyes. "You told me Palforma is scent-bonded to Zia."

"Let me speak plainly. It's against Talin law to scent-bond. Because bonded partners can't be apart for long or they'll die of a disease we call Ending, an emperor in the past made bonding taboo. Then it was codified into law as illegal. Most Talins believe it's impossible for one of our species to scent-bond with humans. But if it's found out I've scent-bonded I will be stripped of my wealth, titles, and honors. My family will erase me from the clan register, and I'll be outcast at best. Imprisoned and executed at worst."

Lasha's eyes went wide and her jaw dropped. It took her a few tries before she spoke. "We can't go back to your people! We can't risk your life."

It warmed his heart that her first thought was for his safety, not what might happen to her if they were separated.

"Talins believe humans are in need of almost constant affection and comfort. Because of that, it's common to see Talins hugging or holding humans. It's even acceptable to rub bonding oil on a human as long as it's for no other reason than to soothe the human."

"Huh, that's interesting." She tilted her head and gave him a considering look. "I'm seeing the loophole in your laws. No wonder Palforma picked Zia and you went to such an effort to find me on this backwater, nasty planet. We humans, or other species like us, are your only chance for affection. Aren't we?"

"Humans are the preferred species," he responded, skirting past the ownership/pet issue.

"So you guys deliberately seek out humans?" she asked, her cheerful expression from earlier changing to one of hurt. "Does sex or age matter, or would any human work?"

He didn't like that question at all. "I value you for more than simply being human. You're a beautiful soul, Lasha. With your songbird voice and will of steel, you're a unique and beautiful human."

"Oh, that, uh, that was…" she blinked up at him, as if caught off guard by his statements. "For a warrior, you're awfully poetic."

"Is that good or bad?"

Before she could answer the shuttle shuddered and the overhead lights flashed a warning. The bumpy but quick flight was over, and they were docking. The ship was quick to move the passengers off the shuttle, and the three of them were checked in and assigned cabins by a well-organized attendant.

Their cabins were across from each other, and Tamerin didn't object when Lasha insisted they follow Ilee and the hover-cart into their room. The cabin door hadn't even finished sliding closed before Ilee was wrenching open the travel case and gently lifting Relee's head.

"We made it," Relee whispered as she flopped several limbs out of the case but didn't make any further move to get out. "Praise the Great Makbee. We made it out!"

"We did," Lasha agreed. "And now we all get to start over."

Now that they were assured Relee was fine, Ilee urged them to leave so Relee could rest. Tamerin didn't object. He could see Lasha was fatigued and he desperately wanted her to rest while he held her to his body.

They were all safe now, and he and Lasha were looking at a lifetime together. He couldn't believe his luck. Lasha was right. They all got to start over.

CHAPTER 16

"It's too bad Relee can't walk with us," Lasha commented as they stepped back into their cabin. "It'd be nice to be with someone who moves as slow as me."

A loud purr rumbled out of Tamerin. "You're moving better and further every day. And we visit Relee and Ilee after every walk, so you get to see them, even if Relee can't leave the room."

No other Talins were on board the Slow Star, but plenty of Vicpor passengers were. They weren't worried about the ship turning around, but they also didn't want anyone raising questions and potentially causing problems for Relee. Deciding on caution, Relee didn't leave the room she shared with Ilee.

Not that she was interested in walking around the ship. She might not have been on death's door like Lasha when Tamerin bought her work contract, but Relee was still malnourished, underweight, and suffering from several chronic issues. She mostly slept and ate as she recovered from her year as a worker on Glakor.

Lasha was doing much better, but her stint in the extreme cold of Glakor had caused her to relapse. The occasional coughing fit that broke through Ilee's medications would leave her lightheaded and hurting, but she was getting better.

When she felt up to it, she and Tamerin walked the ship. By intergalactic standards, the Slow Star wasn't a very large vessel but it was still big enough that Lasha couldn't make it a full loop without needing rest.

Other than eating in the communal dining hall and their walks, she and Tamerin spent most of the time cuddled in their cabin. He'd become as big a fan of Ugarian soap operas as she was. He'd even sounded an angry rattle when a scene ended in an avoidable tragedy.

When they didn't feel like watching the soap operas, he would read to her, like back in the room on Glakor. Mostly he'd read from the Talin histories, but sometimes she'd talk him into reading some Ollie fiction or Hulg poetry.

Occasionally Tamerin would ask her to sing. At first she assumed he was doing it to give himself a break from reading, but by the third day she understood he enjoyed her voice. It gave him the same satisfaction as his reading gave her. That made her eager to share her music with him. She sang anything from folk music her parents taught her to the more upbeat songs she and her friends had composed back on Wimol.

It still boggled her mind that Tamerin didn't have music in his life. How did a civilization never develop music? But then again she was getting to know the Talins as Tamerin read more to her. The Talins were a species focused on goals and practicalities with all of the positive and negative aspects that focus created.

"I'm excited that Relee and Ilee already got messages back from Declow Station. Both of them have jobs waiting with the Delorta!" she commented, dropping face down on the bed with a sigh. It wasn't that she was tired, but after spending so much time rarely being allowed to talk, conversations with Ilee and Relee left her brain feeling oddly fatigued.

"Both of them have strong skill sets and don't mind living in a cold environment," Tamerin pointed out. "The Delorta come from an ice-planet and keep their station at low temperatures. That can make it hard for them to find enough skilled labor. The Delorta themselves can't successfully carry or raise offspring anywhere but their homeplanet, so they constantly need an influx of workers to fill the gaps when breeding groups want to return home to start a family."

"I wish my great-great-great-great grandparents knew about the Delorta before they settled on Wimol. I'm sure they would have traded a cold environment for equal pay," Lasha said as she flipped over on her back and settled her head on a pillow.

Tamerin sounded an affirmative rumble as he checked the room display. He did this several times a day to make sure there weren't any new ship-wide announcements. She'd never met someone so prepared for something bad to happen. Far from being bothersome, his actions made her feel safe.

"Should we read until your next meal?" Tamerin asked after he'd finished with the display. He took the one step needed to cross the room and settled next to her on the bed.

The cabin had been small to begin with. After Tamerin pulled both bunks out and latched them together, they made a nice big bed but left almost no room to walk around. The cabin was more bed than anything else, but Lasha wasn't going to complain. The bed was the best part of the place anyway!

When she didn't answer right away, he spoke again. "Or would you like to sleep?"

Lasha wasn't interested in either of those options, but how spoiled was she? Not long ago she'd been on death's door and now she was bored.

She settled on a nice neutral answer. "Whatever you want to do."

"Whatever I want?" he repeated.

"Sure," she said, rolling her head to look at him. "We could—"

Tamerin rolled on top of her, cutting off her next words. "I want you," he growled, his body language going from laidback to intense in a flash. His hips settled between her legs, and she could already feel his cock getting hard inside his flesh pouch.

Relaxing under him, she met his gaze. She liked where this was going.

"You can have me," she agreed readily. "We've been on the ship for days, and you didn't seem interested. I thought maybe Talins didn't like to engage in sex often."

"You'd be wrong," he countered. "I wanted you to rest after your coughing came back. I worried about hurting you. But you walked the entire inside ring of the ship without coughing today."

Grinning up at him, she wrapped her legs around his waist. "That deserves a reward," she insisted.

A slow, sexual rumble came out of him. It was a deeper, sexier version of his purr. "We both deserve a reward, and I'm determined we'll get them."

Ah, she loved that rumble! "Yes, please."

Her legs fell away as he sat back on his heels. Reaching for the hem of her tunic dress, he found it bunched around her thighs.

"I can't wait to buy you better clothing," he grumbled as he worked the garment over her hips and out from under her ass. Before she could move to help, he easily grabbed and lifted her up. Holding her in the air with one arm, he drew the tunic over her head and tossed it to the floor. With that out of the way, he settled her back on the bed.

Now she was gloriously naked.

One nice thing about those tunic dresses and the lack of undergarments available for humans was the easy access.

But no way was he getting away with doing things his way, at least not in the beginning. When he started to lower his head, she put a hand in his face.

"Nope," she said with as much authority as she could muster. "Pants off first."

"I thought I'd see to your pleasure and then disrobe," he answered.

"Disrobe now. I want us both naked from the start," she told him. "And I never get to see you emerge from your flesh pouch. I want to watch you get hard."

He went quiet and sat back. "I'm not sure you want that," he answered.

"What? Why not?"

Absently he rubbed his right hand over his scarred left forearm, running his palm across where his quills should've been.

"I'm not," he paused, looking away, "correct there anymore."

Nope, they weren't going to play that game. Scrambling to her knees, Lasha cupped his face with her hands and urged him to look up.

"I need you to listen to me," she whispered to him. "More importantly, I need you to believe me. I love you. I don't care if you're missing some quills. I don't care if you have scars. I don't care if you're different. Different isn't bad. You scent-bonded to me even though my brain's flawed. Right?"

"You're not flawed in any way," he growled as he brought his hands up to cover hers.

"Exactly," she agreed. "Neither are you. Let me see."

He took a deep breath and then sounded the rumble of stockinged feet running on a hard floor. In this context the rumble had to signal agreement.

When he dropped his hands, she let go of his face and sat back. Without taking his eyes from hers, he got to his feet next to the bed and pulled his Talin-style pants off.

She'd already prepared herself not to react, but when she dropped her gaze she was puzzled for a moment. After a few seconds of staring, she understood what she was seeing.

Tamerin had explained all about the flesh pouch that safely hid their mating shaft and seed sack. It was made up of tough Talin skin covered with tiny "beads" of keratin plating. As the cock filled with blood, it would push until the flesh pouch retracted far enough to snap under and release their dick and ball, but she'd never seen him before the pouch had retracted.

Now she could clearly see that Tamerin's wasn't all there. The left side of his flesh pouch had gaping holes. Some of the holes were big enough that she could see part of his hardening cock and hints of seed sack inside. How his dick hadn't ended up scarred like the pouch was a miracle.

"It's disgusting," Tamerin said reaching down the grab his pants. "I'm sorry I let you see it."

"Freeze," Lasha ordered. To her surprise, he did.

"What? Do you see danger?" he whispered, rolling his eyes around the room without moving his head.

"The only danger I see is a flesh pouch about to get molested," she warned as she moved to kneel on the edge of the bed in front of Tamerin.

With his pants gripped in his hand, he straightened up and sounded the sharp clatter of a surprised rattle. "Molested?"

Keeping her eyes on his, she leaned over and put her face to his crotch. Placing her mouth over one of the ragged holes, she kissed gently.

When Tamerin sucked in a breath, she pulled away. "Did that hurt?"

"No," he whispered. "It felt amazing. I didn't know my pouch was sensitive like that. But it must disgust you to look at it."

"Nothing about you is disgusting," she assured him, leaning in again. This time she didn't stop kissing until she'd pressed her lips to every mark, scar, and opening. As she worked she could see and feel Tamerin's cock getting harder and pushing at the pouch. She was sure it would retract soon, so she needed to hurry if she wanted to have a little fun. Pushing her tongue through one of the holes, she licked at the side of his dick.

"Lasha!" Tamerin cried out and jerked. She did it again, enjoying the way he shuddered and sounded the low thrumming rumble of arousal.

She was about to lick across one of the smaller scars when the flesh pouch retracted with a pop and Tamerin's thick cock and ball spilled out.

"Hello," she greeted his dick and then followed it up with a friendly lick to the bouncing head, tasting cardamom. Before she could do it again, Tamerin dropped to his knees next to the bed, putting them at eye level.

"You're truly not repulsed by me?" he murmured, putting his face close to hers.

"How do I convince you?" she asked with a smirk. "I know! We could tie you to the bed and wait for your cock to settle and the pouch to cover it backup. Then I could tease you 'til you get hard and the pouch pulls back. I can keep doing that until you really believe me."

A violent shiver went through him. "By the Ancestors! *No!* I swear I believe you," he agreed quickly.

"Shame," she responded with a wicked grin. "I was looking forward to *really* proving it to you."

"I'm sure what you're proposing would be classified as torture," he pointed out.

"But the good kind," she countered.

A soft humorous rumble interrupted his aroused thrumming for a brief moment. "Debatable."

Wrapping her hand around the back of his neck, she urged him to join her on the bed. "Enough talk. I think we were in the middle of something."

"As my songbird wishes," Tamerin agreed and gracefully moved onto the bed. Instead of moving back to make room, she rolled on her back and brought her legs up to wrap around him. Soon they were in a similar position as when this whole thing had started. Except this time, they were both completely naked.

Progress!

"I want you in my mouth," she demanded.

"Let me pleasure you first," he argued.

She frowned and then patted the bed. "I've got an idea. Lie here on your side."

Tamerin didn't hesitate to do as she asked. He practically flopped down on the bed facing her, one arm under his head. "Next?"

Lasha stifled a laugh at his eagerness as she lay down with her feet at the head of the bed. Tamerin's sexy thrumming rumble was interrupted by a slow irregular beat of confusion.

"What are you doing?"

"This way we can touch each other at the same time," she explained and then grasped his cock in one hand, using the other to prop up her body a little. It wasn't the most comfortable position, but she'd heard some of the girls gossiping about it once and always wanted to try it.

Tamerin pulled in a sharp breath when she licked over his bulbous crown. She treated him like a dessert she wanted to savor by licking and sucking on him.

He groaned and remained perfectly still before asking. "I'm allowed to touch back, correct?"

"Of course," she whispered to the head of his dick. She parted her legs by bending her knee and making her leg into a triangle. It didn't feel great, but it was tolerable. Cool air washed across her exposed sex, but to her disappointment Tamerin didn't do anything.

"No, this won't work at all," he announced. Then she felt his hands on her hips and he was lifting and moving her. Letting go of his erection, she gasped and reached down to put her hands on his legs to steady herself. He rolled over on his back, taking her with him. When he'd finished moving, she was on her hands and knees, her pussy hovering over his face.

"There, that's better," he declared. "Lower yourself onto me."

Looking down between their bodies, she shook her head and regarded him with a wide-eyed expression. "I can't do that. I might smother you!"

The marbles-clinking rumble of amusement sounded before he went back to thrumming. "Then I'll get to tell the Ancestors I died a good death."

She bit her lip to keep from laughing and tried to dismount. "There is no way I can—"

"Yes, you can," he countered, his strong hands on her thighs keeping her from moving. "I want this. Please, songbird. Can we try? You're so tiny I could easily lift you off if I have any breathing issues." Then he lifted his head and licked down the length of her slit. "But I'm positive your slick is life-giving."

A combination of a gasp and giggle came out of her. "Don't come back to haunt me if this goes wrong," she grumbled and stopped trying to move.

Instead of answering her, he used his grip to urge her pussy against his face. She sank down until his mouth could reach every part of her sex. Without hesitation he started lapping at her. She moaned and shivered a little as his long strokes stimulated her sensitive flesh. It wasn't enough to make her come, but it felt good. Good enough that she forgot about his impressive cock until it twitched and bobbed in her face.

"Sorry," she whispered to his dick. "I forgot about you for a minute. In my defense the mouth north of you is really distracting!"

Tamerin's hands on her hips lifted her briefly. "Are you talking to my mating shaft?" he asked with an amused rumble.

"Well it's big enough to be its own person, so I thought I should address him accordingly," Lasha sassed.

"Very well. Carry on," he responded and then pushed her hips down and buried his tongue in her pussy.

"Tamerin!" she cried out both in surprise and pleasure. He didn't relent and divided his attention between sliding his impossibly long tongue inside of her and sucking at her throbbing clit.

His cock twitched again and she focused on working her lips over the crown. Balancing her upper body on one hand, she used the other to grasp below her mouth. The smell of cardamom was heavy in her nose. No wonder she wanted him in her mouth. He smelled good enough to eat!

Careful to keep her teeth from hurting him, she worked her mouth up and down, coordinating her movements with her hand. Tamerin moaned against her pussy. Then he started thrumming again, making her moan around his dick.

His constant thrumming rumble was like having a high-powered vibrator between her legs. She wasn't going to last long!

Determined to make him climax with her, she worked his cock. It was hard to concentrate but she managed to hold off her orgasm. Then he slipped a finger between her legs, gathered her juices and some of his own bonding oil, and rubbed it on her puckered opening.

Nope! She had no hope of holding out! Pleasure bloomed from that touch, making her moan around his thick meat in her mouth. No longer in control, her hips pushed down against him, demanding more pressure.

Tamerin gave it to her, sliding one finger into her back hole at the same time his tongue slid deep inside her pussy and his chin hit her clit with that thrumming rumble.

She was overwhelmed so quickly she didn't have time to pull her mouth off him before she was crying out and jerking. She didn't bite down on him, but her teeth did graze his head. Far from making him shout in pain, his cock swelled and soon her mouth was filled with his cum even as her own orgasm was making her body shake uncontrollably.

It was impossible to swallow it all. Some ran out of her mouth as she breathed heavily through her nose. Tamerin moaned into her pussy as he kept stimulating her through both their orgasms. Her pleasure continued reverberating through her as she diligently kept working him with her mouth and hand.

Tamerin broke first by tapping her thigh. "Easy, songbird."

Proud she'd outlasted him, she let his cock slide out from between her lips. Before she could even lift one leg to dismount, he easily lifted her, swung her around, and settled her on the bed next to him.

"Well, I guess that works too," she pretended to grumble even as she snuggled herself up against the soft skin of his scarred left arm. They both needed to visit the cleansing unit for a cleanup, but after some cuddles and rest. She'd never felt so boneless before. Dirty and boneless. What a perfect combination!

"Close your eyes for a mark," he murmured to her, his rumble reverting back to the familiar purr. "Then I'll carry you into the cleansing unit and bathe you."

"Thanks, Tamerin," she whispered, her eyes closed and sleep already tugging at her.

"You never need to thank me, songbird," he assured her. "Because you're the only reason I live right now."

CHAPTER 17

Most passenger vessels had observation areas where passengers could gather to watch passing stars or planets. The Slow Star was no different, but as with everything else on the vessel, their observation area was showing signs of wear. Old seats had been patched and repatched. Some of the windows had been replaced by shutters with giant displays over them to give you the image of what you'd see if the window still existed.

One window even had a giant crack in it. When Lasha saw the prominent blemish, she couldn't take her eyes off it.

"Maybe we shouldn't be here," she murmured. "We should go."

"But you were so excited," Tamerin protested. "You said you'd never gotten to visit an observation area. This one is small and poorly equipped, I'll admit. But it's better than no view."

Lasha pointed to the crack. "I'm not interested in dying for a view."

Tamerin looked to where she indicated and then sounded the marbles-clicking rumble of amusement. "That's not dangerous. If the viewing polymer becomes unstable, shutters will close and seal it before any atmosphere is lost. The shutters seal on all four edges and can't be retracted. When that happens the whole unit has to be replaced."

His explanation made her feel better. "Oh, then I guess that's why they put a display up. Must have been cheaper than replacing that window. Still, it's worrisome that they had one shutter deploy. What do you think happened?"

"Micro-meteor probably," he answered. "If you're in space long enough you're going to get hit by one. It's only a matter of time. That's why all ships have resealing veins in their outside panels. I was on a ship that was hit by so many we looked as if we'd deliberately styled a dimpled exterior."

Laughing, Lasha let him lead her to a heavily padded and battered bench. Sitting down, he started up a soft purr and drew her into his lap. She arranged herself sideways so she could lean against his chest and look out the observation window to his left and he could stare through the ones straight ahead.

"There's not much to see right now," he warned her. "But in about four marks we'll be passing by a gas giant that I believe you might find interesting. It glows a bright blue with a ring of orange across its equator."

"You're right, I want to see that," she agreed.

They watched the stars in silence for a while before Lasha voiced the question that had been bouncing around in her brain since last night. "What happened to your arm and shoulder?"

She expected Tamerin to get tense and maybe even a little defensive, but her warrior surprised her. "I was waiting for you to ask me that," he admitted calmly.

The smell of cardamom hit her nose before she felt his head move and his cheek brush against the top of her head. She waited until he'd finished before reaching up and running her fingers through her hair to better distribute his bonding-oil. She found she liked the smell best after it soaked into her scalp and skin.

She felt his lungs expand and contract a few times as he breathed in their combined scents. Then he started talking, his deep voice soft.

"Palforma and I are members of the same clan, but different families. Our clan is famous for producing warriors, so both of us were excited to be accepted into the military despite our age. We hadn't even finished our last growth-shift yet. Most wouldn't have been accepted for another three or four solars."

"You must've been young," Lasha commented, trying to picture a smaller, youthful version of Tamerin. "Why were you and Palforma different from everyone else."

"At the time I thought it was because we showed inherent skills." Tamerin sounded a rattle she'd never heard before. It was reminiscent of the whooshing of a long rope dropping a significant distance with a heavy weight causing it to snap and rebound at the end.

Her guess was it meant derision. "But it wasn't because you guys were special?"

"Training taught me quickly that neither of us was special," Tamerin answered with the derisive rattle again. "Looking back, I know the head of my clan must have made our acceptance happen because we were too young to get in on our own merits. We were happy to go and didn't question it. I remember my parents had reservations and begged me to reconsider. They wanted me to put off training for several solars at least. Maybe study and train at home, but I was determined."

He paused for a minute and Lasha kept silent to let him organize his thoughts.

"I was allowed to do early training with Palforma and several other members of our clan, but when the general training was done, we were all given assignments in different specialties. I wouldn't see Palforma again for many solars. Not until we ended up in the same healing facility."

"No," Lasha gasped. "You were both wounded at the same time?"

"Within rotations of each other," Tamerin corrected. "Different sections of the same war. Now that the war is over, I can tell you my duties. I was trained in espionage. During the Braxin War, my job was to turn Braxin allied civilizations against the Braxin, or at least to convince them not to get involved. It required me to do a lot of stealth traveling near Braxin space or active war zones. Even if I couldn't get the allies to turn, I was good at planting devices or gathering information. I uncovered several plots that were foiled."

"Is that why you got a Muldy medal or something?" Lasha asked, trying to remember something Tamerin had said to her early in their acquaintance.

"Mattil Medal," he corrected her. "But I didn't get it for any of those successful missions. I was awarded it posthumously after my last mission."

Lasha jerked a little and then sat up so she could turn her head and look up at him. "I'm sorry, I believe you're sitting here alive and well. How did you win something posthumously?"

He wrapped his arms around her, urging her to lean back against him. "For five rotations they thought I was dead. The last plot I uncovered was an attempt to destroy a supply convoy. I got on board a ship they were going to use. I tried to sabotage the ship's thrusters, but that didn't work so I sent off an end-all transmission."

She didn't like the sound of that at all. "End-all?"

"When we go off on our own, we're given a device. When activated, a signal goes out to all Talin ships and stations. They're expected to home in on the device and fire, no questions asked."

"Oh shit," Lasha breathed. "You put yourself on a suicide mission."

Wiggling around, she got situated so she could hug her arms around his neck and put her face next to the strip of exposed skin at the base of his neck. "You must have been so scared!"

"Terrified," Tamerin admitted. "I pulled the device out, armed it, and activated it. After I did all that I realized I was going to die, and in that moment I wanted to undo it all. I wanted to live. I wanted to see my parents and sibling again. That's when I..." Tamerin's voice trailed off.

"What?" Lasha urged. "That's when you, what?"

"I questioned my empire," he whispered. "Why were we fighting this war? The war with the Braxin started over a small solar system without a single life-sustaining planet. What was so important about that corner of space that we had to sacrifice so many lives to get it? That was the moment I despised Talarian, the Apogee Assemble, the monarch, and most of all my clan. From the moment I'd been pulled from an artificial womb, I'd been told I needed to think of the empire first. Then I had to consider my clan and my family. But I was never to think of myself."

"That's some serious indoctrination," Lasha commented.

"It was. Looking back, I can see it all clearly," Tamerin agreed. "At that moment all my illusions were shattered. As I waited to die, I didn't look forward to meeting my Ancestors or entering the Domicile of Souls. All I could picture was my sister's face, and I selfishly wanted to see her again. I didn't want to die an honorable death. I wanted to live a fulfilling life."

"What happened?" Lasha pushed. "How did you survive?"

"With an act of treachery," Tamerin said succinctly.

"Good," Lasha pronounced.

Tamerin jerked. "Good? I said I committed treason and you applaud me?"

"Did you murder babies?" she asked.

"Of course not," he answered, sounding a confused rumble.

"Did you slaughter a bunch of noncombatants?" she questioned.

"Why are you asking me these questions?"

"I don't care what you had to do to survive as long as you didn't hurt a bunch of innocents while you were doing it," she explained. "If you had to do something your empire wouldn't have liked, then fuck them. It's been my experience that those who start wars are never the ones who have to suffer through them."

"You pack a lot of wisdom in a small body," Tamerin murmured. "Let me finish telling you my story and then you can decide if I'm still worthy of you or not."

"You can finish, but it won't change my mind," she assured him. "You're worthy. Now hurry up and tell me what happened. Did you turn off the end-all?"

"After I'd activated it, I stood there staring at the cursed end-all box for way too long," Tamerin described. She could picture him perfectly still and holding the box while all those thoughts swirled around in his head. "When I decided I wanted to live, I smashed it into pieces."

Lasha shook her head. "I can't believe that worked."

Tamerin's voice was grim. "It didn't. The signal goes out to all nearby Talin ship, station, or outpost. They know to lock long-distance weapons and sends them to that location. The incoming projectiles were going to hit no matter what I did to the box. I smashed it to feel better, though I knew it was pointless."

"So what did you do next?" Lasha asked. "Did you warn those on the ship?"

"I'd been hiding in the aft section of the ship, three compartments fore of the port engine room when I figured out what was going on and activated the end-all. The Braxin running the ship were burning hard toward the Talin supply convoy. They still thought they were running undetected. They didn't know I was there. The ship had been stripped down so there weren't any escape pods or shuttles. Not even a life-box. But it was one of those standard O-head vessels so I sprinted for the control room."

"What's an O-head vessel?" Lasha asked, feeling a little confused. She pictured a ship in the shape of a lollipop. Or maybe a penis with a mushroom head? No, this was a serious story, she needed to keep her thoughts out of the gutter.

"An O-head vessel has a support hatch running from the main body of the ship to the control room, but nothing else. That way they can haul dangerous cargo, and if anything goes wrong, the crew simply seal the hatch and flush the atmo out of the support hatch. That creates a vacuum of safety between the cargo and crew in the control room."

"Oh," Lasha exclaimed with a nod. "That must be for hauling stuff like uthar minerals. Those things break containment all the time and create ghost ships."

"Exactly," Tamerin agreed. "I had some master plan of getting to the control room, sealing myself inside and blowing the connecting hatch."

"You were going to turn the control room into an escape pod," Lasha said with approval. "Even if it didn't have independent systems, you would at least survive for a day or two. Right? That's good thinking."

"It would've been if the control room hadn't been full of Braxin. I hit the door display as I lunged inside, locking myself in with four Braxin. They are fierce fighters and as big as an average Talin. As I looked at them, I knew this was my end. But at least I was going to die fighting instead of waiting to be blown up."

"But you didn't die, so you must have won the fight," Lasha guessed.

"Yes and no," Tamerin answered.

"Tamerin!" she protested.

Rumbling out a sound of amusement, he continued. "Three of them turned and attacked me at once. Thankfully, none of them had any weapons, but they have claws and impossibly thick hides. I broke off many of my quills and a few of my claws got ripped out during the fight. I'm not sure how much damage I took because that's not when all of this happened." He pointed to his scarred left arm. "I took down one of the Braxin but was losing to the other two with the last one standing back watching. Then the single Braxin not fighting went to the ship's controls and changed course. That distracted the two I was battling but not enough to give me the upper hand. I remember they were shouting at that male as they hit me. Demanding to know why he'd turned the ship away from the convoy."

"Did they have the kind of instruments that would pick up the incoming projectiles?" Lasha asked.

"Their system registered the projectiles as meteors, but anyone with half a brain would know what the indicators truly meant. As the Braxin I was fighting yelled at him not to turn the ship, he was accusing them of lying."

Lasha shook her head. "Lying? This is getting more complicated than a Ugarian soap opera plot. What happened next?"

A soft rumble of amusement briefly interrupted Tamerin's purring. "Then the projectiles found us. The Braxin had turned the ship so they hit the engine end. The thing was a massive hauler so it didn't disintegrate the entire vessel, only the back third. The front storage and control room sections went hurling off in different directions."

Lasha slumped a little. "You got so lucky that Braxin turned the ship," she whispered. "What did the other Braxin do? Did they hurt him?"

"When the ship was hit, the control room took damage leading to several electrical fires and small explosions. One of the Braxin I'd been battling died and I sustained the worst of my injuries. I blacked out for a while."

"And when you woke up you were the only survivor?" Lasha asked.

"No, the Braxin who'd turned the ship was still alive," Tamerin told her. "And he'd killed the one other Braxin who'd survived. He did it to keep me from being executed."

Lasha jerked a little in surprise. "But why would he do that? I mean, I'm glad, but why?"

Tamerin went silent. He was still purring and when he leaned over, she put her head close so he could rub against her. But he didn't rub. He buried his face in her hair and breathed in deeply.

Staring out at the dark space beyond the viewing windows, Lasha waited patiently for him to find his words.

Finally, Tamerin started talking again. "His name was Nelk and the ship belonged to him. He hadn't been told they were going on a suicide mission. He thought they were taking supplies to a refugee camp. The Braxin are like Talins. They don't have conscriptions. You're supposed to want to join the military. To uphold the honor of your species even unto death."

"But Nelk was different?" she guessed.

"Yes. He didn't believe in war or fighting, and when the war kept going, he dedicated his life to helping the Braxin who'd been displaced. He'd gotten suspicious when they wouldn't let him see the cargo but let it go because he was eager to help citizens displaced by the conflict. He was an honorable male."

Lasha got the feeling that was high praise for a Talin to give a non-Talin. "I'm surprised he killed one of his own."

"He was angry over being lied to by his fellow Braxin, and I never told him what my job was or about the end-all box," Tamerin said, sounding a muted rattle of buzzing wasps. It was the sound of anxiety and maybe sadness. "He thought I was an average civilian who'd snuck on the ship to find out where it was going, which was partially true. At the time, I wasn't carrying any weapons. The lack of weapons made him think I wasn't a soldier. He saw me as trapped in this war, like him. Forced into things I didn't want to do."

"He wasn't entirely wrong," Lasha whispered. "In a way you were both lied to. You realized it after you activated the end-all box and he found out when the missiles launched."

"I suppose so," Tamerin agreed, his voice a low, rumbling murmur. "I don't remember much of our time together. I was in a lot of pain and he couldn't do much for me. The control room was hurtling through space, and if we hadn't been found by a passing freight hauler, we both would have died."

"What happened once you two were rescued?" Lasha asked.

"The freight hauler was owned and run by Leemrons," Tamerin continued. "Their people and the Talin Empire have several trade and diplomatic agreements in place. The moment they saw I was Talin, they went out of their way to aid me. They even changed direction to the nearest Talin outpost to get me help. They put me in their med room and gave me some medications that dulled the pain, but they didn't have any staff capable of dealing with my injuries."

"But what about Nelk?"

"They secured him with restraints in one of their cargo areas," Tamerin explained. "They probably thought they'd get a reward for turning him over."

"You let them do that?" Lasha protested. "He helped you."

"That's not where the story ends," Tamerin said with a glass-marbles-clinking rumble of amusement before going back to purring. "I was in and out of it from both the medication and the pain. When I figured out what was going on I demanded they release him. They were confused and alarmed, but I told them he was working for the Talin Empire and needed to be released on the next station so he could make his way back to Braxin-controlled space."

Lasha beamed at him. "That was clever. Did it work?"

Tamerin tightened his hold on her briefly in response to her compliment. "Of course. They weren't going to question it and potentially ruin an information pipeline. Stopping at the closest station delayed me being treated by a Talin healer for an extra three rotations. That's one of the reasons the damage to my arm and flesh pouch couldn't be fixed."

Lasha reached around to grab Tamerin's quill-less arm and pulled it to her chest. Hugging it tightly, she whispered, "Not damaged, just different. Like me."

"Different," Tamerin corrected himself with a loud purr and then continued. "The ship docked at a large station and let him off. I still had my belt pouch and Ident Cube on me, so I bought an information square off one of the Leemron crew, loaded credits onto it and gave it to Nelk. It wasn't enough to pay him back for saving me, but it was all I had access to at the time."

"Did he say anything to you before he left?" Lasha asked.

"He thanked me." Tamerin sounded that muted-anxious-buzzing rattle again. "I was the reason his ship was destroyed. He was forced to kill one of his own people to save my life, yet he thanked me. He must have realized I was a lost soul because he gave me a last bit of wisdom. He said to decide what was most important in this universe and cling to it. I thought a lot about that while I was recovering."

"What did you decide was the most important thing?" Lasha asked.

"I wanted it to be my parents or my sister," he murmured. "But I couldn't talk to them. I couldn't be honest about what had happened to me during the war and my change in perspective. I never went home after I recovered because I couldn't face them now that I lacked faith in the Talin Empire."

"You don't think they'd understand?" Lasha asked. "They'd been reluctant for you to go to war in the first place. Hadn't they?"

"I couldn't risk it," Tamerin explained. "What if I bared my soul, told them everything, and they turned on me? I was struggling to make it through each day already. I wouldn't have survived their dismissal."

Lasha's heart broke for this entire species. They had so much yet not enough at the same time.

"Did you ever decide what you wanted to cling to?" she pushed, interested in finding out what Tamerin had centered his worldview around.

"You."

His one word made her jerk, and if she hadn't been sitting so securely on his lap, she would've tumbled onto the floor.

"Me?" she squeaked out. "I mean, I love you and everything, but I'm not a worldview!"

"But you are," Tamerin argued. "Your strength and compassion are something everyone could learn from. You left your colony so you wouldn't be a burden, even if it meant making your life worse. Then you spent years being mistreated by Vicpors, yet you were quick to help Ilee and Relee despite the danger to yourself. Many civilizations could do worse than follow you as an example."

Deeply moved, Lasha blinked back tears. "I, uh, that's…" she blew out a breath, unsure how to respond. "Fuck, Tamerin. No one's turned me into a living philosophy before."

This time when he sounded his amused rumble, it was so loud that it was a jar of marbles clinking together instead of a bag. Huh, that must have been the Talin version of a boisterous laugh!

He brushed his lips against hers before talking. "It's only fitting because I worship you!"

CHAPTER 18

"I'm going to miss you!" Ilee said as she carefully tapped her pincer against Lasha's forearm. Normally Vicpors would impact hard enough to make a clacking sound, but Ilee knew to be gentle.

"You two are the only Vicpors I'll ever consider true friends," Lasha assured them. "You have to promise to send an update after you've settled in on Declow. As soon as I know where I'll be, I'll message you my transmission coordinates."

"Please do," Ilee agreed eagerly. "If we get reassigned somewhere else, I'm sure they'll forward the message."

"I wish you could have taken this ship with us," Relee whined.

"Sorana might be on the edge of Delorta and Talin boundaries, but it's nowhere close to Declow," Tamerin reminded her. "We'd be traveling very far out of our way to go there."

"I know," Relee said, holding up her pincer to bump against Lasha's forearm and then Tamerin's. "But it feels like you two are the only family Ilee and I have now."

Lasha's heart went out to Relee. Although Lasha had been useless to the other humans on Wimol, they'd still loved her. It was horrible to think about the way Relee had been treated by someone who should have cared about her the most.

"We are family," Lasha agreed. "We're just living in different places. We'll send lots of messages. Maybe one day we can even find a safe station or planet in the middle to meet again."

Relee's body almost vibrated with happiness. "That would be excellent!"

The warning to board sounded again. Because Kilkurn Station was set up to accommodate ships of any size, the sisters didn't need to take a shuttle to board. Only a few stragglers were left on the loading ramp.

"You guys need to go," Lasha urged. "It'd be silly to have gotten lucky to arrive on Kilkurn just before your ship is leaving only to miss boarding because we couldn't say goodbye."

"You're right," Ilee said, picking up the two bags that contained all of the sisters' possessions. Ilee had to leave most of her equipment and personal belongings behind, but Lasha knew the Vicpor had no regrets. What were belongings compared to freedom for both her and Relee?

The two turned and hurried down the ramp. "I'm going to miss them a lot," Lasha murmured to their retreating backs.

Tamerin stepped up behind her, his warm presence a balm to her sadness. "I'm still here."

Craning her neck, she looked up at him with a smile. "And that's the only reason I'm not crying."

"Don't be sad, songbird," he murmured to her. Leaning over, he rubbed his cheek against the top of her head. The familiar smell of cardamom perfumed the air, chasing away her gloom. She'd never get tired of Tamerin's scent.

Tucking herself firmly against him, she relaxed into his bulk. "As long as you're here, I won't be sad," she promised.

They stood there until the doors closed and the ship left. It was quiet in this section of the station. Lasha didn't mind simply existing while she processed all the profound changes to her life in the last few weeks. Tamerin never stopped holding her or purring, and he didn't push her to talk.

He didn't speak again until the next ship started to dock. "We should see about renting a room. Our ship won't arrive for another rotation."

"I guess so," she agreed with a sigh. Looking around for the first time. Although they were ensconced in a quiet area, she could see beyond a large arch a clear picture of the busy station. "I've never been here before."

"Kilkurn is owned by a Leemron conglomerate," Tamerin explained as he slung their bags over his shoulder and bent to pick her up. "It's the largest station in this sector and boasts many excellent amenities."

She stepped back and held out her hand before he could scoop her off her feet. "I want to walk."

"Very well," Tamerin agreed, but she could tell it was grudgingly. He took her hand in his and led her away from the docks. "We should be able to finally purchase appropriate clothing for you here."

Lasha looked down at her tunic dress. "I like what I've got on. These are comfortable to move around in."

"But they aren't made of the right material," he argued. "You should be wearing much softer things. And you need better slippers and an omnie to keep you warm instead of the badly fitting coat. And tools for grooming your mane and better cleansers."

Apprehension made her bite her lip. She ignored him calling her hair a mane and focused on the important part. "That's a lot of extra stuff. I'm fine with what I've got now. I promise."

Tamerin stopped their progress and faced her. Unwilling to bother the large and intimidating Talin, the foot traffic seamlessly flowed around them without a single annoyed sound.

"I'm not as rich as a member of a merchant family, but I have plenty of wealth. Buying a few items here won't impact my accounts, but it would make me happy to see you outfitted correctly. And it would give me pleasure to see you wearing nicer things."

His little speech made her melt. How had she gotten so lucky? "Okay, maybe a few things," she allowed.

"As much as you need," he corrected.

"Then we're in luck because I don't need much," she quipped as they started walking again.

They bantered as Tamerin rented a room, stored their bags, and guided her to the section of the station with shops. Lasha had only seen so many things for sale one other time in her life, during the trip to Glakor—the last happy moment before she'd started the job that nearly killed her.

But that station paled in comparison to Kilkurn.

"Wow," she breathed. "This place is huge!"

"I told you it was the largest in the sector," Tamerin reminded her.

"I know, but I don't have much experience to go by," she responded with a grin. "Show me around! I want to see everything."

"Certainly, my songbird."

The first place he guided her into was a clothing shop. As with many places that sold garments, this one had a seamer machine with patterns and color options you could pick from. Unlike the ones she'd seen before, this machine had a massive catalog featuring clothing for hundreds of different species.

Tamerin tapped at the machine's display, bringing up six images of clothing options. "These are the ones that will fit you," he explained.

Lasha leaned forward to examine them. They all looked like versions of a wrap-style garment where you put it on like a coat then tied one side at the hip on the inside and the other side tied at the hip on the outside. It reminded her of some styles of clothing she'd seen in Old Earth vids.

Because they looked as comfortable as the tunic dress she was wearing now, she picked the style that went all the way to the ankle with a high collar and long sleeves. It looked the warmest, and she never wanted to be cold again.

"That one seems bulky," Tamerin noted. He pointed to one that ended at the knee with three-quarter sleeves. "This one might be more comfortable."

"Fine," she agreed, trying to cover her irritation. Why did he ask what she wanted if he was going to pick for her?

He sounded a rumble so brief she wasn't sure, but she thought it might have been a humorous one. "We'll get them both."

She was quick to protest. "I don't need two more outfits. I've got the three tunics already."

Ducking his head down, Tamerin rubbed a cheek on the top of her head. "We're buying at least five garments here today. Four wraps and one omnie."

"That's a lot of clothes," she grumbled.

"It's really not," he countered. "Most of the humans I know have boxes of outfits."

She blinked up at him. Then held her hands body width apart. "Boxes?"

He rumbled out a negative sound and held his hands extended out as far as he could stretch. "Not small boxes. Big boxes."

"Wow, damn," she muttered. She didn't know a single human who had more than a handful of practical, heavy-duty garments for work and one or two nice ones for special occasions. The amount of clothing Tamerin described was insane to her. "You have to be lying. No human has that many credits."

"The Talins who care for them have the credits," Tamerin explained.

"Ah, now the universe makes sense again," she joked. "I was worried there for a second. How many humans live with Talins?"

"I can only give you a rough number," he warned her. "But I believe it's somewhere around fifteen thousand now."

"Fifteen thousand?" she questioned with an incredulous cry. "Are you kidding me?"

His soothing purr filled her ears. "I know it's not many, but we are also actively searching out more humans," he assured her.

"No, that's not what I mean," she said. "That's more humans than I've heard about living in one place, ever. Not since Old Earth stopped supporting life anyway. Well, we did have a colony on Mars that supposedly had thirty thousand people, but it collapsed only a few years after Old Earth."

He sounded his glass-marbles-clinking-together rumble of amusement. "Oh, I see. Well, they aren't all gathered together. They're scattered over my homeplanet, Talarian. Some live on Talin colonies, and a few are on Talin space stations."

She nodded. "I guess if you guys let us work side by side with you, we don't have to live in the segregated colony-communities like we do everywhere else. It's nice that Talins are willing to let us integrate."

Tamerin went very still and silent. No rumble. No rattle. No shifting from foot to foot or reaching for her to hug. Hmm, what had she said to make him tense?

"Tamerin? Are you rethinking buying all this stuff?"

"No, not at all, we're still getting everything," he answered. "I was thinking about your integration comment."

"Sure, what about it?" she asked, looking back at the images on the display.

"Humans don't perform hard labor among us," he explained, his words coming out slowly as if he was being careful about how he said things.

Huh, what was that all about? He probably didn't want to scare her off by making life among the Talins sound too hard.

"I'm not surprised you don't need us for manual labor. Most civilizations willing to spend the money on high-quality bots don't need anyone to do hard labor," she agreed, wanting to reassure him that she wasn't worried about being put to work. "And you guys are a huge empire. I've never even seen one of you on Glakor before, but you showed up and everyone jumped to do your bidding. That's a seriously powerful rep. It's just nice that you guys let us humans settle there. I really think someone should go to all the human colonies and see who wants to move."

He purred as he spoke. "Some Talins are seeking out human colonies. Mostly the ones Zia and a few others have told us about, but it needs to be done delicately."

"Why does it have to be done delicately?" Lasha asked.

"The Ilgorian Federation doesn't like us in their space," Tamerin told her.

Lasha made a face. "Oh, that's a problem. Wimol and a bunch of other human colonies are all in Ilgorian territory. But I'm sure you guys can get special permission to visit," Lasha argued. "The Ilgorian Federation isn't that strict. The Ugarians who let my ancestors settle on Wimol didn't even ask the federation for permission."

"There's a vast difference between helpless refugees and members of a powerful empire," Tamerin argued.

Lasha shrugged. "Sure, but you have an in with Zia. She could also go alone to talk to the communities and see if they want to migrate to Talarian."

"That's not the only issue. There are, uh, trade-offs to living among the Talins that some humans might not like."

"Oh yeah, that's true. You guys are downright draconian about the affection and bonding thing. It's sad that if we meet up with other Talins, you can't admit you like me," she responded, feeling her heart sink a little. It occurred to her that among Talins, their true relationship had to be kept a secret.

She didn't like being anyone's dirty secret. But she also didn't want Tamerin to get in trouble. Still, it stung.

"I can admit to liking you. I can't admit I've scent-bonded with you," he reminded her.

Her emotions went from tanking to flying with that one sentence. "And scent-bonding means you love me. Right?"

"You doubt it?" he asked, wrapping his arms around her. "Talin scent-bonding is more powerful than human love. I've heard of humans declaring their love for each other and then separating after a few years. I even heard they would find other partners. I can't do that. If we're separated for too long, I'll die."

Gasping, she reached up to cup his face with her hands. "Die?"

"It's called Ending. When bonded partners are separated for too long, we die."

She remembered him telling her about it now but hadn't thought it applied to their relationship. "But I'm human."

"I would still die," he warned her. "You being human doesn't make my need for you any less."

A strange combination of fear and elation filled her. Their relationship had progressed fast, and her feelings of affection for him were all confused together with her feelings of thankfulness for her rescue. But she was sure of one thing; she'd never let him die.

"You're safe," she promised. "I'd never leave you. Not if I can help it, anyway."

"I promise the same."

This moment felt heavy and meaningful, despite being surrounded by patrons in a busy seamer shop. "Now and forever," she murmured, pulling his face to hers.

"Now and forever," he echoed. She pressed her lips to his. He opened his mouth, inviting her to deepen the kiss. The world faded away and all that mattered was the two of them.

Satisfaction filled her. As far as she was concerned, they'd just gotten married.

"Are you ever going to finish with that machine?"

The angry voice made Lasha jump and Tamerin sound the hard-projectiles-being-rapidly-fired rattle. They both turned to see a cat-like Leemron standing there with a ripped garment in her hands.

The Leemron was already backing away before Lasha spoke.

"We'll finish quickly," Lasha said as she turned to the seamer machine and looked for a button that might cancel their order. Sometimes these systems used the same type of display so she could make an educated guess even though she couldn't read it.

"We are putting in a large order," Tamerin growled out, making the Leemron jerk back into a rack of premade items. Nothing fell, but the rack shook violently from the impact. "This machine won't be done for some time. Go find another."

"Damn Talins think they own the universe," the Leemron grumbled even as she hurried away. Several other seamer machines sat on the other side of the shop, but the Leemron didn't spare them a glance. Instead she left with the garment tucked under her shaggy arm.

"We don't own it yet," Tamerin muttered under his breath. "But when we do there'll be no place for rude fur-lickers in our universe."

Lasha tried hard, but a giggle-snort bubbled out of her. Tamerin looked down at her and made a rumble that sounded alarmingly like large wheels bumping slowly over a cobblestone road.

"What sound was that?" he asked her.

"Same question back at you," she responded this time with a full laugh.

"It was a questioning rumble," he explained and made the sound again.

"Well mine was because I tried to hold in my laugh and then kinda sneezed it out my nose," she explained. A huge grin stretching across her face. She felt happy and carefree.

"You can sneeze a laugh?" Tamerin asked with the clattering rattle of surprise.

"Today we both learned I can sneeze-laugh," she agreed and then dissolved into a fit of giggles. "I wish Zia was here. This is hilarious!"

Tamerin started tapping on the seamer machine's display again. "We'll be leaving for Sorana soon, and you can tell her all about our exchange and discovery," he reminded her.

Before she could respond, he pointed to some nearby fabric samples hanging from the side of the machine. "Pick which colors you like," he instructed. "We'll finish this order and go eat a meal while it's being processed."

Feeling light and bubbly, she pivoted in place and started going through the samples. Ten years ago she'd never imagined being in a place like this deciding on luxurious garments. Her life had gotten very lucky! Now she needed to pick out at least one green item to keep the luck and happiness going.

CHAPTER 19

There were lots of places to eat, but Tamerin was adamant that they go to a specific place. When they entered, she looked around expecting to see some kind of unique or opulent furnishings, but everything struck her as ordinary and mundane.

The decor was the same as every other place on the station. Small round tables surrounded by sturdy stools filled the space. Serving bots scuttling between tables beeped to warn everyone as they moved.

Bemused, Lasha didn't say anything until Tamerin had them settled at a table in a far corner. Then he tapped the display set into the table and started reading the menu to her. That's when she understood why they were at this restaurant specifically.

"Some of this is human food!" she exclaimed. "How is that possible?"

"Occasionally Talins and their human companions will travel through Kilkurn Station. Because humans have special dietary needs, this place agreed to accommodate us. They added several dishes to the menu specifically for humans," Tamerin explained.

"You guys keep surprising me." She was sitting next to Tamerin so she pressed herself up against his side. "I don't know any species that would go to so much effort for humans. Unless there was some kind of trade or power dynamic in the exchange."

Tamerin purred. "I'd do anything for you, songbird."

She loved it when he called her that. Humming softly, she ignored decorum and wiggled herself under his arm and onto his lap.

When he realized what she was doing, he sat back to make it easier for her to get situated, keeping up a soft purr.

"What would you like to eat?" he asked once she was sitting sideways on his thighs with her head resting on his shoulder.

Reaching out she drew his quill-less arm to wrap around her front. He let her move him as he ordered for them. With his free hand he unclipped his Ident and tapped it on the table, then pressed his palm down to match the Ident to his biosignature. The display flashed to acknowledge he'd paid for the meal.

"Tell me about your life," she demanded now that they had nothing to do but wait for the food. "I've told you tons of stories about growing up on Wimol. But you haven't told me much about what your life was like."

"Where should I start?" he asked.

"Let's start with the basics. How many siblings do you have?"

He sounded an amused rumble. "I can tell you how many children most Talin parents have, two."

"That's interesting," she murmured. "Is it a biological thing or cultural?"

"It's the law, actually," he answered. "Our population is under strict control. After marriage each couple is expected to donate their genetic material to a cresh. The cresh will use artificial wombs to produce one male and one female child. Then the cresh will raise the child until they're ready to return home and begin working and learning from their family or clan."

"That, uh…" She didn't want to say it sounded horrible or cold or clinical, but she thought it was. "No live birth, huh?

No Talin is going to lose their figure popping out some kids," she teased.

He was silent for a moment, and she realized she'd said something inappropriate. "I'm sorry. I shouldn't have made a joke like that. Did some kind of disease make it necessary to use artificial wombs?"

"Talins can't get pregnant unless they're scent-bonded," he explained, his voice quiet. "It's not a surprise that artificial wombs were invented at the same time scent-bonding when out of style."

"But what if someone really wants to have their own kid?" Lasha asked.

"They can't," he answered simply. "Not any longer."

Then she remembered. "Because scent-bonding is illegal. Giving birth if proof you broke the law. That's harsh. I mean, I'm not sure I want to have kids, but I'd be pissed off if someone took my choices away."

His purr got louder. "I'll make sure those laws don't touch you," he promised.

She wanted to ask if Tamerin wanted kids, but the food arrived and distracted them both.

"I know that's not real saffron rice," she murmured as the server bot unloaded the plates, platters, and bowls of food. "But it smells like it, and that's all that matters."

"It has a human-safe composition," Tamerin assured her. "It won't hurt you."

"Too bad no one's figured out how to synthesize chocolate," she murmured as she reached for the bowl of faux-saffron rice. It had off-white cubes in it, probably synthesized chicken. One bite told her this was some of the best-manufactured protein she'd ever eaten. Someone had gone to great lengths to design and test these products so they had the right flavor and consistency. They might not look entirely correct, but the taste made up for that.

"Cho-co-late?" Tamerin asked, stumbling over the Old Earth word. His INT hadn't been able to translate it because there wasn't anything comparable in Talin.

Truthfully, no language could translate it because no species produced anything as wonderful and special as chocolate.

"It was another type of food from Old Earth," she said dismissively. Holding up a spoonful of saffron rice and chicken, she offered it to him. "Here, try this."

He took a sniff before delicately nibbling a small bite at the edge of the spoon. He was quick to pull his head back. "I don't think those flavors agree with the Talin palate."

His reaction made her giggle a little, especially when he reached for a canister of water and took several healthy swallows.

"Thanks for giving it a try." She ate what was left on the spoon before putting the bowl down and reaching for another. "What's this?"

"That's jorjuk," he explained and then pointed to several other dishes she didn't recognize and named them. "These are Talin dishes that are all compatible with human digestion."

"You tried my dish, so I'll try yours," she declared as she stared at the stew-like food. "How do you eat this?"

"Bring the edge of the bowl to your lips and tip some of the contents into your mouth." He pointed to one edge of the dish. "This spot is open with curved edges on either side to keep the food from flowing too quickly and splashing onto your face."

"Clever." She wasn't as careful as Tamerin as she tipped the bowl, so she got a big mouthful of thick broth. The texture wasn't disgusting, but it was unusual. It was also bland, reminding her of unflavored, synthesized protein mash.

She took another sip and this time she let several chunks flow into her mouth. One item in the mix reminded her of an Old Earth potato. It wasn't bad, but it could use some salt at least. And cumin. And black pepper. And a pinch of cayenne. That's all and it would be perfect.

"Do you like it?" he asked with an inquisitive rumble.

"I could eat it." There, that was a diplomatic answer. "Do you guys have any kind of table spice that you sprinkle on your food after it's been served?"

"Yes, we have dried and ground up ki seeds." Leaning forward he tapped at the table display. No sooner did he sit back than a server bot hurried up with a small bowl full of a coarse, dark brown powder. "I'm fond of it, but many find it too powerful of a taste for them."

Lasha reached out and took a pinch of the ki seeds and sprinkled it on her tongue. She was pleasantly surprised it was slightly like turmeric. Without consulting Tamerin, she scooped up a good amount of the ki seed and mixed it in with the jorjuk.

The next taste confirmed the ki seed had helped a lot. Tamerin had been quiet throughout this, and when she looked up, she realized she might have ruined the dish for him. He said he was fond of it, not that he wanted it to be added so generously.

"I'm sorry!" she apologized, looking down at the bowl in her hand and then back up at Tamerin. "That was super selfish of me. I already had my dish, and then I acted like your food was mine too."

"It's all for you," he answered. "I ordered everything for you, and I only planned to eat after you were finished."

His pronouncement stunned her for a moment. While no one had starved on Wimol while she'd been growing up, there hadn't been an abundance of food. Meals were never missed or skipped, and it was inconceivable that anyone would wait for everyone else to finish before eating whatever was left over.

Taking a deep breath, she let it out slowly before speaking. "You've probably never been truly hungry in your life, so you can't understand the importance of this gesture to me. But I need you to eat with me because food and love go hand in hand in my culture. Fixing it. Serving it. And eating it with others."

His purr got loud enough to make another patron look over and clack his tail on the floor in annoyance. Tamerin met the patron's eyes and growled and bristled the undamaged quills on his right arm. The patron was quick to pick up his dish and find another table at the other side of the room.

Lasha grinned. "That's one way to do it."

"Do what?" Tamerin asked, turning his attention back to her.

"Nothing," she said and then used her spoon from the saffron rice dish to dip into the jorjuk. "Here, have a bite. See if I added too much ki for you."

"Normally we don't eat this with a spoon," he pointed out before accepting the bite.

She returned the empty spoon to the bowl. "I want to feed you but I don't want to make a mess. Well, do you like it?"

"This is acceptable," he agreed after swallowing. His words might have lacked enthusiasm, but by the sound of his purring, he'd liked being fed by her.

"Great," she responded in a dry tone, amused by his response. "Now this."

She broke off a piece of black flat bread and held it to his mouth. He opened but then closed his lips around her fingers. She let go of the bit of bread as he swept his textured tongue across her finger and thumb. A shiver that had nothing to do with the restaurant's ambient temperature went through her.

Pulling her hand back, she was quick to offer him another bite of flatbread. His purring was loud and would dip into the slower, longer thrumming rumble of arousal when her fingers were in his mouth. Then it would speed back up to the purring rumble while he chewed.

She really liked that thrumming rumble. And the feel of his tongue on her fingers. And his warmth that seeped through their layers of clothing.

Really, she loved everything about him and this moment.

Her heartbeat increased as he accepted the next bite and did the same swipe across her fingers with his tongue. She'd never had something so mundane become sensual before.

"Now you," he insisted, taking a piece of the flatbread and holding it to her mouth.

As he'd done with her, she closed her mouth around his clawed fingers. He remained perfectly still as she tasted both the bland flatbread and the cardamom flavor of his skin.

She couldn't help herself. She used her tongue to move his fingers apart and then sucked on his large index finger as if it was his shaft.

The purring stopped all together as the slow thrumming took over his rumbling completely. Sitting on his lap she could feel the pulses of that thrumming rumble all through her body, especially her clit. She imagined her sex was pulsing to the same beat as his rumble.

"Your mouth is so hot," he whispered as he pulled his fingers free.

"Maybe we should go to our room," she suggested, feeling a little light-headed.

"We haven't finished our meal," he argued, picking up another bite of flatbread and dipped it in the jorjuk before offering it to her. She moved her head to the side to refuse the food. He lowered his hand, his sexy rumble quieting for a moment.

"We can finish later," she urged, desperate to feel his mouth and hands on her naked skin.

"You started this little game here," he responded, his voice merciless. The erotic rumble started up again with its delicious vibrations, making her squirm a little in his lap. "So we'll finish it here."

CHAPTER 20

Lasha gaped at him. Did he mean…no, he couldn't mean to make her orgasm here in public?

A glance around showed the establishment about a quarter full with several tables between them and the closest patron. With his back to the wall and the table in front of them, they were as sheltered from view as they could be in such a public place.

Still, this wasn't something she'd ever done before.

Setting the food down, he put his hands on her waist and lifted her. She thought he'd changed his mind and was going to stand her up so they could leave. That was good. They didn't want to get in trouble for public indecency, if that existed on this station.

She wasn't disappointed. Really she wasn't.

But moving her off his lap wasn't his intention. Using his immense strength, he easily shifted her until she was straddling one of his thighs and facing him instead of sitting sideways in his lap. The tunic dress rode up high on her legs, exposing her from mid-thigh down and bunching around her ass and hips.

"There, that's better," he murmured. She couldn't touch the floor with her feet so she went to lift one leg to set it on the top rung of the stool only to realize how much this new seating was going to affect her.

No undergarments meant her bare pussy was rubbing against his leg. His thrumming, pulsing rumble vibrated all of him, including the limb she was resting most of her weight on. She felt her core weeping from the sensation.

She bit her lip to keep from moaning. How did the male take her from zero to almost dripping wet so fast?

"Did you say something, songbird?" he whispered.

She looked up to see the sides of his face were shiny, oil seeping from the scent glands in his cheeks. Unable to resist, she reached up and ran her hand over his left cheek, gathering the oil on her fingers. Loving the smell and feel of his oil, she brought her fingers to her mouth and spread it across her lips.

Now it was his turn to sound a low moan and drop his head closer.

"Please do that again," he begged.

Without hesitation she brought both hands up and rubbed the sides of his face. His eyes closed as he voiced a low groan, his sensual rumbling becoming more intense. When both hands were covered in his oil, she rubbed them on her neck. His eyes fluttered open to watch her, his breathing growing ragged.

"I thought to tease you," he whispered, "but you've turned my weapons against me."

Swooping down, he crushed his mouth to hers. With a needy whimper, she parted her lips and let Tamerin invade her mouth with his tongue.

As they kissed, she ground her sex against his leg. Everything felt so good. The slick fabric of his pants coupled with his hard, armor-plated leg underneath was the perfect combination. The fabric kept his leg from being too rough on her delicate flesh but the texture of his armor plated skin gave her the friction she needed.

She moaned into his mouth. The smell of cardamom was thick in the air, and all she could hear was his lusty rumbling.

When the kiss ended and they finally pulled apart, her heart was beating as if she'd been running. "You're such a good kisser," she breathed.

"Only because you've taught me," he responded. Grabbing her hips, he slowed her movement. "Not too fast, songbird."

Making an incoherent angry noise, she let his hands keep her movements much slower than she wanted.

Something over her shoulder caught his eyes. Tensing up, he stilled her hips completely and bared his teeth at someone behind her.

"Turn away," he said to someone behind her. Then he sounded the fired-projectile rattle of aggression for emphasis. "For your own safety, go anywhere else but here."

Part of her wanted to turn her head to see who might have been there, but the larger part urged her to bury her face against Tamerin's neck to hide.

"I thought perhaps there was an open invitation to this coupling because you decided to perform in a public place," an unfamiliar voice commented. "I apologize for misunderstanding." Then footsteps leisurely walked away.

"Hoquins," Tamerin muttered. "Always hoping to join in others' fun."

"Maybe we should—" She started to suggest they leave but was cut off when he started that thrumming purr again. "Oh, don't stop," she whispered.

Lowering his head, he pressed his lips to the skin behind her ear, giving her several light kisses. Then he gently nipped the shell of her ear, making pleasure zing down her spine. Who knew ears were erogenous zones?

Shyness disappeared as desire pushed her to moan. "Do that again, please."

With great care, he tugged at the lobe of her ear with his sharp teeth. She jerked every time. It felt so good she couldn't remain still. After he'd done that several times, Tamerin whispered to her, his warm breath tickling the skin of her inner ear.

Words left her. She made incomprehensible pleading sounds, hoping he'd understand.

"Are you going to sing while you come for me, pretty songbird? I'm going to warn you, I'm the only one who gets to hear the way you sing when you climax. You need to stay quiet or I'll stop."

"Don't stop!" She whimpered then pushed her face against the base of his neck. That strip of vulnerable skin was against her mouth, so she licked it.

Her lick made him jolt. One of his hands came up and cradled the back of her head, holding her in place.

"Do that again, songbird." His words were half demand and half plea.

Far from making her feel trapped, his hand made her feel guarded, safe, and secure. She was surrounded by the sound, smell, and feel of him. Tamerin swamped every sense she possessed, except taste. To change that she flicked her tongue out, running up the length of his exposed flesh.

His hips jerked and he hissed out a breath. Something hard hit her gently in the belly. Tiling her head down, she saw Tamerin had come free of his flesh pouch and managed to tear open a round, disk-sized hole in his pants.

She didn't know a cock could be that strong.

Torn between climbing onto his shaft or keeping up the grinding she was already doing, she let loose with a breathless whimper.

Reaching down, she tried to take him in hand, but he was quick to intercept it, gently placing her fingers back on his face.

"I'll climax the moment you touch me," he growled. "And I have plans for later in our room. I can wait. You will not."

Lasha never thought she was that kind of person, but his commanding tone and strong, but gentle grip on her head were doing amazing things for her. Her entire world narrowed down to Tamerin and her looming orgasm.

Relaxing her face against his neck, she panted and resumed rubbing her sex hard against his leg. God, it felt so good!

Tamerin's throbbing rumble intensified. "You smell so good, songbird," he whispered, his breath hot against her ear.

"When we get back to the room, I'm going to lay you out on the bed, pull your legs apart, and feast on you. Even after you come again I won't stop. I'm going to hold you down and make you scream. Only then will I sink my shaft in you and fill you with my seed."

Panting, gasping, and whimpering, she opened her mouth and bit down on that little strip of exposed, soft, Talin skin. He groaned, his thrumming rumble never pausing or missing a beat.

"Yes," he moaned, tilting his head to the side to give her better access. "Use your human teeth on me. Bite me, rub on me, use my body for your pleasure."

Even as she bit down again, her orgasm crashed over her. Her jaw locked down on his skin, muffling her wail. Tamerin jerked from the pressure but then moaned. His hand never moved from the back of her head.

"You're beautiful, my songbird," Tamerin whispered to her, still holding her head against his throat. "Every part of you is perfect and mine. Even your pleasure is mine."

His possessive words made her body tremble more as she kept rubbing against him to make the orgasm last. She'd been called pretty but never beautiful. No partner in the past had denied themselves so they could please her.

Tamerin's attention and devotion were beyond anything she could have hoped to experience. She wanted to tell him how much she loved him and that he was perfect too, but she couldn't unlock her jaw from his throat. Not that his hand on her head would let her move her face. He liked her teeth sunk into one of the most vulnerable places on his body.

When his vibrating, thrumming rumble became too much for her oversensitive clit, she unclenched her jaw and tried to move her body off him. Between muscles that had turned to jelly and his strong arms, she remained exactly where she was.

"Please," she sobbed. "Stop. Too much."

His aroused rumble gave way to his soothing purr and his arms quickly lifted and shifted her body on his lap. Soon she was sitting sideways again, her head resting on his smooth, hard pectoral keratin plate, her breathing ragged.

She was covered in sweat and his bonding oil. He probably had a wet spot on his pants where she'd rubbed herself to climax, and his cock was still jutting up and begging to be touched.

"Are you well, Lasha?" Tamerin asked, his purring interrupted for a moment by the lower bass drum of a concerned rumble.

"Amazing," she breathed. "That was, uh, amazing. Really, really amazing."

Yeah, her brain was mush.

"I'm happy to hear it," he murmured. She could hear the pride in his voice. He knew he'd wrecked her. "When you're ready, we'll finish our meal and return to our room."

She rolled her eyes down to take in his straining dick. She wanted to touch it. Suck on it. And she didn't want to have to wait.

"Or I could take care of you here," she offered. "I could sink down to the floor and take you in my mouth. The table would hide me from view and the place still isn't that crowded."

Besides, not a single serving bot or manager had come over to demand they leave. The Hoquin hadn't hesitated to approach them and ask to join. Maybe public sex was common here? And it wasn't fair she got to have such a good time and he didn't.

"No, sweet songbird," Tamerin cooed. "I promised you another session back in our room, and I want to wait for that. I want to smear bonding oil all over your body. You'll sing my name as I fill you with my seed."

His words made a shiver of anticipation go down her spine. To her surprise she was up for more. So much more. "Oh, in that case, let's go."

Tamerin's arms kept her on his lap. "You need to eat and then we'll leave," he reminded her. "That will give my mating shaft time to calm and retreat back into my flesh pouch. When we're back in the room you can reawaken him with your touch."

His lusty thrumming rumble wasn't helping her concentrate on the food.

"You'll still have a hole in your pants," she argued. "We should go back to the room right now so you can change."

"After my mating shaft is back in my flesh pouch, I'll simply shift my belt pouch over the hole. No one will be the wiser. Now stop stalling," he insisted.

"Please," she whined with an exaggerated pout, but it didn't do any good.

"Eat," he commanded, holding the now lukewarm food up to her face. She accepted it because the sooner they finished the faster they'd get to strip down and do this again.

That was the first meal Lasha ever ate where she actually wanted something more than the food!

CHAPTER 21

With all the clothes Tamerin bought her, they were forced to buy a second bag that he refused to let her carry. It made her feel a strange combination of guilty, greedy, and adored. She tried to focus on the adored part instead of the other two uncomfortable emotions.

She vowed she'd adore him right back! Hadn't she spent a good amount of time with her lips wrapped around his impressive cock, showing him the same amount of mercy he'd shown her at the restaurant?

The answers to that was *yes* and with *no mercy*! It had been fun to hear him begging her for release by the end. She never did stop teasing him. When he'd had enough, he simply flipped her over and took what he'd wanted after making her orgasm again. And again.

A girl could get used to this!

As they made their way through the port section of the station, Lasha felt so happy she wanted to skip and sing. She thought about all the things in the second bag. The wrap garments he'd bought her were the softest things she'd ever owned. The omnie he'd mentioned turned out to be a coat with nano-infused faux fur on the inside that adjusted automatically to keep her toasty warm. It was the height of luxury.

And the colors! The wrap she was currently wearing was a dramatic burnt orange and the other wraps were a sapphire blue, amethyst purple, sunflower yellow, and emerald green. Despite her protest, Tamerin had bought one in every jeweled tone they offered.

He'd agreed to limit his purchases to one omnie. She'd picked out a gorgeous, deep burgundy one with black embroidery at the hem and cuffs. He'd insisted she get the style with a high plush collar that reached almost to her ears.

The seamer didn't have patterns for human undergarments, but she wasn't bothered. All this warm softness against her skin was an opulence she never expected.

The only thing that bothered her was the fact that the tunic dresses and wraps weren't practical for work. When she'd pointed that out to Tamerin, he'd gotten gruff and simply said, "We can always buy other things if these garments don't work out."

His sudden change in attitude made her quick to drop the subject. It was obvious the thought of her working distressed him. Although she was determined to figure out some way to be helpful and pay him back, there was no rush at the moment. She was still recovering her strength, and he admitted he didn't have a permanent home picked out. They were both in transition.

She felt like they had all the opportunities in the universe!

"This should be worn like this," he commented, adjusting the collar of the omnie so it was closed. The collar was tall enough that it covered Lasha's entire neck, with the soft top of it brushing her jaw every time she moved her head.

"It's like I'm being snuggled," she said with a grin. They'd been on their way to board the next ship on their journey to Sorana when the corridor had gotten chillier. He pressed her into putting on the omnie. Now that she was wearing it, she was glad he'd insisted. "Thanks, Tamerin."

"I'm determined to see that you never suffer from cold again," he declared. "And our ship doesn't leave for many marks yet. We have plenty of time to traverse the docks."

"I'm almost sad to leave Kilkurn. This place has been fun," she commented with a grin.

"We can always come back for—" He was interrupted by someone calling out his name.

"Tamerin?"

The voice made both of them turn to find another Talin walking out an open doorway. From all the documents Tamerin had read to her and the images he'd shown her, she knew this Talin was female. Other than the minor gender differences such as female Talins lacking quills, Talins were exceptionally uniform. They seemed to shy away from items that would identify their wealth or status. This female could be a high-ranking general or a first-year assistant chief. Lasha had no way of knowing.

"Glendan?" Tamerin responded with a surprised rumble. "I'm surprised to see you so far from home."

"My family bought stock in a new colony, and I was sent to check on our venture," she explained while her eyes darted back and forth between Tamerin and Lasha.. "I was…I mean…" a loud purr suddenly sounded from her. "Did you get a human?" she asked, excitement coloring her voice.

Unsure what the protocol was, Lasha decided to be friendly. "Hello, my name is Lasha."

"Hello, little Lasha," Glendan cooed. "You're omnie is very nice. Is it new?"

Blinking at the strange question, Lasha nodded. "Tamerin bought it for me yesterday."

"I'm sure he's bought you lots of things now that you're healthy," Glendan agreed.

Lasha startled. "How did you know I was sick?"

An amused rumble came out of Glendan. If Talins had facial expression, Lasha would swear the female sent Tamerin the same kind of aren't-they-adorable look her parents used with each other when Lasha was a young child.

"Your mane is short," Glendan pointed out with confidence, eyeing Lasha's spiky black hair. "The only reason that would happen is if you had been very sick or wild-caught."

"Wild-caught," Lasha repeated, feeling uneasy. "What does—"

"We should go," Tamerin interrupted her question. "Or we might miss our ship."

Glendan sounded a sympathetic rumble "Are you going home to be with your sister? I know most others have cut ties with her and your entire family because your parents refuse to hide what's happening. It's noble, but foolish."

She felt Tamerin stiffen at Glendan's comment. "What do you mean? What's happened to my sister?" he demanded.

The sharp clatter of a surprised rattle came out of Glendan. "You don't know? She's dying of the *Fading*." Glendan whispered that last word, as if it was a nasty, dirty thing to say.

Tamerin's rattle of shock echoed down the corridor. "No!"

"I'm afraid it's true," Glendan replied. "There's probably no point in you rushing back to Talarian. I'm sure she'll be gone before you get there."

Lasha watched Tamerin's jaw clench and his fingers curl into tight fists. He was trying hard to keep his composure.

"Tamerin?" she asked as she reached for his clenched left hand. His fingers loosened enough for her to hold hands as he focused his gaze on her. "We can book passage to Talarian, right? We might be able to make it."

"You don't understand, songbird. I can't take you there." He sounded devastated.

"Why can't you take her to Talarian?" Glendan asked and then dropped her eyes to Lasha. "It's wonderful there, with plenty of other humans you can meet and many shops where Tamerin can buy you things. Our capital even has several parks specifically designed for humans!"

Lasha ignored how weird that all sounded and tugged at Tamerin's hand. "Let's find a ship going in the right direction," she insisted.

"There are things...I can't..." He sounded a frustrated rattle when he couldn't find the right words. "This can't be happening."

Lasha understood. When Alsi had died back on Wimol, the community had been so devastated that every day was a struggle to even do the most mundane tasks. If Tamerin needed to tell her something about the Talin homeworld or problems with his family, they could talk about it on the way.

"We're going," she declared. "You don't let family suffer alone."

"Oh, aren't you adorable with your uncontrolled human emotions," Glendan crooned. Ugh, Lasha really didn't like this Talin. Serious creepy vibes. And was that an insult?

Whatever, they didn't have time for Glendan, the weird witch of Kilkurn Station.

"It was nice to meet you, Glendan," Lasha said even as she pulled hard on Tamerin's hand. "We have to go. Have safe travels."

Glendan said something else but Lasha couldn't hear it. She was busy pulling a reluctant Tamerin down the hall. Not that she could have moved him a single stride if he wasn't willing, but he walked as if in a daze.

"Reolina can't be dying," he whispered as they walked. "She can't be. She was always the stronger of us. We're the same age but she kept me safe when we were growing up in the cresh."

"I can't say it's going to be okay," Lasha stated grimly as she kept urging Tamerin to walk. "But we need to focus on what we can do right here, right now."

He didn't respond. By the look in his eyes and the rumble that sounded way too much like someone's muffled sobbing, she guessed he was lost in his own grief. She got him to the ticket kiosk and then realized she needed him to do this part.

Frustrated at her inability to do even the simplest task, she turned to Tamerin.

"Find a ship to take us to your homeworld," she ordered, pointing at the kiosk's display.

Tamerin blinked uncomprehendingly at the display for a few seconds before he started tapping.

"There's one cargo ship run by a Leemron company, but it's leaving very soon," he told her. "Another leaves in five rotations."

"Book us on the Leemron cargo ship," she ordered, unclipping his Ident and waiting for the familiar symbol to appear indicating the kiosk was ready to take payment. When it did she tapped the Ident to the right place and then urged Tamerin to press his hand to the same spot. Finally the display flashed to indicate a successful booking. After clipping his Ident back to his belt, she led him away from the kiosk.

"Which dock?" she asked, looking around at the three different directions they could take to the docks.

Tamerin didn't answer. When she looked up, he was staring off into space. She'd lost him again. She could empathize. If she'd heard Zia or Isla was dying and she might not make it to them in time to say goodbye, she'd be devastated.

Going on instinct, Lasha jumped at Tamerin. With his familiar lightning quick reflexes he caught her in his arms and held her tightly to his chest, a soothing purr rumbling out.

Rubbing her fingers over one of his scent glands, she put her lips to his ear hole and whispered. "I don't know where to go, Tamerin. You need to take me to the right ship. Can you do that?"

He hugged her tightly for a beat but remained silent. For a moment she worried he wasn't going to respond, but then he let out a shuddering breath and started walking.

It was good Tamerin was strong enough to carry her and their bags while still traveling swiftly because they got to the ship just as the warning lights started flashing. Tamerin was forced to jog down the ramp and only slipped through the hatch a moment before it slid closed.

He wasn't even breathing hard.

Unwrapping herself from his grip, she slid down his body until her feet hit the floor. He didn't let go, so she was forced to turn in the circle of his arms to see what kind of vessel they were on.

What she could see of the ship was utilitarian, plain, and worn. Looked like they'd booked passage on an older cargo ship. It was common for a hauler to take on a few passengers if they had the space. It was easy money. The tickets must have been cheap, and the accommodations would be serviceable but not lavish.

"Could be worse," she muttered to herself as a Leemron walked up to them.

"Are you two our passengers?" the Leemron asked. By the look of the longer, stripped fur, this individual was female.

"I sure hope so," Lasha said as the ship shook slightly. It was warming up the engines to leave the station. There was no turning back now unless they wanted to go through the lengthy cool-down procedures.

"We only had one bunk free, so you two are going to have to share," the Leemron warned her without a hint of humor. "Follow me."

Stepping out of Tamerin's arms, Lasha grabbed one of his hands and tugged him into step beside her as the Leemron led them deeper into the ship.

When the Leemron had said bunk, she wasn't exaggerating. They were housed in a communal sleeping area with four other bunks. The Leemron tapped the wall next to their bunk and it opened.

"You can put your stuff in there," she explained. "Then key it to your hand. After you leave, the first officer comes through and blanks out the keys of the passenger lockers, so make sure you remember everything. If you leave it behind, it belongs to us."

"That sounds fair," Lasha agreed, earning her a sniff of approval from the Leemron.

"You're a logical one. What species are you?" she asked.

"Human." Lasha wasn't surprised by the Leemron's response.

"Never heard of your kind before," she said, rubbing a paw-like hand over one of her cat ears. "But let's share a drink at meal time."

"I'd like that," Lasha agreed. She knew from experience that when a Leemron said "share a drink" they meant it literally. They'd both be sipping out of the same cup that looked more like a tall bowl than anything else.

At least the Leemron wouldn't expect her to lap up the drink. That would end up being a messy failure.

The comms on the ship blipped, and then a garbled voice made an announcement that Lasha's INT couldn't make heads or tails of. By the look on the Leemron's face she understood everything coming out of the distorted speakers.

"I've got to get back to work," the Leemron said, wiggling her whiskers in annoyance. "This captain is very demanding. I'll come by for first meal and walk you two to the galley."

"That'd be great, thanks," Lasha said as the Leemron hurried off.

Now that they were alone, she turned her attention on Tamerin, who still seemed a little out of it. She tugged one bag off his shoulder, stowed it, and then grabbed the second one. He kept purring and watching her move, but it was obvious he wasn't really following what was going on.

"Will you cuddle me?" she asked, tugging him to their assigned bunk. There wasn't anything else to do and physical contact might make him feel better.

Without a word he sat sideways on the bunk, resting his back against the bulkhead. Then he lifted her into his lap, so she could snuggle against his chest.

"Please," he whispered. "Please sing for me. My chest hurts."

She guessed that was the Talin way of saying he was sad. She started with the lullabies she'd sung him before and then moved onto love songs. When she ran out of love songs she started singing everything she remembered, even if she'd forgotten some of the words. Everything was in Old Earth languages so she was confident he'd never know where she was winging the lyrics.

She didn't know how long they stayed like that, but eventually his body relaxed a little and he was taking deep, even breaths. When she stopped singing and tilted her head up to look at him, his gaze met hers and he started purring.

He was back from whatever dark place the shock had driven him to.

"I don't deserve you," he murmured, rubbing a scent gland into her hair.

She pulled in a deep breath as the familiar smell of cardamom perfumed the air.

"Probably not," she agreed with a cheeky grin. "But I'm sticking around anyway."

Instead of sounding a humorous rumble, he remained silent. "I can only hope."

Well, didn't that sound ominous! Before she could ask what he meant by that, the Leemron was back to take them to first meal.

CHAPTER 22

Lasha stood at the end of the ramp waiting anxiously for Tamerin to return. They were docked at a Talin station, but both of them had been warned the stop would be brief. The Leemron ship was only here to offload a few containers of cargo before continuing on to Talarian.

With so little time, Lasha hadn't wanted Tamerin to leave the ship and risk getting left behind. He'd insisted he needed to go onto the station to buy an important item. What it was she didn't know, but the time was ticking by rapidly.

"Come on," she muttered, pacing in the small area at the open hatch. "Hurry up, big guy!"

What could have possibly been so important to risk their spots? Sure, they could buy passage on another ship, but that would cause more delays. He'd been so distressed the last few days he hadn't let go of her for more than a few minutes at a time. They cuddled in bed, walked the ship hand in hand, or sat with her on his lap. Except for time in the cleansing unit, they were always together.

To help ease his anxiety, Tamerin used the ship's comms to send an expensive message to his parents that he was on his way. They'd probably get to Talarian before the message bounced through all the relay stations, but Lasha was sure it made him feel better to have sent it.

Considering all that, he'd still decided to leave the ship causing Lasha no end of worry.

"He doesn't have much longer," Torman warned her. She was the Leemron Lasha had befriended on the first day on the ship. They'd shared drinks several times now and swapped stories about unrelenting bosses.

Nothing was so bonding as having worked for assholes.

"I know," Lasha replied, looking over her shoulder at Torman. "I'd hate to have to step off, but I might not have a choice."

"Eh, you don't want to go to the Talin homeworld anyway," Torman assured her. "Those Talins are all stuck up. As if they don't crouch down to take a shit like the rest of us."

Lasha snorted. "Maybe, but my Tamerin isn't like that."

Torman dipped her long, furry ears sideways, the Leemron equivalent of a shrug. "He's a quiet one, so I'll take your word for it. But my advice is to leave Talarian as soon as you can. I don't know how Tamerin got permission to take you there, but I wouldn't trust it if I were you."

Now she had Lasha's full attention. "What do you mean, permission?"

"Those Talins are picky about who gets to land on their planet," Torman explained. "When we land they're going to have their people unload us at the port. We aren't even allowed to leave the ship."

"They do that with all outsiders?" Lasha pushed, worried she might not be allowed to leave the ship like the Leemron crew.

"They even do it with their own people!" Torman exclaimed. Nothing was more distasteful to a Leemron than treating a member of your own species badly. The universe was a cruel enough place already, and Leemrons believed one should take care of their own species above all else. There was no such thing as a homeless or orphaned Leemron.

In truth Lasha was a little surprised by Torman's claim, as it seemed extreme. "They don't let their own people come home?"

"I don't understand all of it. From what I've heard you have to own property on Talarian or have family willing to let you live with them or you can't stay there," Torman explained. "There are no hotels or any other type of place to rent. And even if you have property, there is a limit to how many people you're allowed to house there. They deliberately keep the population density low on their homeplanet."

"That explains why Talins are colonizing all over the place," Lasha murmured. "They have to or their family won't have any place to live."

"Exactly," Torman agreed. "Occasionally diplomats from other species will visit, but those are very carefully planned. I hope for your sake Tamerin has submitted all the forms and made all the arrangements. If not you might get imprisoned before they deport you."

A shiver of fear went down Lasha's spine. She didn't like the sound of this at all. "Wait, I met a Talin who said there are lots of humans on Talarian," Lasha argued.

"I've never seen one. But I've only seen what's visible from an open bay door. I've never gotten to tour the planet," Torman confessed. "Just keep your guard up, my friend."

Touched by Torman's concern, Lasha tipped her head down and presented the Leemron with her forehead. Torman leaned forward and gently touched her furry forehead to Lasha's, a sign of friendly affection among Leemrons.

"What do you—" Lasha's question was cut off by the sound of pounding feet. Turning, she saw Tamerin sprinting up the ramp. Sudden and profound relief made her feel a little dizzy as he covered the last quarter of the ramp and only slowed as he got to the hatch.

No sooner had he stepped into the ship than the warning lights went off.

"You cut that way too close!" Lasha admonished him even as she wrapped her arms around his broad form in a tight hug.

"My calculation was exemplary," he argued. "I made it back in time. Didn't I?"

"Sure," she agreed. The sound of the hatch closing behind Tamerin made her grin. "But let's not do that again."

"Why are our bags sitting in the hall?" he asked. He must have spotted them behind her. She didn't bother looking over her shoulder or letting go of him.

"If you didn't get back in time I was going to grab them and leave the ship," she explained. "I wasn't going to leave you behind."

"My sweet songbird," he murmured. "I feel honored by your care."

"You shouldn't," she retorted, pulling away. "I simply didn't want to end up on a strange planet without you."

His rumble of amusement made her grin. "Let's stow these," he suggested, leaning over to lift the two heavy bags in one hand as if they weighed nothing. She'd been forced to carry each one individually, and he picked both up at the same time with no effort.

Stupid universe with its unfair strength distribution.

She wanted to take his other hand but noticed he was holding a small package. Interesting.

"Was that what you had to go buy?" she asked as they walked toward their shared accommodations.

"Yes."

She waited for a few beats. He didn't expound. She couldn't tell if he was teasing her or had slipped back into the devastated melancholy he'd suffered on and off since hearing about his sister.

Before she could figure out what to say, they were back in the room, and he was shoving their bags into the locker.

"Might as well leave the bags packed. We only have another rotation of travel," he pointed out.

"Yeah, I can always pull one of the tunics out later," she agreed. She'd taken to sleeping in the tunic dresses while they shared a room with members of the crew.

With the bags stowed, Tamerin sat on their bunk. She expected him to take up his familiar position against the bulkhead and invite her to climb onto his lap, but he didn't.

Instead, he sat on the edge with his legs apart and drew her between them. He grabbed the package from where he'd tossed it on the foot of the bunk.

"You have to promise never to take this off," he said as he opened the mysterious package.

"You risked a trip to the station for something for me?" she asked, trying to figure out if she was more upset or flattered.

"It's important," he assured her.

Crossing her arms over her chest she frowned at him. "Then what is it?"

After the conversation with Torman, she expected him to pull out some kind of identification device. Nothing as old or ridiculously expensive as an Ident Cube, but maybe a specialized data crystal or small information square. The box was the right shape to hold the kind of information square used by some of the overseers on Glakor.

She didn't expect what was revealed when he flipped open the lid to the flat box and presented it to her. Uncrossing her arms, she brought both hands to her mouth to cover her gasp.

"I can't accept this!"

Tamerin put it closer to her. "Why not? I specifically purchased it because it had most of your favorite colors."

Lasha had no words. Nestled in the box was the most beautiful jeweled necklace she'd ever seen. Covered in red, orange, and yellow stones, it gleamed in the harsh artificial light of the cabin.

"It's too beautiful," she whispered. She started to reach for it but then pulled her hands back. She didn't dare touch it. She might drop it or break it by accident.

"It's not more beautiful or precious than you," Tamerin assured her. "I bought it for you. Would you please put it on? It's important to me."

"Is this a bonded thing?" she asked, finally raising her eyes from the jewelry to meet his gaze. "Does it signify we're together?"

"In a manner of speaking," he hedged.

Some kind of cultural thing was going on that he was reluctant to tell her about. Unwilling to press him for answers right now, she lifted the necklace out of the box and held it up to the light. It was perfect. Each stone was a unique color or size, and all of them were flawless.

It looked so delicate she worried she'd damage it with simple handling. "I might break it. Maybe we should save it for special occasions."

"Every day we are together is a special occasion," he said, taking the necklace from her. He held it between his hands as he tugged, showing her how deceptively sturdy the jewelry was.

"See, it won't break. It's well made and meant to be worn every day. I wouldn't buy you something flimsy." He showed her the clasp. "And this can't accidentally come undone. It's a lock keyed to my biosignature and I'll key it to you also. Hold out your hand."

She held her hand out and he gently took her thumb and pressed it to one side of the delicate-looking lock. Then he pressed his thumb against the other side until it emitted a slight chime.

Standing up, he unlatched the necklace. "There, now you can take it off any time you want. But it would make me happier if you always wore it. Even in bed."

Reaching out, he put the necklace on her. The chime sounded again as it latched at the back of her neck.

It didn't feel cold at all, and despite the stones, the weight was negligible. Because it sat right at the hollow of her throat, she couldn't see it. Unable to believe he'd given her such an extravagant gift, she ran her hands over the smooth stones.

"I'm going to treasure this," she promised. "And if we ever have to sell it because we're short of funds, I promise I won't cry. Much."

He didn't react to her attempt at humor, only drew her into his lap.

"Promise not to leave me," he whispered, his voice desperate.

"I can't predict our future, but I promise never to leave you willingly," she answered. It was the best she could do in a universe that didn't care about love or devotion.

He didn't say anything more, simply started purring as he held her.

To help him deal with whatever internal demons he was fighting, she started singing.

Tamerin knew he was making a huge mistake by not telling Lasha that once they entered Talin-controlled space she was officially his pet. According to Talin law she would never be allowed to go free. From now on, a Talin would own her.

He was such a coward.

At first he'd kept the truth from her because they were going straight to Sorana. He'd thought he could break the news to her slowly at the colony where humans walked around freely and didn't have to wear collars. With Zia there and happily scent-bonded to a Talin who technically "owned" her, Lasha would see it wasn't a big deal.

When he'd found out about his sister, his brain had stopped working. By the time he realized his mistake he'd irrevocably ended her freedom. It would be nearly impossible to keep it a secret once they got to Talarian, he didn't know how to undo the damage.

He might not have outright lied to her, but he'd lied by omission many times.

If someone had done the same thing to him, he'd be enraged. He'd want them dead. Would his sweet songbird want him dead when she found out? Would she demand to be taken away from him?

When he'd first met Zia and realized Palforma hadn't told her the entire truth, he'd thought his cousin all kinds of foolish. Now he understood why Palforma had kept the truth from Zia, even though she'd inevitable found out.

When you scent-bonded a partner, your logic got muddled. He'd witnessed what happened between Zia and Palforma, yet he'd still done the same damn thing.

Maybe he could mitigate the damage somehow?

Humans were so prized among Talins they were mostly kept within the safety of private property. It was uncommon to simply run across one in public even on Talarian. It was unlikely they'd see one while traveling from the port to his parents' estate. His family didn't own any human pets, so Lasha wouldn't encounter any there.

Perhaps if he prepared her for the way Talins would treat her, she might not figure out what was going on. He had no intention of staying on Talarian long. All he had to do was get the two of them safely to Sorana after he finished the official mourning ceremony with his parents.

Mourning. The word threatened to sink him back into a dark place where he had to contend with a world that no longer included his sister.

To distract himself, he focused on Lasha.

"The Talins you meet might treat you oddly," he started, interrupting Lasha's singing.

"Oddly?" she questioned. "You mean like that Glendan person we met at Kilkurn?"

"Yes," he agreed, relief making him eager. "Yes, exactly like her."

"She acted like I was a kid," Lasha murmured. "It was weird."

"Most Talins won't think you're very intelligent," he explained. "I know you're clever, but they'll assume you have the same cognitive abilities as a Talin child."

Her response surprised him. "As long as they aren't mean, I don't care."

He barely stifled his surprised rattle. "You don't?"

"A lot of species think humans are dumb because we don't have a viable homeplanet," she explained dismissively. "It's one of the reasons it's easy to exploit us."

"No Talins I know will be cruel or unkind toward you," he rushed to assure her. "Many of them will even offer you candy." He felt her perk up.

"Candy?"

"They are little, soft, colorful balls of flavored sugar," he explained. "Some are covered in seeds. I think they're patterned off Old Earth concoctions, but they've been around since the first wave of humans came to Talarian."

"Huh, you guys really do think we're kids," she exclaimed with a laugh. "How long ago did the first humans immigrate to Talarian?"

Ignoring the word immigrate, he was quick to give her only the bare facts. "About five hundred years ago. An advanced squad found about eighty humans abandoned and starving at an Orlock mining facility. The Talin empire had just won a war against the Orlock Empire and were claiming all their imperial wealth. The advance squad and the humans they found got along so well that other Talins went searching for humans left behind when the Orlocks retreated toward the end of the war."

"I remember hearing about that war from a guy who moved to Wimol colony when I was young," Lasha commented. "The group of humans his great-great-grandmother was with had to move from Orlock-controlled space to a colony on an Ilgorian-owned planet because the war was getting so close to them."

"We're finding out now that many humans ended up in Ilgorian territory," Tamerin admitted. "Otherwise we would have offered them a home on Talarian. The Ilgorian Federation and the Talin Empire don't get along, but neither side wants war. So we stay out of each other's space."

"That would explain why I'd never even heard of Talins before I got to Glakor," Lasha murmured as she rested her head back on his chest. "Will anyone be upset that I have this super expensive necklace?" she asked, fingering the collar he'd bought her and the whole reason he'd gotten off the ship.

Looking down, he eyed the collar. The Talin station the cargo ship had briefly stopped at had a shop that sold goods for human pets. He'd run to the shop, demanded to see the nicest collars they had, and grabbed the one with the gems he thought Lasha would like the best. Lasha was now wearing the latest fashion in collars. Not only encrusted with gems, but with a tracking device hidden in the lock.

"No Talin will give the necklace a second look," he promised her. In fact, if she wasn't wearing it, there'd be a lot of talk. Humans had to wear collars as part of the law. The only time it didn't apply was when they were young or had a medical issue.

"That's good," she murmured. To his surprise, she sounded like she might be on the verge of drifting off to sleep. "I promise not to take offense to anything said, but they can't be mean to you either."

Tamerin leaned his head down to rub his scent gland over the top of her head. "Don't worry about me, songbird. My skin might be scarred, but it's still tough."

He couldn't understand what she mumbled, but a moment later her breathing deepened and evened out. She'd fallen asleep.

"Rest, songbird. Soon we'll be on my homeworld, and I'll do the best I can to make sure everything works out well."

CHAPTER 23

Lasha could tell Tamerin was nervous as they waited for the cargo ship to open its hatch. Torman had warned her the Talin port authorities would make them wait until their security and biohazard bots had scanned the entire ship before letting any doors open.

She'd thought Torman exaggerated, but it had been several hours, and they were still waiting for permission. Maybe this was a good introduction to Talin culture. She still wasn't sure if she entirely believed everything Torman had told her about Talarian, but it looked like the Leemron hadn't embellished.

The warning light finally flashed and the hatch slid open at the same time the ramp deployed. Tamerin grabbed their two bags and slung them over one shoulder. Then he crouched to pick her up and balance her on one hip like a child with his arm providing a seat for her bottom.

With a surprised exclamation, she wrapped her arms around his neck

"Tamerin!" she admonished. "I can walk."

He sounded a soothing rumble before he started walking. "Let me carry you, please."

She couldn't imagine the kind of emotional turmoil he was dealing with. If holding her made him feel better, she should let him. Even if it made her feel a little uncomfortable. She hadn't wanted her first steps on Talarian to be via Tamerin.

"Fine, but if I feel like you're getting tired, I'm going to demand you set me down," she responded. "I'm not letting you wear yourself out by carrying me."

"I'll never tire of holding you," he whispered into her ear.

"Step carefully. The ramp could be slippery," a voice called. They both looked down to find a group of ten Talins standing at the base of the ramp.

"Is that your family?" she whispered. Gah, she really didn't want his family's first meeting with her to be like this. She looked like a little kid!

"No," Tamerin explained grimly as he walked down the ramp. "That's the leadership of the port authority."

By the tone of his voice, Lasha got the impression this wasn't standard procedure.

"Welcome home Tamerin of the Kiferian Family, member of the Ibek Clan," one of them said as she stepped forward. "I know you have pressing matters to attend to, but I have no record of this human going through a checkup or decontamination process."

Checkup? Decontamination? Wow, these Talins were paranoid about bio-contagions.

"I was sick, but it wasn't contagious," Lasha explained, feeling silly having this conversation while she clung to Tamerin like a child. "And I've had all the standard inoculations and Universal Standard Health Precautions."

Only after she'd spoken did she realize she might have gotten the two of them in trouble. What if subordinates weren't allowed to speak unless directly instructed? Could Tamerin get blamed for her rudeness?

Was disrespect a punishable offense on Talarian?

She opened her mouth to apologize when every single Talin in the group focused their gaze on her and started purring at once. It was disconcerting enough to leave her speechless.

"I'm glad you're feeling better, little one," the female said in the same kind of indulgent tone Glendan had back on Kilkurn. "But it's very important that all humans are registered and go through the proper process."

She wasn't surprised about the registration process. It had been the same for the company that recruited the most desperate and then sold their work contracts to places like Glakor. She just hadn't expected it here because she didn't have a job yet.

"I've already filled out and filed all the necessary documents," Tamerin explained. "I'd hoped I could have a healer see her in the privacy of my parents' home to keep her trauma to a minimum. She almost died of her illness and is still not fully recovered."

When had he been filling out and filing information about her? Not that she could have helped, but he should have told her all this documentation was required to bring her to Talarian.

"Ah, that explains the short mane," the Talin said with the rumble that sounded like a bunch of people snapping their fingers—comprehension. She made a mental note to ask Tamerin why Talins associated short hair with illness.

Another Talin stepped forward and addressed the Talin who'd been talking. "Manorian, we should let them go. If she's still recovering then being exposed to the elements might be detrimental to her fragile health."

Elements? The weather here was pleasant and warm, similar to Wimol. While they'd been waiting for the hatch to open, she'd even taken off her omnie when Tamerin had told her the outside temperature. How could any of them consider this mild weather *detrimental*?

These guys were turning out to be almost as overprotective and adorable as Tamerin, and they didn't even know her!

"Yes, exactly," Tamerin hurried to say. "I worry about her relapsing."

"But where is her omnie?" another Talin asked from further in the small crowd.

"I didn't need it," Lasha explained. "I don't feel cold."

"You should wear it anyway," the Talin insisted, stepping forward to stand next to Manorian. "Human bodies don't regulate their temperature very well at the best of times, and if you have a weakened system, you could become chilled before you realize it."

Even though she thought all of this was nonsense, Tamerin set her down and pulled her omnie out of one of the bags. After shaking it out, he held it up so she could slip her arms in. Only after she was snuggled into the garment did the group seem to relax a bit.

"There, isn't that better?" the male asked as he rummaged around in his belt pouch. Pulling his clawed hand out, he held a bright-colored ball out to her.

"Nojolian, don't feed her that," the female next to Manorian shouted and slapped the treat out of her hand. "Some of the medication we give the humans are made less viable if we give them sweets."

Instead of getting angry, Nojolian made the stockinged-feet-running rumble of agreement. "I wasn't thinking. Thank you, Hagarian." Then he looked at Tamerin. "I'll send some sweets to your family's home and she can have them once the healer deems it safe."

At this point Lasha was fighting to keep her mouth from gaping open. "Um, you guys do realize I'm an adult human? Fully grown and all that."

Again the group focused their attention on her, and the purring got loud as Manorian spoke. "Why yes, little one. You're a very handsome adult female."

How did you respond to a compliment like that? "Uh, thanks? You're a nice looking adult Talin."

Everyone except Tamerin rumbled out the marbles-clinking sound of amusement.

"Aren't you just adorable!" Hagarian exclaimed and then addressed Tamerin. "I have a very amusing male. We could introduce these two and see if they might be interested in breeding together. He's a little older, but still very active."

Woah, hold up. Breeding?

Even though it might be considered rude, Lasha turned her back on the group to face Tamerin. When she crooked her finger, he leaned over so she could put her lips next to his earhole.

"What the fuck?" she whispered, caught between being amused and horrified. "I know we have to keep our relationship a secret, but I didn't think other Talins would be trying to set me up on blind dates with their human friends! Get me out of here before I say something irrevocably rude."

"Act overwhelmed and shy," Tamerin suggested. "That will make it easier to get away from the group."

Lasha raised an eyebrow. "How shy?"

"Ask me to hold you again and hide your face in my neck," he instructed.

"So act like a toddler," she muttered, fighting an eye roll.

"If that is how they act, then yes," Tamerin agreed.

She stifled a laugh and half turned so when she spoke the others would easily hear her. "Tamerin, would you carry me, please? I'm tired."

While they'd had their private conversation, the group had dissolved into an argument over what males she should meet or if she might like to meet females instead. While they watched, she held up her hands like a small child. As if he was the parent, Tamerin crouched and lifted her, just like he'd done earlier on the ship.

"Poor thing, she's probably a overwhelmed from meeting all of us," Hagarian commented. "I'll send some soothing tea to your family's residence. Make sure your staff lets it cool before serving it to her."

"And keep her away from your sister," Manorian ordered. "She shouldn't be exposed to such a shameful ordeal."

Lasha had to bite her tongue to keep from snapping at Manorian. How dare she say something like that? How could these Talins be so kind to her and callous to one of their own?

It boggled her mind.

Tamerin's body was stiff, and she couldn't tell if he was breathing. He was probably fighting the urge to say something nasty too or maybe even getting into a fight. The last thing they needed to was to get involved in an altercation that might delay getting to his sister.

Nestling her face against the slip of exposed skin on his neck, she worked on keeping her voice childlike and needy.

"I want to lay down. Can we go?"

Her words had a magical effect on the group of Talins.

Hagarian grabbed the bags off Tamerin's shoulder. "Come this way."

"Your family sent a private ground transport for you," Nojolian said as the entire group fell in step around them. "It's not far. Do you need me to carry her?"

"She shouldn't be jostled," Manorian argued.

"Yes, you're right," Nojolian agreed and then hurried ahead of them. "Let me make sure the ground transport is warm inside."

The entire group clucked like hens as they gave Tamerin advice on how best to care for her while she recovered. One of them even suggested she be allowed to lie in a large nest with other humans because that would make her feel comforted.

This was by far the most bizarre situation she'd ever encountered.

Soon they were ensconced in a ground transport large enough to have accommodated half a dozen Talins. The moment the transport door shut, Tamerin sighed out a long-relieved breath. The ground transport started trundling along, easily navigating the wide streets.

"Your species is weirdly intense," Lasha commented as she stared at the passing city. Talin architecture seemed to favor obelisk shapes and dark stone building materials.

The next thing that struck her was how perfectly orderly the city was. Not just the buildings, streets, and walking paths, but the individuals going about their day. As she watched she almost felt like the Talins she saw were pacing themselves perfectly with each other as they walked.

Could people walk in a queue form?

She saw no poorly maintained building nor even litter laying around. All the Talins she saw were outfitted like Tamerin, wearing pants gathered at the knees in various muted colors. They also all had thick belts, each with an Ident Cube on one hip and a pouch on the other. A few of them had the same giant dagger Tamerin owned secured to the backs of their belts, but that was the only obvious difference she saw.

She caught sight of one belt with what looked like a crest hanging from it, but she couldn't be sure. If it ever felt appropriate, she'd have to ask Tamerin about this city and Talin fashion. She was fascinated. She'd never met such a uniform species.

Before long the self-piloted ground transport turned into a sprawling estate surrounded by thick, high walls made of black stone. When they rounded a corner and no longer had dense bushes obscuring their view, Lasha got her first look at Tamerin's family home.

It was a palace. That's the only way she could describe it. It reminded her a bit of Old Earth images she'd seen of the Taj Mahal mausoleum. Unlike the black stone used everywhere else, this house was built of gleaming white stone, with silver domes at the top. She'd never seen anything so opulent.

No wonder Tamerin hadn't been concerned about spending money on her. His family must be insanely rich!

Before the vehicle even came to a full stop, a male hurried out from inside the mansion.

"Tamerin, you're back. Hurry, hurry!" the guy urged as he forcefully pulled the ground transport's door open. Unlike Tamerin's more rust red color, this Talin's color was a dark-sand tone. His shoulders were so wide he had to turn slightly to fit his upper body through the door of the transport. As he reached for Tamerin, she noticed most of his quills were broken off close to the base and the ends were jagged. Huh, what would cause that?

Then he saw Lasha and froze with one arm still extended to grab Tamerin. "You have a human!"

The strong impulse to wave her hands and shout "boo" forced her stifle a laugh as the stranger sounded a rattle of surprise.

"This is Lasha," Tamerin explained. "Lasha, this is Novilum. He's a cousin of mine but belongs to a different clan. We were born and raised in the same cresh."

"Hello, little Lasha," Novilum purred. "That's a very nice omnie you're wearing. Are you hungry? I could have my chef prepare something and have it sent over."

"Aren't we in a hurry?" she reminded him.

Novilum jerked back at her words and then finished his original move to grab Tamerin. With a hand around Tamerin's elbow, Novilum roughly pulled him out of the ground transport. She scrambled out after them but was slow and didn't catch the beginning of what Novilum said.

"... a human here? Your sister is on death's door! Ignoring the fact that it's reprehensible to expose a delicate human to this, but what if the committee hears about it? They could take Lasha away!"

Lasha wasn't sure what Novilum was talking about, but one thing was certain, he didn't want her here because he didn't want her to see death.

Some civilizations hid their dying relatives, forcing them to spend their last days alone and without the comfort of friends and family. Talins must be like that, but Tamerin wasn't following that rule. He was desperate to comfort his sister and that filled Lasha with pride. Despite social pressures, he was going against the grain to support family.

She wasn't going to let Novilum make Tamerin feel bad because of her!

Shoving between the two of them, she faced Novilum. "Don't talk to Tamerin like that. If you're not going to be supportive, go away."

Novilum sounded a rattle of surprise and backed up a little. "There are many things you don't understand. I'm only trying to keep both you and Tamerin safe."

Grabbing Tamerin's scarred left hand, she tugged him toward the still-open door Novilum had burst out of. "We're going to see Tamerin's sister."

Sounding an agitated rattle, Novilum fell into step behind them. "This is such a bad idea."

Lasha came to an abrupt stop once she was inside the door. There was no discrete foyer or greeting area. The front door led right into a massive room lit by high, ornate windows. There was a little furniture at the far end of the room, but most of the grand area was left empty. Along two of the walls were built-in shelves that displayed various items. Most she didn't recognize but a few she knew were expensive crafts from Hulg. One of those pieces of artwork could have clothed and fed the entire Wimol human colony for a year.

Shaking off the distraction of the family's wealth, she turned a circle. Four doorways led off the main room, and she had no clue where to go from here. So much for taking charge.

"This way," Tamerin murmured as he picked her up and cradled her against his chest. He purred as he walked them through a doorway to their right and down a long corridor. He took them to the one open door at the end.

The first thing Lasha noticed when they entered was how dim the room was. Unlike the rest of the house, this room's windows were shuttered, and the only source of illumination was a tiny glowing sconce over the door.

The only thing in the room was a single narrow bed, and they hadn't even given Reolina bedding. She was lying on her side with no pillow or blankets, staring blankly ahead. Her body looked too small for her frame, as if she'd been starved. Her keratin plates had gaps between them and her face looked sunken.

She didn't react to their presence, not even moving her eyes.

It broke Lasha's heart!

Wordlessly Lasha pushed to be put down. Tamerin stopped purring and set her on her feet. Without hesitation she rushed to Reolina and knelt by the too small bed. Carefully she took Reolina's hand in hers.

"My name is Lasha," she whispered to the sick Talin. "I'm going to stay with you until the end. You won't be alone, I promise.

CHAPTER 24

Tamerin had seen images of what Fading did to Talins, but he wasn't prepared to see the effect the deadly disease had on his sister. This was not the vital female he'd grown up with. This was not the sister who'd protected him from the other children in the cresh because he'd been the smallest in their class. The figure lying in this bed had almost no resemblance to Reolina.

He was so stunned he'd forgotten he was holding Lasha until her little hand pressed on his shoulder. Setting her down, he expected her to flee from the room, but instead she went to his sister.

To his absolute shock, she settled on the floor next to the bed and grasped Reolina's hand. When Lasha spoke, it took him a moment to register what she'd said. Then he realized Lasha had promised to keep Reolina company.

His sweet songbird had a generous soul, and he couldn't think of anyone more worthy of her kindness than his sister.

"You can't stay here!" Novilum protested.

Lasha glared at the incredulous male. "You don't get a say in anything I do."

Novilum turned to him. "Tamerin, you can't mean to let this happen."

Tamerin opened his mouth, but words didn't come out. He felt overwhelmed by sorrow and unsure what to say to either Lasha or Novilum.

"Tamerin," Lasha called to him softly. It was a relief to focus his eyes on her. "I need you to find some pillows and soft blankets. Can you do that? And do Talins have comfort foods they feed the sick? I'd like some of that brought here if possible. Please?"

Orders. Tasks. Yes, he could do those things.

Without another word he hurried out of the room to gather the items Lasha requested. It didn't take long, but when he returned with his arms full of bedding and a canister of libit, Reolina's favorite drink, he was greeted by chaos.

Both his parents were in the room with Novilum, and the three of them were trying to gently drag Lasha away from Reolina.

"Stop it! Let go!" Lasha was yelling, her fingers white from how hard she was gripping Reolina's hand, her feet pushing at the floor to help her resist. His parents held her other hand and Novilum was pulling at the back of her omnie. None of them were using much pressure because they were afraid of hurting Lasha. But her weaker human build would give in to their gentle consistent tugs eventually, and everyone in the room knew it.

"No!" Lasha yelled out again and this time kicked his mother in the thigh.

"Human, you can't be in here!" his mother protested, the blow from Lasha's slippered feet probably felt like a nudge to his mother's Talin hide.

Then Lasha saw Tamerin. "Make them leave me alone!" Lasha wailed. He could see she was losing her grip on Reolina's hand.

Her demand shook him out of his stupor, but before he could even take a step forward, Reolina moved.

Without any of her normal grace, she shook off Lasha's hand and grabbed the small human around the waist with both arms. With effort she lifted Lasha's slight form onto the bed and tucked the human behind her. Then she rolled over to face everyone else in the room and raised up on one elbow. She gave a weak war rattle and raised a hand with her claws fully extended. Her entire body was shaking with the effort.

"Leave the human alone," she demanded. Her strong voice belied her weakened state, and he wasn't sure her bleary eyes could even focus on any of them.

"Reolina!" Lasha exclaimed, wrapping arms around his sister's neck to give her a hug from behind. "Don't hurt yourself. You need to rest."

"Who are you, little human?" Reolina asked gently. "And why were they trying to take you somewhere?

"Oh!" Lasha exclaimed and then grinned. "Um, hi! I'm Lasha. I'm here with Tamerin, and I didn't want to leave you."

"Tamerin?" Reolina murmured, her unfocused eyes wandering the room. "Brother?"

Lasha motioned him to step forward, her expression impatient, as if what was happening wasn't some kind of miracle.

His mother Japhinan looked at his father. "This isn't possible."

"Yet it's happening," Tamerin said from behind them as he stepped around to get to the bed. Once there he dropped unceremoniously to his knees, putting his head level with his sister. "Hello, Reolina. I'm here now."

"I'm sorry," Reolina whispered as she rolled onto her back.

"Tamerin, tell her not to be sorry," Lasha instructed as she held her hands out for the bedding he brought. "Tell her that you love her and want to be here. That if you'd known we'd have gotten here sooner."

"I think you've said it all," he answered, handing her the bedding. With her mounds of pillows and blankets, Lasha proceeded to make a nice nest for his sister.

"Still, you should say it too," she whispered as she tucked the blankets around Reolina. "And why the hell is it so bleak in here? This isn't how you treat family!"

"It's thought to be a mercy to those dying of Fading," Reolina answered for him, blinking slowly as if she was struggling to keep up with what was going on around her. "We are believed to die faster if all forms of stimulation are removed. It's supposed to lessen our suffering."

"For a smart species, you guys are dumb," Lasha muttered to herself. With her little, gentle hands, she put pillows under Reolina's head, finished covering her body with soft blankets, and draped the extra over the foot of the bed in case they were needed later.

"Reolina?" Luminarean croaked out, taking a step closer to the bed. Tamerin had forgotten his father was still in the room along with his mother and cousin.

"Yes, Father?" Reolina answered, her voice getting weaker. Both Luminarean and Japhinan stepped closer to the bed.

"You're talking. You haven't talked in rotations," his father said. "We didn't think you were capable of speech any longer."

Lasha startled and looked at Reolina. "You haven't? Is it bad you're talking now? Oh, God, am I making it worse?"

Tamerin watched water leak from Lasha's eyes. Crying. The humans called it crying and they did it when they were in physical or mental pain. He knew she wasn't injured. Everyone in the room had been extremely careful even as they'd tried to force her to move. She was crying because of emotional distress.

She was crying for Reolina and they didn't even know each other. Tamerin marveled at the human capacity for compassion.

"No, my sweet songbird," Tamerin assured her with a loud soothing rumble. "This is a good thing. Once Talins suffering from the Fading stop talking they don't start again."

"Songbird," Reolina whispered. Exhausted from her interactions, Reolina closed her eyes as she spoke. "I want to hear the songbird."

"I'll sing for you," Lasha promised. "And Tamerin will talk to you." She raised her eyes to pin his parents and cousin with a fierce demanding gaze as she continued to speak to his sister. "And your family will all be here to help you get better."

Because you never said no to someone with the power to perform medical miracles, everyone was quick to agree.

CHAPTER 25

"If we're all going to be spending time with Reolina, I'll see about having a bigger room prepared," Luminarean said and then hurried out.

His mother was quick to follow her husband's lead. "I'll help you, Luminarean. And I need to contact…" her voice trailed off as she caught up with him in the hall.

Tamerin knew part of the reason his parents were so quick to leave was because they were overcome with emotions they didn't want to display in front of everyone. His father would probably hide in an empty room and his mother in her office to deal with this sudden change of circumstances.

It wasn't every day a family member was pulled back from the brink of death.

That left only Novilum. He was standing in the middle of the room staring at Lasha like she was some kind of new species he'd never seen.

"I guess the rumors are true," he murmured thoughtfully.

"Rumors?" Lasha asked.

Tamerin could tell his cousin hadn't meant to say that out loud.

"Nothing," he responded and then looked down to meet Tamerin's gaze. "I'll talk to the house chef and check the delivery schedule. We're going to need to order specific items to accommodate a human."

With that he left. Lasha looked at Tamerin with a questioning expression.

"What was that all about?" she asked as she reached out to take Reolina's hand again. Holding it in both of hers, she kept her eyes on him.

"It's complicated, perhaps another time," Tamerin answered.

She accepted that with a nod and then leaned over Reolina's supine form to whisper in his ear hole. "If she's dying, shouldn't we contact whoever her scent-bonded partner is? Or did that person die already?"

It took a moment for Tamerin to figure out what Lasha was saying. "No, my sweet. There is no scent-bonded partner. No laws have been broken here. Reolina has the Fading, not the Ending."

Lasha wrinkled her nose. "Neither of those names are great. But I think I need a reminder. What's the difference between Fading and Ending?"

"No one entirely knows why the Fading happens. Some Talins will suddenly lose the will to live. They'll stop eating, stop working, and one day they'll lie down and never get back up. That is Fading.

Lasha's mouth turned down in a frown. "But this doesn't happen to Talins who scent-bond?"

"All the records indicate that when Talins are scent-bonded, they can't succumb to Fading," Tamerin agreed.

"Then you're safe?" Lasha asked and Tamerin realized one of the reasons she was voicing all these questions.

"Yes, my sweet songbird," Tamerin assured her. "With you in my life, this won't happen to me."

Lasha looked relieved and then guilty as she gazed down at Reolina. "Should we call one of your healer people?"

"It's unlikely any of them would come," Tamerin said.

"Because Fading is so shameful," Lasha muttered with disgust. "How stupid is it to think of a disease as being shameful. If this is Fading, what is Ending?"

Tamerin didn't comment but continued to explain. "Ending is when a scent-bonded couple are separated for too long. It's different from couple to couple, but eventually they both succumb to Ending. It's a painful way to die."

"They were impressed she was talking and moving," Lasha commented, still whispering as if not to disturb Reolina. "This means she might get better. Right?"

"Her talking at this stage is unheard of," Tamerin admitted. "Normally by the time someone suffering from the Fading gets this bad, they stop responding to everything. Not even severe pain will cause a reaction."

"Then I guess it's good your parents and Novilum decided to be so obnoxious and try to drag me out of the room," she declared with a small grin. "Maybe a threat to someone else is a way to pull Talins out of the Fading."

"This might have been a special circumstance. What made Reolina react probably won't work on others," Tamerin pointed out.

"I know," Lasha answered, sounding subdued. "I'm just angry no one tried to help. How could anyone think it's acceptable to put someone who's suffering in a dark room and wait for them to die? It's wrong. They're wrong."

Tamerin felt the need to defend his family. "My parents and cousin were trying to protect you. Their actions had good intentions but were misguided. It's thought that humans are emotionally fragile. They didn't want you to be mentally scarred by Reolina's state."

"Yeah, I can understand wanting to shield kids from death, but I'm an adult. I'm staying," she warned him. "You can't make me leave either."

"I wouldn't," he answered quickly. "I know better. I'm fully aware that you aren't like other humans. That you have a reservoir of strength to match any Talin. I'm honored that you care for my sister as much as you care for me."

"I love you, Tamerin. And I can see you love your sister." She put a hand over his mouth before he could respond.

"Yeah, yeah, I know. Talins don't love like humans. Let me use the word anyway. Okay? I know you love your sister and I love you. That means I love her too. So let me be clear—even if this turns out bad, I'm staying 'til the end."

He wanted to argue but quashed the impulse. "If that's what you want."

Lasha's expression turned determined. "It is what I want. Your dad is going to get a bigger room and chairs, and we're all going to talk to her and spend time with her until…"

Lasha's voice trailed off so Tamerin spoke for her. "Until Reolina recovers or joins the Ancestors."

"Yeah, that," Lasha agreed, her eyes going watery. "But maybe Reolina will be the one who breaks the pattern and survives."

"I want to have hope," Tamerin admitted, "but I'm terrified I'll be disappointed."

"I have enough hope for both of us," Lasha promised, and then her eyes slid to the floor. "Kneeling like that's bad for you."

He stood. "I'll fetch a chair."

"No," she objected and pointed next to her on the narrow bed. "Sit here. It'll be tight, but we can make it work for a little while."

With her urging he found himself sitting sideways on the bed with Reolina's legs resting on his lap and his back against the wall. Lasha leaned against him, still holding Reolina's hand.

"There, that's better," she murmured.

Then she started singing, and the dim, barren room didn't seem so desolate any longer.

CHAPTER 26

Luminarean moved Reolina into a much larger room with a massive ornate bed fit for four Talins. The room also had several of the backless chairs the Talins favored with small tables between them and a long bench stretching almost the length of one wall. The windows were all unshuttered and cheerful sunlight streamed through the room all day.

It was one hundred percent Lasha approved, and she made herself at home.

Over the next few days, Lasha rarely left Reolina's side. Every time Reolina stirred, Lasha made her interact. She would push until Reolina responded to her. But Lasha wasn't content with words. She'd beg, cajole or bully Reolina into drinking. By the end of the second day, Reolina was taking small sips of water on her own.

By the third day she ate a morsel of food.

Tamerin's sister wasn't dying on her watch!

Everyone hailed it as a miracle, but Lasha only saw it as steps in a longer game. Next she was going to make Reolina sit up. Then she was going to walk. Although she didn't say it,

Lasha was convinced Tamerin's sister was going to live. She was so sickly that it would probably be a long time before she was fully recovered, but Lasha knew it was only a matter of time and effort.

"Would you sing for us again?" Japhinan requested as her husband came into the room and settled into the seat next to her. "Luminarean didn't get to hear you this morning, and you sang that new song."

Lasha frowned a little. "New song?"

"You said it was about a race," Japhinan elaborated.

Sitting on the bed next to Reolina, Lasha tried to remember what she'd sung that morning. Then she almost laughed. She'd forgotten the words to the song halfway through and had made them up. Some were even nonsense words that sounded good with the melody. It wasn't as if it mattered since no one could understand what she was saying. When Japhinan had asked her what the song had been about, she'd said a race between a horse and goat.

Now she was being asked to repeat it! This was a lesson in humility.

"Let's pick a different one," Lasha suggested. She'd have to come up with more cohesive lyrics for that song later. Otherwise it might change every time. She looked at Tamerin. "You've been reading out loud for a while, so you get to pick."

He was sitting on a chair next to the bed clutching his sister's hand. Lasha had made a rule that someone had to be in that chair at all times and holding Reolina's hand. Everyone but Tamerin had complained, but none of them tried to get out of it.

"Can you sing the one about the two people meeting in a crowded room?" he requested. He knew it was a love song, but she told everyone else it was about a negotiation.

"I was reading longer than Tamerin," Novilum protested. "I should be allowed to pick. I want the song about the drunk man who goes home to the wrong domicile."

Laughing, Lasha nodded. "I can sing both. Meeting song first and then drunk song."

"I want the sunrise one," Reolina requested.

"New order," Lasha announced. "Sunrise song, meeting song, and then drunk song."

"And then you should take a break," Tamerin added.

"Yes," Reolina agreed. Her voice might still sound weak, but she was carrying on full, albeit short, conversations. It was immense progress. "Have you seen the garden yet?"

Lasha smiled at her. "I'll take a break and see the garden if you promise to eat a whole meal with me."

Reolina hesitated before answering. "I can try."

"That's all I ask," Lasha agreed, feeling excited.

"I'll make sure the evening meal has all your favorite foods," Luminarean promised.

"And food for Lasha," Reolina interjected.

"They always have food for me," Lasha was quick to tell her.

"Your favorite food?" Reolina asked.

"Oh, well," Lasha floundered and looked over at Tamerin who sounded an amused rumble.

"We're working on that," he said. "Lasha's got some particular tastes, and the chef has been flummoxed by some of her requests."

Flummoxed was a polite way of saying the chef had refused to fix anything Lasha requested until she got confirmation from two different healers that none of the ingredients were harmful to humans.

"Make her cook Lasha what she wants," Reolina demanded before closing her eyes and resting her head back on her pillows. "Sing now? Please?"

"Of course. I'll sing as long you want me to," she promised. Ignoring the playlist they'd agreed on moments ago, Lasha launched into a lullaby Reolina had said was her favorite.

Closing her eyes, Lasha sang, going seamlessly from one song to another while she let her thoughts wander.

Good to their word, Tamerin's parents and cousin spent a lot of time talking, reading, or just being with Reolina. What Lasha hadn't been prepared for was how fascinated Tamerin's family would be with her singing. They couldn't praise her enough. She'd never felt so popular. Or important.

Luminarean had even said Lasha's singing had brought Reolina back from death.

Reolina might have survived on her own, but everyone was crediting Lasha with Reolina's recovery. It was hard to keep her head from swelling at all the compliments she was getting. The human community on Wimol had been loving and kind, but most of them had seen Lasha as a burden. With Tamerin and his family, she felt like a gift.

Even after Reolina was better, Lasha was going to ask Tamerin if they could stay on Talarian. She still expected to visit Zia and Palforma, but she wanted to come back to this estate and this family. She didn't want to give up being unique and special in a good way.

Lasha hit the last notes of the love song she was singing and opened her eyes. She was startled to find two unfamiliar Talins in the room—one male and one female.

Without her realizing it, Tamerin had gotten up from his seat. He and Japhinan were standing stiffly on either side of the strangers, so they must not be intruders. Not that she expected that to happen much on Talarian. The Talins were far too organized and focused on civic duty to resort to crime very often.

"What amazing sounds you make, human," the female said, sounding the stocking-feet-running rumble. In this context, it had to mean approval because there wasn't anything to agree to.

Lasha was feeling really proud of her Talin sound interpretation skills!

"Um, thanks," Lasha said. "My grandmother taught me."

"I've heard of humans who can make these sounds, but I've never met one," the male commented.

"Everyone I grew up with could sing," Lasha said with a shrug. What was she supposed to say to these two? And why wasn't Tamerin talking or making introductions?

When she looked at him, she noticed how stiffly he was standing with his hands balled up into tight fists. Something was wrong. He wasn't happy to have these Talins here, but apparently he couldn't do anything about it.

Standing up, Lasha gave a little bow. It's something Oglee would've liked and not a motion that most species would take as anything but a sign of respect.

"My name's Lasha of the Chandra family, and um, I guess the Wimol Clan." There, that sounded both respectful and formal. Then she looked at Tamerin. "Or should I say I'm part of your clan?"

Tamerin purred loudly but remained silent.

"Don't be silly. Humans don't have clans," the male said. Lasha didn't know what to say to that so she didn't respond.

"We've come for an important reason," the female said, taking a step closer to Lasha. "I'm Assembly Citizen Delinian, the head of the Ibek Clan and representative to the Clan Assembly. I have the power to demand Tamerin sell you to me, but I don't want to be forced to do something that extreme. Instead, I'm going to borrow you to help my brother. He's like Reolina."

The woman's eyes skittered over to where Reolina lay propped up in the bed, watching all of this as silently as the rest of the Talins in the room. Then, as if ashamed she'd looked at the recovering woman, Delinian dropped her gaze before refocusing it on Lasha.

Standing tall, Lasha crossed her arms over her chest. Suddenly she felt powerful, strong. She had something this formidable Talin wanted. Something they couldn't force. Sure, they could always do unpleasant things to her, but she had full confidence that these Talins wouldn't want to hurt her.

No, this was a game of intimidation, and Zia had taught her how to handle that.

"I know I have no power here, but I have control of one thing, myself. Even if Tamerin could sell me to you, that doesn't mean anything. If you want me to help, you have to ask nicely."

Her words caused shocked rattles to sound from almost everyone in the room. It was loud enough to cause her to jump and wince. Guess no one talked to the head of a clan like that.

The moment the rattles died down, Lasha spoke again. "And if I help, you have to promise to do everything I ask."

"It's not your place to demand things," the male said with an angry rattle.

"Quiet, Satorian," Delinian murmured without looking away from Lasha. "I think we might have to concede to Lasha's demand, my husband."

"This is unprecedented," he grumbled.

"But if it works, that means we have a cure for the Fading. Isn't that worth a little humility?" she asked, and Lasha got the feeling she was speaking both to Satorian and the rest of the room.

"Helping family is the most important thing," Lasha agreed. "Is your brother stable enough to travel?"

"Probably," Delinian answered, obviously a little confused.

"Then bring him here," Lasha invited. "This room is big. We can fit another bed. Or he could share this bed with Reolina, it's giant."

"Hey, are you giving half my bed away?" Reolina asked, her soft voice full of humor. "First you bully me into living and now you're going to make me share?"

Her comment made most of the Talins in the room sound marble-clacking rumbles of amusement.

"Bring Pakorium here?" Delinian said, looking around the room. "But it's so bright here?"

Lasha nodded her head. "Exactly."

"It goes against all conventional wisdom," Satorian muttered.

"How's that wisdom been working so far?" Lasha asked, raising an eyebrow. She couldn't believe how bold she'd become.

Japhinan stepped up to stand next to Delinian. "Lasha is new to Talarian and moving her from familiar surroundings so soon after arriving might be detrimental. Besides we have a larger room we could move both Pakorium and Reolina into, and they can both have standard-size beds."

This bed was standard size? What would they consider a big bed, something the size of a house?

"They don't have to share a bed," Lasha conceded. "But you have to visit them."

She gave Delinian and Satorian the same list of demands she'd given Tamerin's family. "You have to talk to them. Read to them. Spend time with them, even if all you do is listen to me singing."

"But what good would that possibly do?" Satorian objected.

"Lasha and my family called me back from the gray abyss," Reolina stated. "At first it was only Lasha, but then all their voices pulled at me."

Lasha understood exactly what Reolina was saying. It pushed her to quote one of her mother's favorite phrases. "The body won't fight to live if the spirit has given up. We have to care for both."

There was absolute silence in the room, and everyone stared at her with unblinking eyes. It was unnerving and suddenly all her courage fled. She looked to Tamerin who'd stepped far to the side to give his mother room to stand next to Delinian.

Giving into what had worked at the port, she held up her arms and made grabby hands like a toddler. Without hesitation Tamerin crossed over and picked her up, supporting her butt with one arm so she could loosely wrap her legs around his waist and her arms around his neck.

"You did well, songbird," he whispered before running a scent gland over the top of her head. The smell of cardamom perfumed the air, making her relax in his hold. It felt weird to go from feeling so self-assured to anxious and needy, but she wasn't like Zia. She didn't have boundless confidence, only spurts of it.

"What has happened?" Delinian asked with an anxious rattle, which sounded like a muted version of the buzzing-wasp rattle of annoyance. "Have we overwhelmed her? Will she still work with my brother?"

"Tell her to bring him here," Lasha whispered to Tamerin even as she buried her face in his neck. "But they have to do what I asked. And bring a few of his favorite things and the softest, nicest bedding they have."

"She says he can still come but the rules she stated earlier apply. One of you must be in the room at all times ready to read or talk or interact in some way."

"Yes, we will," Delinian agreed.

"And the stuff," Lasha reminded him.

Tamerin purred for her as he spoke to Delinian. "And Lasha demands you bring anything Pakorium has a sentimental attachment to as well as the softest bedding you can find."

"Fine, yes, we'll do all of that, but she must save him," Delinian declared and for the first time Lasha heard desperation in her tone. She wasn't as cold or clinical about her brother's illness as she was pretending to be.

Picking her head up from where it was resting on Tamerin's neck, she met Delinian's eyes.

"I can only try. I can't promise," she warned the head of Tamerin's Clan.

"That's all I ask," she agreed and then turned on her heels and hurried off with most of everyone in the room following close behind.

"What just happened?" Reolina asked from the bed. "Did a little human just stand up to the leader of our clan?"

"And won," Tamerin said as he tightening his hold on her for a moment. "We've been graced by the Ancestors to have Lasha with us."

Rearing back a little so she could look him in the face, she frowned at Tamerin. "Speaking of humans on Talarian," she said dryly. "Don't think I didn't notice the part where Delinian threatened to force you to sell me. I thought you nullified my work contract."

Tamerin went stock still, tension radiating off his body again. "I did," he assured her. "There are things I should tell you. I might not have been as forthcoming as I should've."

That sounded bad. "What things?"

"Let's go into the garden," he suggested.

Lasha looked over to Reolina who sounded a weak but understandable tink-tink-tink rumble of agreement. "I'm fine. Novilum is going to read the latest information distribution document from the Apogee Assembly, and I'm fascinated to find out what they've decided concerning the Inol trade deals."

Without hesitating, Novilum slid into the vacant seat next to her bed and held up an information square. "I have it right here. I look forward to discussing the ramifications."

"Sounds riveting," Lasha teased.

"We'll be back," Tamerin promised before he walked out with her in his arms.

CHAPTER 27

Tamerin didn't stop until he was deep in the elaborate gardens that took up a hectare of land behind the estate. They couldn't see the house or perimeter wall from here. They couldn't even hear the sounds of the city.

Sitting down on a lone bench surrounded by flowering trees, he settled her in his lap and started purring. Sitting sideways across his thighs, she held his scarred hand in both of hers and looked at him expectantly.

"You're in Talin-controlled space, which means you're owned now," he started, his words rushing out as if his chest was under pressure. "No human is allowed to be free. Even if you weren't a slave or indentured servant with a work contract, you'd still be owned. Officially I own you because I brought you here. That was the paperwork they were requesting at the port, your ownership documentation."

Going quiet, Tamerin braced himself.

Remembering how angry Zia was with Palforma when she'd realized the truth, Tamerin expected Lasha to at least jump off his lap and put distance between them. He wouldn't have held it against her if she'd raged at him, hurling abuses he deserved.

But she didn't do either of those things. She sat on his lap in serene silence, her expression deep in thought. He tried to give her time by focusing on the arguments he'd use to convince her to stay with him. The promises he could make about when they would leave, even if he had to break some laws to get them off Talarian.

Palforma was good friends with Commandant Holian, a male with massive amounts of resources. He owned an entire colony, and even Searin, Prime Son and potential heir to the throne, listened to him. If nothing else, Tamerin was sure Holian could secure Lasha's freedom even if Delinian tried to intervene.

Scenarios and plans erupted in his head, some practical and some ridiculous. More than a few ended with him being left behind. The more he thought, the greater his anxiety became. Within only a few submarks his chest had got tight. He wasn't sure he could breathe properly anymore.

"This doesn't make sense," Lasha finally said, her tone calm and contemplative. "Slavery is illegal here. Remember when we helped Ilee and Relee? Abhorrence of slavery was something you said Talins had in common with the Delorta."

"Humans aren't slaves. They're pets," Tamerin explained.

"There's a difference?" Lasha looked genuinely curious, and there still wasn't any anger in her tone or expression.

"A huge difference," Tamerin assured her, a glimmer of hope easing some of his anxiety. "Slaves are meant to work for their owners. Pets never labor. Their only job is to thrive."

"And to provide Talins with the love and affection they've stripped out of their culture," she added. "Now I see why our relationship has to be such a secret. You're really not supposed to fuck the family dog."

Tamerin blinked both at the Old Earth word he didn't know and Lasha's use of such a vulgar term. "What's a dog?"

Lasha snorted out a laugh. "It was a common and beloved pet back on Old Earth, but they were only pets, not sapient beings like Talins and humans."

Tamerin latched on to the one part of her statement he could explain. "Talins acknowledge that humans have some intelligence. A small percentage of us are aware that humans are just as smart as Talins. But when the first Talins met the first humans hundreds of years ago, some conclusions were drawn and laws were made that were never changed."

She gave a little gasp and touched her neck. "This isn't a necklace. It's a collar. Isn't it?" she asked, her eyes going wide. "That's why the latch locks. I thought that was weird, but I figured it was to keep it from getting lost or stolen."

Miserable, Tamerin made a rumble of agreement. "I got you the nicest collar I could find."

"That's why I couldn't come with you on the Talin station. I would have seen collars that looked like collars," she continued, sounding hurt. "You did that on purpose. This wasn't simply you neglecting to tell me things. This was deliberate. Why, Tamerin?"

Her wounded expression made all the anxiety come right back. "I'd hoped to ease you into the truth," he admitted. "If we hadn't found out about my sister we would have gone straight to Sorana. You wouldn't have experienced any collars or threats. No one would have treated you as you've been treated here."

One corner of her mouth tipped up in a half grin. "That would've been a shame."

"I know and I..." his words trailed off as he registered what she'd said. "Shame?"

"I like it here," she said, her grin blossoming. Her dark eyes twinkled and her flat, white, human teeth flashed in the sun. "I mean I don't like you keeping important information from me, but other than that, this place is great."

"It is?" Tamerin asked, blinking.

"I've never felt so important," she exclaimed. "I probably helped Reolina! I helped! Back home, Isla was the one everyone turned to when they were sad or upset. Zia was who they talked to if they needed something fixed. I was never important. But here I can do things others can't. I love it here!"

It took a full submark before Tamerin's brain caught up with what she was saying. "You're not going to leave me?"

A horrified look came over her face, and she let go of his hand and wrapped her arms around his neck. "No! Tamerin, never! We're scent-bonded, right? Leaving you means I kill you. I love you, you big, dumb, spiky male. I'll never love anyone like I love you. And unless there's something really wrong with your brain, you don't kill the ones you love."

"I am a big, dumb male," Tamerin agreed with an amused rumble. Holding her tightly to his chest, he breathed in the combined scent of his bonding oil soaked into her skin.

"Don't forget spiky," she whispered against his neck.

"Big, dumb, spiky male," he repeated dutifully. "I'll have a special crest commissioned for myself."

"Good," she responded, laughter in her voice. "Because you better not ever question my love again."

"Never."

CHAPTER 28

When they got back from the garden, Lasha wasn't surprised to find Reolina's sick room completely changed. Now two beds sat in there, both of them massive by Lasha's human standards. They were arranged on opposite walls with a double row of seats set up to visually divide the room into two sides. The long bench was gone, and small benches had been added. Extra tables had been placed next to the guest bed, all of them piled high with miniatures of ships and buildings.

It looked like someone liked models, how adorable!

Large, fluffy square pillows lay strewn all over the floor with dozens of them piled up on the floor at the foot of each bed. Almost no floor was left uncovered.

Lasha was confused. "Are the pillows some kind of comfort thing? So Talins don't need to walk on bare floor?"

"Those are all for you. These are the most expensive kneeling pillows you can buy," he explained. "It looks like they bought every one they could find."

"Kneeling pillows?" she asked in a low tone to keep the other Talins in the room from hearing her question.

"For humans comfort when they kneel or sit on the floor next to their master," he explained.

"Yeah, uh, no," she said with a frown.

"I didn't buy them," he was quick to point out. "I'm sure Delinian only wanted to provide you with things she thought you might like." He nodded to one of the benches covered in piles of clothing. "Those are all human wraps and omnies, and you're the only human here. They're gifts for you, my sweet songbird."

Lasha looked over the messy stacks of items. "That's nice of her but silly. I don't need all that."

"Lasha?" Reolina called out weakly.

Forgetting about all the new things in the room, Lasha rushed to Reolina's side. "What do you need?"

"I don't need you, but that boy does. He's as bad as I was," she said with an anxious rattle. "Please go work your magic with the boy."

Apprehension hit Lasha, making her freeze in place. She'd deliberately not looked at the person in the second bed when she and Tamerin had walked into the room. She wasn't sure if anything she'd done had really helped Reolina or if it had all been a fluke. What if Pakorium died even with her singing and talking to him?

Then Tamerin was there, sweeping her up in his arms and purring.

"He'll die if you do nothing," Tamerin told her, accurately reading her state of mind. "At least you can comfort him in his last days."

Right, yes, that had been her original intention with Reolina after all. Comfort and companionship. She could do that.

"Down please," she murmured to Tamerin.

Once she was on the floor she walked slowly to Pakorium's bed. She was shocked at the state of the Talin and now understood why Reolina had referred to him as a boy.

"How old is he?" she asked as she climbed onto the bed and settled herself in a cross legged position next his hip. This let her facing the head of the bed to better talk or sing to him.

"He's in the phase we call adultette," Delinian said as she entered the room, her arms full of items and followed by several more Talins all equally burdened. "It's the age where we leave the cresh and join our families to learn the family or clan business."

"About the equivalent of sixteen Old Earth solars," Tamerin volunteered helpfully.

"No one is supposed to get the Fading so young," Delinian continued, setting everything she was holding on one of the benches. The others did the same, and now all the benches were full of items. It was a good thing there were plenty of seats because the benches were all tables now.

"I thought brothers and sisters were born at the same time," Lasha commented, taking in Pakorium's sightless gaze.

"My first brother died during the Pangal Insurrection before he could marry and provide for heirs," Delinian explained as she came to stand next to the bed. "In such circumstances, my parents were expected to produce another male child so our population numbers don't become skewed, but they handed his care to me. I checked on him in the cresh as he grew. I reviewed his learning plans and progress. He came to live with me last solar when he left the cresh. What you see here is my fault."

Although Delinian's statements were delivered in an emotionless and factual tone, Lasha heard both loss and love there. Talins might not be able to show it, but they wanted to love as deeply as any human.

Taking up Pakorium's right hand in both of hers, she was startled at how cold he felt. Even Reolina had radiated heat. "Hello, Pakorium, my name's Lasha. We're going to be spending a lot of time together. It's important that you listen to me. You don't have to talk. But if you feel like it I'd love to hear your voice when you're ready."

"You should sing to him," Delinian demanded, stepping closer so she loomed over Lasha.

Lasha looked up, not intimidated at all. This Talin might be big, tough, and powerful, but the only feeling she inspired in Lasha was sympathy.

"I will. But we're going to talk to him for a little while first," Lasha answered and then issued a demand of her own. "I want you to sit next to the bed and take his other hand."

Delinian paused for a second, probably dealing with the fact that she was about to take orders from a lowly pet human.

Then she grabbed one of the backless chairs and rounded the bed. Thumping it down, she sat and reached for Pakorium's hand. Realizing she wouldn't be able to reach him from the seat, she stood up and gingerly sat on the bed. Once she settled in a similar position as Lasha, she took Pakorium's hand in her own.

"Now what?" Delinian asked, looking at Lasha.

"Now we talk," Lasha answered. "Look at Pakorium and tell him how much you love him."

"Love is a human thing," Delinian declared dismissively.

Lasha almost sighed at the stubborn Talin. "Fine, tell him the reasons you're proud of him. Talk about all the things you'd miss if he died."

"Yes," Delinian agreed. "Yes, I can talk about those things. He's very adventurous. His cresh was on the edge of a river and when he was very young—"

Lasha interrupted her. "Don't tell me about it. Talk to him."

Delinian looked down at her brother. "But he can't hear me."

"You can't know that for sure," Lasha argued.

"Very well," Delinian answered stiffly. "Do you remember the time you fell into the river because you wanted to get a closer look at the troof fish? You were swept so far down the river it took us a mark to find you. Everyone was extremely concerned. We thought we'd find your little broken body caught in a hydrodam or cast aside on an embankment. But no, you managed to swim to a small inlet where you were trapping the troof fish for further study. You were so young but already fascinated by the natural order of the world around you."

As she spoke, Delinian's stiff posture started to relax slightly and words began to flow better. To add to the encounter, Lasha started softly humming one of the many love songs she knew. Love songs had been her grandmother's favorite, so they made up at least half of all the songs Lasha had learned from the wonderful woman.

"I know you didn't want to join the military," Delinian continued. "I shouldn't have pushed you so hard. Even though I promised you could do the minimum service length and then start a second career in the sciences, I should have let you join grandmother's clan as you'd asked."

As Delinian talked, Lasha got a clear picture of why Pakorium was afflicted by the Fading despite his young age. Because the Ibek Clan was famous for producing exceptional warriors and military leaders, Delinian was determined her brother would hold up the clan's reputation just as she had.

But this young male wanted nothing more than to study and research. He had no interest in the empire, expansion, or war. He didn't even like the practice fighting classes he had to take at the cresh. Then he came to live with his sister and his life revolved around training and applying to the most prestigious specialties in the military.

Lasha's heart broke for Pakorium—a Talin with all the privileges but no freedom.

Now that she'd started talking, Delinian kept it up without any further encouragement.

"Drink," Tamerin commanded handing her an open canister. She accepted it and sipped the cool water as Tamerin placed a chair next to her side of Pakorium's bed. When he sat, he was facing his sister but reached his arm out to rest a hand on Lasha's thigh. She appreciated his silent support.

"Thanks," she murmured, handing the canister back. Tamerin finished off the contents and then set it on the floor.

"I'm here," he reminded her. And it was that simple. He was there to help her as she helped others.

How perfect was her Talin?

She gave him a quick smile before focusing her attention back on the sick Talin. She went back to hummed while holding Pakorium's hand. Tamerin kept up a quiet conversation with Reolina, reminiscing about their childhood, experiences in the military, and thoughts about the future.

Lasha was so lost in her humming, she jumped when Pakorium's fingers unexpectedly twitched in her grip. Delinian sounded a loud rattle of surprise and stared down at the hand she was holding.

"He moved," she breathed. "He hasn't moved in rotations. Not even when we had to lift him from the bed to the carrier to bring him here."

"I felt it too," Lasha assured her. "This is good. Keep talking. He has a long journey to find his way back to us. You need to make sure he doesn't get lost again."

"Yes, yes of course. I'll talk without stopping for as long as it takes," she declared, breathing rapidly. "Do you hear me, Pakorium? You can't get rid of me. I'm going to tell all the stories about you falling into mud pits or losing control of your specimens in the cresh kitchen."

Lasha smiled even as tears pricked her eyes. This might work after all.

Two days later Lasha was staring dumbfounded at a room so jam-packed with items there was no open space, only paths to move around the stacks of elaborately carved boxes. "What do you mean this is all for me?"

"Word about what's happened here has gotten out," Tamerin said as his eyes looked over the massive number of boxes. "I was told many families have been sending you gifts in hopes you will help their loved ones suffering from Fading, but I didn't expect this much. The problem is so much worse than anyone realizes."

Lasha turned to him, her hands on her hips. "This is so bad. Are all these people doing the same thing with their family members as your parents did to Reolina?"

Tamerin didn't meet her gaze. "Yes."

She didn't say anything, just waited for him to drop his eyes to hers. "Spill," she demanded.

"Spill what?" he asked.

"Don't act like you don't understand my slang in context," she retorted.

Tamerin looked away. "You have to understand, this is difficult to talk about."

Reaching out, she wrapped her arms around his waist. "Come on, big guy. Just tell me."

Tamerin rumbled out a deep, soothing purr as he hugged her back. "We're taught from a young age that Fading only happens to weak-willed Talins. It's better if they die. It's so shameful no one wants to admit that they have it. When it's discovered, the family will go to great lengths to hide it. I've even heard rumors that soldiers will deliberately do dangerous things if they think they might be developing it. They'd rather allow themselves to die in battle than let anyone know."

Lasha couldn't believe it. "Don't you guys have doctors or scientists to figure out how to fix this?"

"The stigma is too great," Tamerin told her. "Most healers won't even visit someone suffering from Fading. One of the only healers I know who even researches it was labeled as unprofessional. She struggles to stay on Talarian and might end up losing her family's support and be forced to move to a colony or station."

"You were telling me when we first got here that no one would treat Reolina." Lasha sighed. "For some reason I thought it was a local issue. Like the healers here at the capital wouldn't touch it. But if your people won't even study it, you guys fucked yourselves good."

He didn't even pretend not to understand. "In this regard, yes."

Something occurred to her, making her let go of him and step away. "Did you have it? When I was first recovering in the room you rented on Glakor, I had a dream someone was talking to me about not wanting to eat and that maybe I could fix it. Was that you? Are you Fading?"

Fear made her grab hold of his hands hard enough to hurt her softer human skin. Tamerin dropped to his knees in front of her and purred.

"You saved me," he whispered. "I'd lost interest in food, which is always the first sign. But then there you were. There's a rumor almost everyone denies but secretly believes; humans can keep the Fading from happening, like Novilum commented. Seeing what you've done for my sister, now I believe humans can also cure the Fading. You and your species are the saviors of ours, even though we thought it was the other way around."

Breathing through the terror that had spiked through her body at the thought of Tamerin dying, Lasha stepped close to his kneeling form and wrapped her arms around his neck. His head nestled against her chest, and they both shuddered a little.

"You're not allowed to die," she commanded, her voice a little shaky. "I love you, so you can't leave me."

Lasha felt warm oil soak into the front of her wrap and the familiar smell of cardamom filled her nose.

"Never," he promised.

Shouting from down the hall made them both startle. Tamerin lunged to his feet and put himself in front of her, quills up and claws out. Then realizing there was no threat, he straightened up. It was Delinian shouting from the room Pakorium and Reolina were sharing.

"I thought Pakorium was doing better." Her voice quaked as she spoke. "We only left him for a minute. Quick, we have to say goodbye."

Running down the hall with Tamerin right behind her, she almost crashed into the family's chef as she carried a heaping platter of food and drinks.

"Sorry," the Talin said. "Assembly Citizen Delinian requested all of this be brought to Pakorium immediately. She was very adamant about it."

Then she moved around Lasha to enter the room. Following the chef in, Lasha found Pakorium sitting up and weakly looking around. Delinian was kneeling next to his bed, speaking rapidly while at the same time purring loudly.

"...and you're going to study under the head researcher there. But if you don't like that we can find you another spot. It's not a problem. I only wanted to secure that one because you always seemed more fascinated by biology than any of the other sciences. Of course there's also the xeno-biology department. You don't need to be limited to Talarian specimens."

Lasha had to hold back tears as she listened to Delinian list all the places Pakorium could study or work if he wished. It was clear Assembly Citizen Delinian, head of the Ibek Clan and Clan Assembly representative, had learned her lesson and was going to let her younger brother live the life he wanted.

This was the best possible outcome.

CHAPTER 29

Lasha had mixed feelings about both Reolina and Pakorium doing better. It had been ten days since Pakorium had woken up, and he was already able to walk a few steps on his own. Reolina could now make it out to the garden. The two of them were eating and drinking almost like normal Talins. Lasha couldn't be more pleased.

But she could also see her tenure as caregiver and entertainer coming to an end. It wouldn't be long before Pakorium moved back to his sister's estate to finish recovering. Then he was off to study his choice of subject. He'd talked to Lasha at length about the different types of microorganisms living in Talin bodies. It seemed that might be the specialty he picked.

After he'd started talking, Delinian had to resume her work with the Clan Assembly, but she made sure to visit Pakorium every day. She was quick to sit on the edge of his bed, hold his hand, and discuss anything he wanted.

It warmed Lasha's heart that these powerful Talins might pretend love was a human emotion, but they could learn to show it to each other just the same. All they needed was a push in the right direction.

Or maybe *shove* would be a more accurate word.

Reolina was also talking about resuming her duties. She ran a small but successful security business for remote Talin colonies. When she'd realized she was Fading, she hurried home so she could say goodbye to her parents before she died. Now she wanted to get back to work. She also mentioned looking into some rumors she'd heard about some humans living and working at a space station in Ilgorian Federation territory. It would take some diplomatic work, but she could probably get permission under the guise of selling her services to the station.

"Before you go looking for them, you and I should have a talk," Lasha cautioned her.

"Oh yes," Reolina agreed. "I heard you were wild-caught. You would have many insights into taming a human who hasn't been a pet before."

Ignoring the words she didn't like, Lasha focused on keeping her expression neutral. "Lots and lots of insights. There's time yet. We'll have a nice conversation about it before you leave."

"I look forward to that," she answered eagerly. Reolina probably didn't realize Lasha was going to school her on the etiquette of honesty when trying to convince humans to travel to Talin controlled space. Lasha wanted the two species to come together. Both groups brought important things to the table, but the power imbalance was way too severe to simply brush aside.

She could easily forgive Tamerin for what he'd done, but another human might not. The last thing she wanted was for a fellow human to end up trapped as a pet if they didn't want to be.

"I've heard even more gifts have arrived for you," Pakorium commented.

"The room is completely full now," Tamerin told him. "If anything more arrives we'll have to start putting it in a separate room."

"I wanted to send it all back, but Tamerin said I can't do that." She wrinkled her nose. "I don't want to insult anyone, but

I can't use all this stuff. There are more clothes, bedding, and shoes in there than I could use in a lifetime."

Lasha didn't comment that she couldn't bring herself to even look in the room. Every box of items in there represented someone in need, and it broke her heart.

"Do you think you'd be willing to visit any other sick Talins?" Reolina asked.

"I'm not sure," Lasha admitted. Knowing she was now considered a pet, Lasha was reluctant to leave the safety of the Kiferian Family estate. Here she was full of courage. Here she could even command an Assembly Citizen to do things and browbeat Talins into comforting each other. Now fully aware of her status, Lasha found the idea of leaving the safety of the estate a little terrifying.

Guilt at not helping other suffering Talins was eating at her.

Biting her lip, she looked at Tamerin. He sounded a loud purr. "One rotation at a time, songbird," he reminded her. "Today we're here with Reolina and Pakorium."

That had turned into Tamerin's favorite saying with her—one thing at a time.

One day at a time.

One step at a time.

One song at a time.

It was a lot easier to focus on that mantra than the overwhelming number of Talins beyond the estate walls dying in dark rooms without any comfort or kindness.

"Could you sing that adventure song again?" Pakorium requested. "I'm tired but scared to sleep."

Both Pakorium and Reolina had confessed that sleeping was difficult. They were both terrified that they'd fall back into the Fading if they succumbed to slumber. Lasha's singing seemed to help keep them grounded.

"Of course," Lasha agreed and launched into the requested song.

When she was done it was obvious Pakorium had drifted off. Feeling proud of herself, Lasha stood up to stretch. She needed to take a break. She'd never sung so much in her life as she had since arriving on Talarian.

"I think I might go for a little walk," she whispered to the room. Novilum, Japhinan, Satorian, Tamerin, and her two patients were all present and watching at her. "Anyone want to join me?"

"I think I'll read to Pakorium," Satorian said, picking up an information square and sounding a quick, quiet purr. "It's not as effective as your singing, but I think it will help him sleep peacefully."

Lasha now understood that most Talins purred for humans, even if they didn't really know the person, but they rarely purred for each other. It was another example of how much they needed to up their affection game.

"Good idea," Lasha said with a nod and then looked at Reolina.

"I'd like to come," Reolina agreed as she got out of bed unaided. Novilum hurried to her side but she waved him off. "I'm slow, but stable."

Japhinan stood up. "I'm going to check on the comms to make sure no pressing issues need my attention. I'll come back to eat the evening meal with everyone in four marks." Then she focused her gaze on Lasha. "Chef is convinced she can make synthesized chicken vindaloo that will taste correct this time."

Lasha grinned. "I can't wait. Her last attempt wasn't too bad."

"It was disgusting," Reolina argued.

Pointing a finger at her, Lasha mock growled. "Don't insult my food or I'll tickle you again."

Apparently Talin armor plates thinned just before they were about to shed them. Lasha had accidentally found one of those spots on Reolina's shoulder and made the poor woman jerk and almost fall out of the bed. She'd said it felt like powerful tingles were radiating down her arm.

Lasha had been careful not to touch it again but was merciless with her threats.

"It's the most delicious rubbish I've ever eaten," Reolina amended quickly and then sounded a quiet, clinking-marbles rumble of amusement. She was on her feet now and moving toward the door.

Stifling her laugh, Lasha gave up defending her taste in food. "If you were human, you'd love the stuff."

"We can scientifically test that," Pakorium whispered from the bed.

"Sorry we woke you up," Lasha murmured.

"I was barely asleep," Pakorium assured her. "But now I'm thinking about experiments. We simply gather ten pets together and let them sample it. It would prove your eating choices are an oddity even among humans."

The word *pet* threw Lasha off her stride for a moment, but she recovered quickly. "When the chef finishes perfecting the food, we should."

By now Reolina was out of the room and down the hall, and Tamerin was waiting for her by the door.

"I'll be back. Don't get into trouble while I'm gone," Lasha called out before skipping up to Tamerin and taking his hand.

"I like it here," Lasha confided to him as they trailed after Reolina and Novilum.

"I'm glad," Tamerin replied with a loud purr. "My family adores you and Delinian would give you anything you asked for."

"Oh, even if I ask for an entire ship of my own," Lasha teased.

"Don't say that to her, or she'll get you one," Tamerin commented, making Lasha stop in her tracks.

"You're kidding, right?"

Tamerin sounded a negative rattle. "Not at all. Our clan is one of the more powerful ones, and Delinian is the head of our clan. Her husband is from the second most powerful family in our clan. The two of them command a massive amount of wealth and power. If you asked for a ship all they'd do was request you specify what type of ship you want."

"That's, uh, nice?" How was she supposed to react when finding out someone would buy her an entire ship?

Swooping down, Tamerin picked her up without breaking his stride, cuddling her against his chest and purring. "Don't fret, songbird. I only wanted you to understand how welcome you are here. When you're ready, we can talk about picking a wing of this house or building one of our own on this estate."

"I think I'd like a house of our own," she answered promptly. "I want to stay here for a while before getting back on a ship. Do you think Zia will be mad if I don't visit her right away?"

"Probably," Tamerin said and then sounded a clinking-marbles rumble of humor. "But no one can stay mad at you for long."

"No, you're mistaking me for my friend Isla," Lasha argued. "No one could ever stay mad at Isla no matter what kind of mischief she got herself into. I was just the dumb one everybody felt sorry for."

"Who called you dumb?" The question was voiced in the form of a demand, loud enough to echo down the hall and catch the attention of Reolina and Novilum exiting the sprawling house ahead of them.

Clutching her tightly, Tamerin swung around to find Delinian standing behind them with a Talin Lasha had never met before. Delinian's claws were out and she was breathing hard as she sounded the aggressive projectiles-being-fired rattle.

Oh, she was pissed.

"It was nothing," Lasha said quickly, hoping the Talin hadn't heard more of their conversation. "I was just saying everyone thought I was dumb growing up because I couldn't learn to read."

"You can't read?" the other Talin asked.

"Um, no. I can't," Lasha confirmed as she focused on this stranger. The first thing she noted was the forest green, knee-length tunic the woman was wearing. It was belted at the waist with the typical wide Talin belt, and Lasha could see the hint of the normal Talin trousers peeking out from under the hem of the tunic. It was the first time she'd seen a Talin wear anything on their upper body besides military armor.

As curious as she was about the outfit, Lasha was far more startled by the petite stature of this stranger. She was small for a Talin, probably only about six feet or so. The stranger had a surprisingly slim build. Lasha had gotten used to all the Talins she met being massive and brawny, so this woman struck her as delicate looking.

Before Lasha could ask who this woman was, Delinian spoke up. "If you can't read it's the fault of your dam and sire, not you. Or the Talins who owned you and your family. We don't blame the weapon for missing the target, we blame the gunner. I want the names of your former owners. I'll make sure they are investigated by the Committee of Pet Welfare. There is a minimum education standard for humans, and they have clearly flouted the rules. Never fear, Lasha. I will get you justice."

Wow, when Delinian decided to be protective, she went all the way.

"She was wild-caught," Tamerin explained before Lasha could figure out how to respond to Delinian.

It was a fight, but Lasha managed to keep from grimacing at the term *wild-caught*. But really, come on! That made it sound like Tamerin found her running around in some woods wearing fur and scrounging in the dirt for wild roots.

Tamerin's explanation caused both women to sound loud, soothing purrs.

"You poor thing," the small Talin proclaimed. "That explains your hair and how small you are."

You're one to speak, lady, Lasha thought. *I bet everyone around here towers over you too!*

"Still, if anyone here ever calls you dumb, you come to me," Delinian insisted.

This was like having a protective big sister. Lasha loved it. "If Tamerin doesn't take care of them, you're next on my list."

Delinian gave a sharp nod of her head. "Just so."

Stepping forward and rummaging around in her belt pouch, the stranger introduced herself.

"Hello, Lasha, I'm Healer Verinan." Pulling her hand free she presented Lasha with two of the familiar sweets Talins liked to carry around specifically to hand out to humans. "I'm told you're well enough to enjoy a few treats."

Lasha accepted the candy and popped them into her mouth. She didn't know who'd engineered them, but they'd done a fantastic job. Sweet, fruity flavor exploded on her tongue as the candies dissolved.

"Thanks," she mumbled, feeling a little greedy for filling her mouth like a ten-year-old with no self-control.

"I've come to talk to you," Verinan continued. "I've heard some stories, and when I found out they were true, I begged Delinian to let me meet you."

Tamerin was still holding her cradled to his chest, and while none of the Talins seemed to think it was weird, Lasha was starting to feel a little socially awkward. Sure, it was nice to be tall, but being held like a baby didn't seem very adult-like behavior.

"Tamerin, could you set me down?" she murmured to him.

He didn't make a sound, but his slow compliance told her how much he objected. She giggled a little when her feet finally hit the ground and he straightened back up. Then she put herself in front of him, pressed her back against his front, and pulled his quill-less arm around so she could hug him to her chest.

There, that was perfect.

"Why did you want to meet me?" Lasha asked, even though she was ninety-nine percent sure she knew the answer.

"What I've been told by several sources now is that you've pulled two individuals back from being deep in the Fading. One was reputed to have been on the verge of death yet you brought him back to us. I need you to tell me everything you've done."

Lasha peered at this Talin with interest. "Are you the one who's gotten into trouble because you're trying to research Fading?"

Verinan must have taken her question as a reproach because she stiffened and her tone became chilly and formal as she answered Lasha's question with another question.

"We use science and reason to look at everything else in our world, why not this? Why are we letting prejudice and superstition overrule inquiry and research?" Verinan clasped her hands behind her back, probably to keep herself from fidgeting or showing nerves. "My work is as important as any other medical study, even more so if we look at the increasing numbers of Talins afflicted. Fading is rapidly turning into the most prevalent disease among us, except no one is willing to face it!"

Her voice got loud at the end of her impassioned speech, and then she blinked and realized she'd made a fuss in the home of a powerful family and in front of an Assembly Citizen.

Before Verinan could start apologizing, Lasha spoke up. "I agree! Everything you said is exactly right! Of course I'll talk to you. I'll do anything you want to help. I was told you're having a hard time keeping your clinic open. People sent me loads of stuff, you can have it. Maybe selling it will help."

"Absolutely not," Tamerin argued. "Those are for you. You've had so little in your life. I want you to enjoy opening all those boxes."

"But this is important," Lasha whined. She had yet to admit to Tamerin the amount of guilt she felt every time she looked at the boxes. Donating them would help alleviate some of that guilt. "And I want to help."

"And you will," Delinian declared with a tink-tink-tink rattle of agreement. "But not by giving away the paltry gifts you've received."

"Paltry," Lasha whispered to Tamerin. "There's a room full of boxes. Full!"

"Here, that is paltry," Tamerin whispered back as Delinian continued to talk.

"I've been approached by many families and individuals begging for Lasha's help. When they couldn't get Tamerin or his family to listen, they came to me. I've been offered staggering amounts of wealth. Some are seeking to buy Lasha outright and others beg only for some of her time."

Lasha hissed out a breath at Delinian's *buying* comment. But Tamerin sounded a soothing purr, and she remembered he'd never let that happen. They were scent-bonded and in love, even if they couldn't tell anyone about it. He'd do everything in his power

"All of these offers made me realize we could open a center dedicated to studying and treating Fading," Delinian concluded. "That's why I agreed to let you come here, Healer Verinan. I'm going to help you fund, staff, and run this center."

"But Lasha would need to spend time there," Verinan protested. "My work has shown little success. Fading is resistant to the medications I've tried. In all the years I've studied it, I've had hundreds die and only three survive. Yet this human has managed to save two with no training and no medication. She's only lived among Talins for a short time. My research needs Lasha!"

Her impassioned speech made Lasha feel both special and a little apprehensive. "I don't know if I did anything that special. I'd be willing to help, but I'm scared you think I'm some kind of genius."

"Of course you're not a genius. You're human," Delinian commented. "But you are important, probably because you're wild-caught. You must have learned some kind of survival strategy or skill that is applicable in this situation."

Lasha barely kept from rolling her eyes at Delinian. "It's called compassion."

Delinian didn't take offense to Lasha's dry tone. "An emotion that will get you into trouble more often than not, but a fitting quality among humans."

That made Lasha bark out a laugh and then focus her attention on Verinan. "I have an idea for the clinic, but think about it before you say anything. Okay?"

Verinan made a quick tink-tink-tink of agreement before going silent and staring intently at Lasha. She got the feeling this Talin did everything with intensity.

"Maybe we should see if other humans might be willing to hang out with me at the clinic," Lasha said in a rush. "Even if what I do helps, there is only one of me and only so many hours, um, marks in a rotation. But if we could get more humans to visit, they could copy what I do and maybe we could save more people."

When no one talked right away, she wished she hadn't opened her big mouth. "Never mind, that was a dumb idea."

"Why would you say that," Verinan asked. "I believe your suggestion has merit."

"You do?" Lasha breathed. "But you didn't say anything."

"You told me to think about it before replying," Verinan pointed out. "I wanted you to know I'd thought about your words before I spoke. We'd probably want to start very small, only four or five patients. I'd need to be able to study everything you do. As we prove this condition is treatable, we can expand if any human pets would be willing to spend time at the center."

"It will be very difficult," Tamerin warned them. "Even after you prove efficacy, the shame and taboo nature surrounding the disease will make Talins worry about letting their humans visit, even if the humans volunteer."

"I guess we'll cross that bridge when we come to it," Lasha commented.

All three Talins stared at her.

"What else would you do with a bridge but cross it?" Delinian asked.

Lasha grinned. "Burn it down. But that's for extreme situations."

Instead of sounding rumbles of laughter, they all sounded brief rattles of agreement. "Yes, that's a good metaphor," Verinan agreed.

"Very good," Tamerin added. "I like this human saying. Cross the bridge and then burn it so the enemy cannot follow."

"Uh, that's not what I said," Lasha objected, trying hard not to laugh.

Tamerin briefly tightened his arm around her. "I know I paraphrased, but it's close enough. And my version is more succinct than saying 'we will cross the bridge when we get to it and then burn it down in extreme situations.' That's much too long for regular use."

That was when Lasha gave up and let loose with peals of laughter.

CHAPTER 30

"Lasha?"

Looking up from where she'd been holding the hand of an emaciated and dying Talin, Lasha blinked at the familiar figure standing in the doorway of the communal sick room.

Sorimun was dressed in the light green, knee-length tunic that all the healers-in-training wore instead of the forest green of fully trained healers. He was the newest member of the staff, but Lasha had liked him immediately.

And it didn't have anything to do with the overflowing handful of candy he'd given her before even saying hello.

Out of all the staff, he was by far the most compassionate and the quickest to emulate Lasha, even if it meant he was doing things "unseemly" for a Talin. He had to be the least pretentious Talin she'd ever met.

"Hi, Sorimun, is it time for drinks?" she asked.

The moment a Talin roused themselves from the Fading enough to be thirsty, they were fed a dense nutrient drink. Verinan had figured out through trial and error that it was best to have them consume small quantities of the drinks often. She'd even worked with a chef to develop something that would be tasty, healthy, and highly nutritious. Not that the recovering Talins could taste it right away. But Lasha admired her dedication to detail.

The five in this room were their second round of Fading patients. All but one of the original five had survived and left the clinic on their own two feet. Unfortunately Lasha couldn't forget the one who hadn't made it. Not a single member of her family had visited her. Lasha had wept as the Talin died and then raged at the family's callous treatment of their own daughter.

Tamerin had held her, rocking her gently and keeping up a soothing purr as she'd alternated between sobbing and screaming. After she'd calmed down he'd wanted her to leave the clinic and never come back.

Their conversation was one Lasha would never forget.

"No, I can't leave. I have to be here. I have to do this," Lasha had argued. *"I thought I was born flawed. I was sure the best I'd ever do was not to be a burden to anyone. But here I'm making a difference. I'm helping!"*

"But at what cost?" Tamerin retorted, filling the small room they were in with his frustrated buzzing rattle. *"I can't watch you go through this again when another patient dies."* She opened her mouth to argue that she was determined to save them all, but he rushed to speak. *"Some will die, my sweet songbird. They will come to us too late with depleted bodies and locked-in minds. You won't be able to save them all, and I won't let you make yourself sick."*

"This one hit me hard," Lasha admitted. *"But someone has to care about these Talins. I'll learn to distance myself a little. I promise. But you can't ask me to stop. And maybe we'll get more humans to come help. But if I quit, no one will let their humans come here."*

"I could make you leave," Tamerin stated.

Lasha knew his threat came from a place of fear for her. *"You could, but you won't."*

His buzzing frustrated rattle abruptly cut off as one of surprise briefly sounded. "How can you know that?"

"Because you love me," Lasha explained. *"And you want me to be happy, and being here makes me happy, even if it makes me sad sometimes too."*

When he went back to purring, she knew he would let her keep working. The conversation made her acknowledge that she needed to work on keeping some emotional distance from these Talins, or she might burn out and be of no use to anyone. She'd seen it happen with the Wimol Colony midwife after losing one too many babies.

Caring but clinical—it was a hard line to keep but an important one.

"A Talin is here to see you, and he brought his human," Sorimun said, pulling her out of her memories.

"Do you think they're here to volunteer?" Lasha asked excitedly.

Sorimun seemed hesitant. "I'm not sure, the human seems agitated, and the Talin won't speak more than a few words at a time."

Huh, that was weird. "Where are they?"

"Waiting in the intake room," Sorimun answered. "I made sure to give the human plenty of candy and left canisters of drinks so she won't get thirsty."

At the moment their clinic consisted of only four rooms: intake, the single communal patient room, storage, and kitchen. Verinan had plans to expand, but despite their obvious success, there was still little enthusiasm for this program.

Lasha consoled herself with the fact that it was still early days. Even if they got more space, they couldn't take more than five patients at a time. Not until she had more humans to help her.

Still, her heart broke for all the Talins out there suffering even as she focused on fixing her little part of the universe.

Looking down, she spoke to the Talin in the bed. "I'm going to leave, but I'll only be gone for a little while. When I get back, you can request any song you like."

The Talin didn't speak, but she could have sworn she felt his fingers twitch a little. That seemed to be the thing that always came back first, the fingers.

Letting go of his hand, she stood up and addressed the room. "I'll be back soon. Sorimun is going to keep all of you company while I'm gone."

"What should I read today?" Sorimun asked, taking the chair in the middle of the room and picking up the information square they kept on the table next to it.

"Read about the battle of Midwash," Lasha suggested. "It's really exciting, especially the part where the future monarch and her husband go into battle together!"

"Excellent choice," Sorimun agreed and tapped on the information square. As he started reading the introduction to the account, Lasha slipped out of the room. It was only a quick trip down a short hall before she stepped into the intake room.

Then she squealed with delight.

"Zia!"

Her childhood friend looked up, even though she couldn't hear Lasha's voice. Zia had special implants in her eyes that connected with her INT. They would translate the sounds into words or symbols so Zia knew if people were talking, walking, or in Lasha's case, screaming!

Before Zia could tap out a greeting in the silent language of the Norka, Lasha was gripping her in a bear hug, ignoring the giant Talin looming over the two of them. Zia got her arms free and hugged Lasha back as tears of happiness welled in Lasha's eyes. She'd missed her friend so very much.

Finally they separated and Lasha was quick to start tapping, not bothering to speak and unnecessarily fill Zia's eye implant with written text.

'I'm so happy to see you! Are you staying long? How is it on Sorana? Is this Palforma? Gosh, he's so big! Sorimun didn't tell me it was you two. Do you have a place to stay? I'm sure Tamerin's family wouldn't mind if you stayed with them. They're really great. I'm still on shift, but in about three marks I can take you over there and introduce you. Or you can go now and I'll have Sorimun send them a message. Oh, and Tamerin will be back soon, so you can't leave until he gets back. You met Tamerin, right? Isn't he the best? Did you bring anyone else with you? I——'

Zia blinked at the rapid-fire questions then grinned and grabbed Lasha's hands to stop her stream of questions and comments. Blushing a little, Lasha pulled her hands free of Zia and playfully slapped them over her mouth, indicating she'd stop tapping.

'I'm relieved and happy to see you alive and well,' Zia started and then pointed at the Talin with her before tapping again. 'You guessed right. This is my Talin, Palforma.'

'I like it when you call me that,' Palforma tapped, sounding a loud purr.

'It's the simple truth,' Zia responded with a gentle smile before focusing back on Lasha. 'But I'm confused. How did you end up on Talarian? The message we got from Tamerin was that he was supposed to bring you straight to Sorana. Almost the entire Wimol Colony is there now. We even have a domicile built just for you.'

Now it was Lasha's turn to blink. 'My own domicile?'

'Everyone gets their own unless they want to live in the dorms,' Zia explained. 'And we're free there. Most of us don't even bother to wear our collars. The only ones allowed on the colony are Talins who agree to keep our secret and treat us as equals. We have to pretend to be pets if anyone from the government visits, but that hasn't happened yet.'

'You can do that?' Lasha asked. 'The Talin government seems way too strict to get away with that.'

'This colony was started by Prime Son Searin,' Palforma explained. 'He's the son of the monarch. He carries a lot of influence so we haven't had inspectors out yet. It will happen, but I'm sure we'll get plenty of warning and be able to prepare everyone for it.'

'So you need to pack up your things,' Zia ordered. 'We came straight from the port and Nalia and Derani told us that if we return with a few marks we can leave today. Otherwise we'll have to wait a few rotations.'

'Look at you using marks and rotations like a Talin,' Lasha teased. 'Half the time I still forget and say hours or days.'

Zia frowned. 'Focus, Lasha. We need to get moving. I'm sorry you had to come to Talarian, and I promise Tamerin will have to explain his change of plans. But if we're going to get you free of this place today, we have to act quickly.'

Lasha took a step back, matching Zia's frown. 'I'm not leaving.'

'What?' Zia used a big gesture to tap that single word, basically showing she'd yelled it.

Staring her in the eye, Lasha tapped slowly, as if talking to someone with Norka newly programmed into their INT. 'I. Am. Not. Leaving.'

A spark of anger gleamed in Zia's eyes. 'Why the hell not? Why would you want to stay on a planet where a committee or authority figure could unilaterally decide to take you away from Tamerin? You do realize they don't see us as anything but pets. Right? We're a low intelligence species to them. Nothing more than an amusing animal to own. A means to gain status and prestige. We're things to them!'

'I'm more,' Lasha argued. 'Tamerin told me what happened to you on Oglin station, and I'm sorry you had to go through that. But I'm not in danger here. I promise.'

'You can't know that,' Zia shot back. 'You could get taken away and given to someone abusive! They could decide to breed you and put you in a cage with some guy who'll rape you. Lasha, you're in real danger here!'

'And your colony could get hit by a meteor tomorrow,' Lasha countered. 'Lots of what-ifs can happen.'

Zia's expression turned thunderous. 'The chance of an undetected meteor is slim. The likelihood of something bad happening to you on Talarian is high.'

Lasha shook her head and kept her expression serene despite the riot of emotions going through her. Like Tamerin when he wanted to make her quit working at the clinic, Zia was acting on an abundance of love, not cruelty.

'Do you know what I do here?' she asked, keeping her tapping fluid instead of letting it get jerky and harsh like Zia's.

'I don't even know what this place is,' Zia admitted, obviously a little thrown by the change of topic. 'When we contacted the Kiferian family estate, they directed us here to find you two.'

'Follow me,' Lasha instructed and then looked at Palforma. 'No rattles, okay? Purring or happy rumbles are fine.'

Palforma's tapping was slow, showing confusion. 'I won't rattle.'

Taking Zia's hand, Lasha led her into the treatment room. She heard Palforma suck in a harsh breath when he saw the patients, but good to his word he kept his back plates quiet.

Sorimun stopped reading as they entered. He watched Lasha closely, waiting for her cue to leave. She appreciated that about him. He was always willing to let her take charge even if she was only a lowly pet.

"I'm sorry to interrupt Sorimun's reading," Lasha said, addressing the room. "But I wanted to introduce everyone to my childhood friend Zia. She's only going to be here a short time, but I knew she'd love to meet all of you. She's deaf, so I'm going to speak for her."

No response came from any of the beds, but that didn't deter Lasha. Boldly she led Zia to the first bed. "Zia, this is Grunlium. She's a skilled structural engineer. She and her family all live on Omeanin Colony, so we're really lucky she was able to make it to Talarian to join us. Grunlium, this is my friend Zia."

'Hello, Grunlium,' Zia tapped and Lasha verbalized. 'It's nice to meet you.'

Grunlium's only response was to move her eyes slightly to focus on Zia. That was the first response she'd shown since twitching her fingers yesterday. Lasha's heart sang with happiness.

After a brief, one-sided conversation with Grunlium, Lasha walked Zia and Palforma to the next bed. They kept this up until they had "spoken" with everyone in the room. Then Lasha looked at Sorimun.

"I'm going to escort them out, but it might take a while. Please continue to read while I'm gone," Lasha requested.

"Of course," Sorimun agreed and then looked to Zia and Palforma. "I'm pleased to meet you both and hope you visit again. Have a fruitful rotation."

With that, Lasha took them back to the intake room. The moment the door closed, Zia started tapping.

'What was wrong with all of them?' she asked, her eyes wide. 'I've never seen Talins look like that. They all seemed so…sickly!'

'They all have advanced cases of Fading,' Palforma answered for Lasha and then turned on her with an angry rattle. 'Dear Ancestors, those poor souls. Why have you put them in such a bright room? Are you trying to torture them?'

Lasha wasn't intimidated in the least. 'I'm saving them,' she answered, her head held high. 'All of the Talins in that room got here four rotations ago. They arrived because four of the five previous patients in that room recovered and walked out on their own.'

'Recovered?' Palforma echoed. 'Were they as bad as these cases?'

'Some were worse,' Lasha told him and then bit her lip. 'One didn't make it. But I'm sure all the ones in the room now will heal. They're all showing signs of doing better already.'

'You're a doctor now?' Zia asked, looking confused.

'No,' Lasha tapped with a grin. 'I'm more like an entertainer. I sing or talk to them mostly. I hold their hands and tell them to come back. I tell them they aren't alone and we'd be sad if they died.'

Lasha watched different emotions filter across Zia's face. Puzzlement, understanding, pride, and finally concern.

'This feels dangerous,' she tapped. 'I didn't know that's what Fading did to a Talin's body, and I feel for those people. But we humans are already a bone of contention. The Reformists and the Traditionalists use us as a way to fight over policy. This could put you in their crosshairs.'

'Doing something important is worth the danger,' Lasha tapped. 'You taught me that.'

A toothy grin unfurled across Zia's face. 'Fuck you for throwing my own words back at me.'

'Fuck you for teaching me such important lessons,' Lasha shot back. Then she grabbed Zia in a hug because she knew her friend understood.

Palforma wrapped his arms around both of them and started purring.

That's when Tamerin walked in. "Unless you want me to dent the other side of your skull, you'll let go of my songbird."

Sounding a laughing rumble, Palforma let go of Lasha but swept Zia up in his arms. Lasha rushed to hug Tamerin. "I've got a lot to tell you!"

"No doubt," Tamerin answered, mirroring Palforma's movements by grabbing Lasha and cradled her against his chest. "But first I need a proper greeting."

"Of course," she agreed and tilted her head a little to make rubbing his scent gland into her hair a little easier. She breathed in the intense smell of cardamom and let out a happy sigh. Everything was going to be okay.

CHAPTER 31

Lasha didn't think she'd find more elaborate gardens than the one at the Kiferian family estate, but she'd been wrong. The monarch's estate was larger, more ornate, and lavish. There was even a lake back here. Not a pond, but a full-on lake!

Wait, was that an island?

Lasha held a hand up to shield her eyes from the sun and squinted. Yup, that looked like an island, with a little house on it. As much as she wanted to get back to the clinic and her five patients, she also really wanted to visit the island with its tiny house. It was probably bigger than she thought, but from here it looked adorable.

"The guy didn't say anything about a lake" she muttered to herself. She had definitely taken the wrong path.

The Talin who'd sent her out here had told her she'd find a small waterfall in the middle of a sand garden, not a lake. But there'd been a lot of intersections and she couldn't read the decorative signs posted everywhere.

It was probably time to retrace her steps—if she could.

"The island used to be a habitat for a human couple, but after they passed no one else wanted to live there."

The human voice startled Lasha badly enough that she gasped and spun around. Moving with no grace, she promptly tripped over her own feet. She caught a flash of a surprised face before she toppled backward into a soft flowering bush.

"Oh, crap! I'm so sorry, I didn't mean to scare you," the woman said, leaning over where Lasha had sunk into the bush with only her feet sticking out. "Are you okay? Wait, no, don't move. If you broke something you could hurt yourself worse by moving. I'll run and get help."

Lasha waved a hand outside the bush to stop the concerned stranger from leaving. "I'm fine, just embarrassed," she promised. "This plant is pretty comfy actually. I think I might take a nap here."

Giggling, the woman held out a hand. "Let me help you out. I'm Sora. I saw you staring at the island and figured you had the same question I had when I first saw it."

Lasha took Sora's hand. "I totally did. Okay, heave!"

Sora pulled Lasha out of the bush. "I give you a seven point five for the pirouette but only a two on the landing."

"But I stuck the landing," Lasha argued as she picked a leaf out of her hair. "That deserves at least a four!"

Sora glanced down at the smooshed plant. "What can I say? I'm a harsh judge and the bush might never recover."

"Fair," Lasha agreed with a laugh of her own. "Do you know where we are? I was looking for a water fountain in a sand garden, whatever that is. But I'm pretty sure I took a wrong turn three intersections ago."

Pointing down a path Lasha hadn't taken yet, Sora nodded. "We need to go this way. You're not too far off. And I promise the sand garden is more interesting than it sounds."

"Want to show me?" Lasha asked, eager to make a new friend. "I'm new to Talarian and I don't know any humans here yet. Well, except for Zia, but she and Palforma left to go back to Sorana yesterday."

"Then consider me a new friend," Sora insisted, tucking her arm in Lasha's. "Were you born among Talins or were you wild-caught?"

"That's such a weird term," Lasha muttered.

"And there's my answer," Sora said with a chuckle. "I was a slave before. Being bought by a Talin was the best thing that ever happened to me. Although it was a little rocky for a while, I have the best life now."

"I was basically a slave," Lasha admitted. "I was born free, but I signed a work contract that turned me into a slave in everything but name."

Sora's voice was sympathetic. "It's tough for us humans to find work out there."

Lasha sighed. "And what we do find often sucks. But I'm like you. I love it here!"

"I'm so glad," Sora cheered and then sobered. "Um, I'm not sure how to ask this. But, um, is your owner, um, do you two, uh…" As Sora stumbled over her words, her face got red and she stared down at the path in front of them.

Because she didn't like the term owner, Lasha almost made a face but caught herself in time. "My Talin's name is Tamerin and I love him."

Sora beamed at her. "I'm happy for both of you. I'm surprised he let you out here on your own. These Talins tend to be overprotective."

"Don't I know it," Lasha agreed. "But the person he met with didn't want me in the room. He said it wasn't healthy for humans to be involved in political discussions."

"And that sounds typical also," Sora said with a grin. "Who is Tamerin meeting with?"

"He's meeting with an aid to the monarch," Lasha explained. "We're trying to get help with our clinic, but we're getting a lot of pushback."

Sora came to an abrupt halt. "Clinic?"

Excited to share, Lasha nodded and launched into an explanation. "Yes! We help Talins who've come down with the Fading disease. We've helped four so far and we have another five showing improvement. But one group doesn't approve. Um, I think they're called Traditionalists? Anyway, they don't like the clinic, so they keep filing petitions to shut us down and have me taken away from Tamerin. Several Talins from the Committee of Pet Welfare have visited, asking me all kinds of stupid questions."

"They don't tend to be the brightest bunch," Sora agreed with distaste. "And they think we're dumb!"

"Right! When they can't see what's right in front of them," Lasha semi-shouted and then realized she was being loud and focused on staying calm. "I really want to expand the clinic, but I need more humans."

"Humans?" Sora asked.

"So I think the Fading is the Talins' version of a really deep depression," Lasha said. "They get so bad that they end up locked in their own heads. But if you interact with them, touch them, talk to them, they can be pulled out."

"That's wonderful news!" Sora agreed. "I've heard of individual humans helping their Talins who had the Fading, but I didn't think we could help multiple Talins at the same time. I mean, when they scent-bond with us it—" Sora gasped and covered her mouth with her hands. Her next words were muffled by her palms. "Shit, I'm not supposed to talk about scent-bonding with strangers!"

Lasha patted her arm. "Yeah, no, don't worry, I'm scent-bonded to my Talin, Tamerin. I get that it's a big secret, but we're good."

"Great, because I'd hate to have to kill you and bury your body in the garden." Sora said it with such a straight face that for a second Lasha thought she was serious, but then Sora burst out laughing.

"You got me," Lasha conceded. "Good one."

"Tell me more about this clinic," Sora urged. "Do you think I could come help? I can't sing, though."

Excited to have potentially enlisted help, Lasha was quick to answer. "You don't need to sing. You can tell them stories or just hold a hand and talk to them."

"And that works?" Sora asked.

"It has so far," Lasha assured her. "And Healer Verinan has noticed that it helps to give them a drug. I can't remember the name of it, but I think it's a type of stimulant. She's been working hard to find ways to help for her entire career and now we're working together."

"I've been among the Talins for years, and this is the first time I've ever heard of anyone trying to treat Fading," Sora commented. "No one even likes to talk about it."

"We want to change that," Lasha said with determination.

"And I'm going to help!" Sora declared. "But would you sing for me while we walk? It's been ages since I've heard a human song."

"All the stuff I know is from India on Old Earth," Lasha warned her. "I never translated them to Universal."

"Doesn't matter. You can always tell me what the lyrics mean," Sora assured her.

"Love story, lullaby, or epic?" Lasha asked.

"Love story," Sora demanded.

As they walked arm in arm through the ostentatious garden, the smell of blossoming flowers in their nose, Lasha sang about two people falling in love.

What a perfect day it had turned out to be. She'd made a friend and found an ally. They might only be humans, but now there were two of them, and maybe even more in the future.

Tamerin left the meeting with the monarch's aid disheartened. The aid had made it clear that while the monarch wanted to help, she couldn't risk the political backlash at the moment. Tensions between the Reformists and Traditionalists were at an all-time high, forcing the monarch to tread carefully or risk alienating half the Apogee Assembly.

Frustrated and discouraged, Tamerin searched for Lasha. He was desperate for the comfort of his little songbird. She'd make him feel better. Maybe he'd ask her to stay when he contacted Holian to explain that their petition to the monarch had failed.

When he spotted the servant he'd left her standing with alone at a door display, he let out a low buzzing rattle of annoyance. "Where is Lasha?"

"Your human with the short mane?" the male asked. "I left her in the garden. She—"

"Sora?" a yell to Tamerin's right made both him and the servant swing around in surprise to see the familiar visage of Prime Son Searin striding toward them. When he reached them he didn't lower his booming voice. "My human isn't where I left her! Where is my Sora!"

To punctuate his words, Searin let loose with a war rattle that shook the potted plants nearby. It was loud enough to make both Tamerin and the servant take involuntary steps back. He'd heard about the famous war rattle of the Prime Family but had never experienced it firsthand.

It wasn't pleasant!

"Y-y-your human?" the servant asked, cowering back.

"Yes! Mine!" Searin roared.

Ducking away the servant pointed to the garden with a shaking hand. "I heard human voices talking about the Sand Garden."

The answer didn't placate Searin at all. "The Sand Garden? You fool! Tano bushes surround the Sand Garden. Sora might not remember they're toxic to humans and touch one of them."

Searin's words made Tamerin rattle with anger. If the other human this male heard was his Lasha, she was in similar danger.

When the Prime Son charged out the door, Tamerin was right on his heels. Instead of taking the well-maintained but circuitous path, Searin charged through ornate bushes, over tall pots full of flowering plants, and treaded over delicate ground cover. Tamerin followed the Prime Son, trusting he'd know the layout of the massive garden.

The sound of humans singing registered in Tamerin's ear holes just as he burst into the Sand Garden behind Searin. Lasha and another human he'd never seen before were sitting on a boulder next to the waterfall at the center of the Sand Garden.

The women had been singing but stopped abruptly and turned to look at them as they'd crashed through a last section of bushes.

"Sora!" Searin cried out as he kept up his momentum and swept her up in his arms.

"Searin? What's wrong? Are we under attack?" Sora asked, clutching her arms around the Prime Son's neck. "We need to get back to the children!"

"No attack," Searin answered, his voice muffled by her hair. "I couldn't find you."

Sora let out a relieved chuckle as Tamerin picked Lasha up and cradled her against his chest. The moment he held her, all his anxiety and frustration vanished, replaced with calm serenity.

"You didn't touch any of those bushes with the yellow flowers. Did you?" he asked as he emptied his scent glands into her hair.

"What? No! Those things are dangerous!" Lasha explained. "They're pretty but the sap will seep in through your skin and make your lungs stop working."

She had known. His wonderful, clever Lasha had already known.

"I didn't get my new friend in trouble. Did I?" Lasha asked. "I thought we were allowed to be in the garden."

Tamerin turned to face Searin. The large male had just finished rubbing his scent glands into Sora's hair and was purring loudly. Sora turned her head and grinned at them.

"Lasha, this is my Talin, Searin," Sora said with a cheeky grin.

"Hiya, Searin," Lasha said without a morsel of the respect due the monarch's son. "This is my Talin, Tamerin. Tamerin, this is Sora and Searin. I was teaching Sora one of my songs when you guys, um, showed up."

Fearful of reprisal, Tamerin was quick to speak, "Prime Son Searin, I'd like to introduce you to my human pet, Lasha. She's wild-caught and new to our ways. Please don't take offense at her familiar address."

"I'm not upset at my Sora or your Lasha," Searin assured him. "I might have overreacted to finding she'd left the manor without an escort."

"I don't need an escort here," Sora protested.

"Right now you need an escort everywhere you go when I'm not with you," Searin argued. "You know how dangerous it is. The Traditionalist extremists would like nothing more than to steal you away from me."

Sora sighed but didn't argue further. This was obviously not the first time these two had had this discussion.

Keeping his stance stiff and his tone formal, Tamerin interjected into Searin and Sora's conversation. "Thank you for your understanding, Prime Son. I've concluded my business so Lasha and I will be leaving now."

"Can you stay for dinner?" Sora asked. "Searin, please ask them to stay. I want to talk to Lasha more."

"Indeed," Searin said looking at Tamerin. "You and your human are invited to stay. The evening meal will begin in only ten submarks. It will be easy to add extra portions to accommodate the two of you."

Lasha's expression was delighted as she looked up at Tamerin. "Can we stay? We can go straight back to the clinic after dinner."

"Clinic?" Searin asked. "Are you sick, Lasha? I have access to the best healers. Do you need me to contact one of them?"

Sora answered Searin, "No, Lasha's not sick. She and Tamerin work at a clinic helping Talins who have the Fading. Isn't that great?"

"Fading?" Searin repeated, his gaze jumping between Sora and Lasha. "What do you mean she works there?"

"Lasha, tell him," Sora encouraged.

"Walk with us," Searin instructed. "And tell me about this clinic."

And just like that, Tamerin found himself carrying Lasha as she discussed their work with the Prime Son of the Talin Empire.

Between Lasha and Sora, Searin didn't have a chance. By the time the meal was over, Searin had agreed to visit the clinic and even give his endorsement.

Tamerin felt obligated to explain the monarch had refused to support the clinic, but Searin had waved off his concern.

"My mother has to be neutral, but my sister and I are allowed to pick sides. Until one of us is formally chosen to be the next monarch, we have a great deal of political freedom. I'll have to talk to Commandant Holian first, but this might work well with the schemes he's been putting in place for the last solar."

Well aware of Commandant Holian's advocacy for both humans and the Reformist cause, Tamerin didn't need to ask what machinations the male was plotting. All he needed to know was that it might allow Searin to openly favor the clinic.

Having the support of the Prime Son would help draw positive attention and more support from other Reformist families and clans.

"I've been thinking," Lasha commented from his lap. Searin had led them into a private area where they'd been served an elaborate meal. Neither male had let their humans sit anywhere but their laps the entire time.

"Yes?" Searin inquired. He'd been nothing but patient and kind to Lasha, despite the way she'd spoken to him when they'd first met. The Prime Son was truly humble and kind.

"I know Fading is this big shameful, taboo thing, but what if we were to come at it sideways?" Lasha asked.

Sora gave Lasha a confused look and asked the question Tamerin was thinking. "What do you mean sideways?"

"Instead of trying to convince people that it's a disease that needs to be treated like any other disease, we talk about how it might have an environmental or epigenetic cause," Lasha offered.

"How would that make a difference?" Tamerin asked.

"Well, if it can be triggered, it's exploitable. Right?" When no one responded to Lasha right away, she continued, "If we don't figure out what causes it, or at least how to treat it, some enemy could figure it out and use it against the Talin empire. You know, like a biological weapon or something."

Tamerin sat in stunned silence for several submarks as he absorbed Lasha's suggestion. He was still thinking when Searin spoke.

"That's brilliant," he praised. "It's an argument even the Traditionalists can't go against because then they'd be advocating for a vulnerable military. You're a very smart human, Lasha."

The compliment made Lasha blush a little as she smiled broadly. "Thanks. You can take credit for it. I know if anyone finds out a human thought it up, they'd dismiss it no matter what."

Searin met Tamerin's gaze. "Put together a research proposal using Lasha's idea. Submit it to me for budget consideration so I can present it to the Apogee Assembly. I'll make sure it gets approved and then I'll put the word out that the clinic needs human pets willing to volunteer there. You'll have plenty of support then."

Lasha was quick to intervene. "I don't want anyone forced to come."

"I'm sure you and Tamerin can come up with a vetting process," Searin pointed out, "including a closed interview where you talk to the other human alone. We can also make sure that if the human doesn't want to be at the clinic we find a reason to reject the owner, not the human."

"That's good," Lasha said with a sigh of relief. "I don't want to cause any backlash."

"There'll be plenty of backlash," Searin warned. "But not for that. The Traditionalists are going to hate this. But even better, they're going to loathe the fact they can't do anything about it."

"And that delights you," Sora commented with a chuckle.

Searin sounded a rumble of amusement. "Absolutely."

CHAPTER 32

Standing up, Lasha stretched her arms up over her head and yawned.

"Are you fatigued?" a breathy voice asked to her right. "You can lie with me and nap. You've created a nice nest, but it's wasted on an old warrior like me."

Lasha smiled fondly at the scarred and recovering Talin. Koraneum wasn't old, but he had been badly hurt when his ship had been ambushed. He'd survived all that only to find out his sister, on a support ship at the rear of the fleet, had perished along with many of his good friends.

Koraneum started Fading soon after. Now he was well on the road to recovery and even teased Lasha that he planned to bottle her songs and sell them. He bragged about making his fortune and buying her a planet. He was surprisingly fanciful and Lasha thought he might have some fun making up stories for her. She should encourage him to write them down. Talins didn't appreciate fiction, but maybe she could change that one Talin at a time.

"I'm not tired," she assured him. "Stretching always makes me yawn."

"Even if she wanted to rest, Lasha wouldn't want to be with you," Junian in the next bed protested as she sounded a weak purr. "She's much too sophisticated. She'd rather relax on my bed so I can explain all the different kinds of singularities to her."

"You mean you can help her fall asleep with your explanations," Koraneum volleyed back, making Junian sound a rumble of amusement.

Lasha loved the relationship these two had developed. She had a strong suspicion they might even enter into a marriage contract together. She'd caught them talking about property and mutually beneficial arrangements yesterday. It had taken some time, but she'd come to realize that was the Talin version of flirting.

Ah, to be in love and whispering sweet words of investments!

Stifling a laugh at that thought, Lasha popped her hands on her hips. "I'm not getting into anyone's bed. Like I said, I'm not sleepy. I've been sitting too long so I need to walk around a little. Anyone want to join me in the garden?"

Within ten days of their talk with Searin and Sora, the Prime Son presented the clinic's proposal to the Apogee Assembly and got approval to donate government-held resources and wealth to the project.

Their small, humble clinic was a thing of the past.

Not only were they in a much bigger building now with a garden and a dedicated medical staff, but hundreds of Talins had shown up with their humans to volunteer. Most Talins were doing it to be fashionable or show their support for the Prime Son. Some truly believed in the cause, and their humans genuinely wanted to help. The clinic had twenty humans who rotated in as often as they felt comfortable or their owners would allow.

Lasha had made some good friends, but more importantly, they'd expanded how many patients they could accept. They could comfortably accommodate fifty Talins coming from all areas of the Empire and all walks of life. They stuck to the five patients per room model and made sure someone was always in the room day or night talking, reading, or if the volunteer was human and willing, singing.

The best part was that it was working. All of them were getting better, some more slowly than others but still with measurable progress.

Keno popped his head in the open door of the room. "Did I hear walkies?" he asked with his ever-cheerful smile, his long light brown hair curling around his shoulders. "Two of mine are almost out the door. Wanna come?"

"Keno!" Helorium called from his bed. "I'll escort you out. Would you like to sit on my lap in the garden? You can cling to me as hard as you like. You won't hurt me."

"Better get a move on then," Keno called out to Helorium. "Or I'll sit in Mansorium's lap."

"Mansorium!" Helorium protested, swinging his legs off the bed. He was unsteady when he stood, and Lasha was about to rush to his side to help. Before she could, one of the Talin medical aids got there first. With the added resources, they had a one-to-one patient-to-aid ratio, and Tamerin assured her they'd be adding more healers to the roster soon.

"No more helping like that, Lasha," Bulorium, the aid, admonished her gently. "We can't risk you getting hurt again."

"It was one bruise," she muttered. A few days ago she'd tried to steady one of the patients, and both of them had ended up on the floor with Lasha at the bottom of their two person pile. After that Tamerin had decreed the humans weren't to touch the patients when they were standing, only sitting or lying down.

Lasha thought it was extreme but probably not an entirely bad idea.

"What bruise?" Tamerin asked as he rushed into the room. "Did you get hurt again? I leave for ten submarks and you get injured?"

Before she could even get a word out, Tamerin dropped to his knees next to her and started running his fingers gently over her body. "Where does it hurt? Healer Verinan is still here. Would it hurt to carry you, or should I bring her here?"

Still standing at the door, Keno burst out laughing, and several patients sitting up on their beds rumbled out sounds of amusement. Tamerin was so focused on her that he didn't even notice.

Getting both his hands in hers, she quieted Tamerin's frantic movements.

"Nothing happened," she assured him. She nodded at Bulorium standing next to a wobbly Helorium. "They were just making sure I didn't get any new bruises. That's all."

Tamerin shifted his gaze to Bulorium. "Well done. She doesn't worry enough about her own safety."

Lasha rolled her eyes. "I'm not out in space going into battle or exploring planets."

"Perhaps not, but your work is just as important," Tamerin responded as he gathered her into his arms and stood up with a purr. "And it's time for your break."

"Can we take our break in the garden?" she asked, knowing better than to demand Tamerin set her down. Holding her was about his comfort, not hers.

"Of course," Tamerin agreed. "But no singing. Let Keno entertain everyone with his antics."

"Hey, I heard that!" Keno sang out and then turned and skipped down the hall. "Last one to the garden has to clean the bird poop off the benches!"

"We have bots for that," Helorium muttered as Bulorium walked with him out the door. "Why would we do it ourselves? Does Keno not understand how bots work? I'll have to explain it."

Lasha held back a snicker at Helorium's remark. Although she knew Keno was joking about cleaning off benches, no one else had realized that he liked to play dumb so the recovering Talins could "explain" things to him. He'd told Lasha that nothing energized a Talin like having an audience willing to listen to a lecture.

"Lasha, Tamerin?"

Tamerin turned so they could see Healer Verinan striding toward them. She was sounding a loud anxiously buzzing rattle. "Commandant Holian is here!"

Tamerin sounded a loud rattle of surprise. "Here? But why?"

"He didn't say," Verinan said and then pointed. "Hurry! He's a well-respected advisor to the Prime Son. We can't afford to upset him in any way."

With that she turned and led them down to one of the rooms set aside for staff meetings.

"Should we be worried?" Lasha whispered to Tamerin.

"I don't think so," Tamerin answered, but she could hear his uncertainty. They didn't get a chance to say anymore before they stepped into a room where Holian and a human woman were waiting for them.

Lasha relaxed the moment she saw the human. No way was Holian was here with bad news if he'd brought a human companion along. Maybe she wanted to volunteer.

Without her needing to say anything, Tamerin set her down then slapped his fist hard against the keratin armor of his chest. "It's an honor, Commandant Holian."

"Um, yeah, super honored," Lasha agreed but didn't slap her hand to her chest. That looked like it would hurt!

The woman with Holian chuckled. "Don't worry about the slapping," the woman said to Lasha. "Most Talins who were in the military do that when he shows up. It's a knee-jerk reaction thing to authority figures."

Lasha took a step forward, liking this human and her lack of decorum. "Doesn't it hurt?"

"I don't think so," the woman responded. "But I'm not a Talin, so who knows? My name's Jinna."

Lasha placed a hand on her chest. "Lasha."

"I heard singing when I first got here. Was that you?" Jinna asked.

"Probably," Lasha admitted. "But I think Marl is here, and she likes to sing too."

"I wish I could sing," Jinna murmured.

"I'm sure you're better than you think," Lasha assured her.

"I sound like a dying inko bird," Jinna stated dryly, making Lasha laugh.

"Would you or your human like some refreshments, Commandant Holian?" Tamerin asked.

Holian eyed Jinna and Lasha. "That would probably be for the best. I thought this would be a quick visit, but I can see that won't be the case."

Tamerin was quick to tap on his Ident, probably sending a request for beverages to the kitchen. Then he looked up and indicated the backless chairs in the room. "Shall we sit?"

Grabbing his hand, Lasha laughingly led Tamerin to a chair. "We shall sit!"

Jinna did the same with Holian, and it was no surprise to anyone when the women ended up sitting on the laps of their Talins instead of on chairs of their own.

They chatted until the drinks arrived, and then once the aide left, Holian spoke. "I'm here for two reasons. One is to relay the information Lasha asked for and the other is to request a favor."

Tamerin startled at Holian's words. "Lasha asked you for a favor?" he murmured and then looked down at his little human. "How do you know Commandant Holian?"

"I don't," Lasha answered, looking confused.

"Let me explain," Holian said. "Lasha asked Zia for help. Zia asked Palforma and Palforma came to me."

"Oh!" Lasha exclaimed. "I'm sorry. I didn't know that would happen. I told Zia not to make a fuss about it!"

Tamerin felt alarmed. "What did you ask Zia to do?"

Lasha looked a little embarrassed. "I wanted to get you a gift, but it's not like I can buy you anything. So I thought I'd get some information for you instead. But I told Zia not to worry about it if she couldn't find anything out."

Her little speech didn't help settle his unease. "What did you ask?" he repeated.

"She inquired about a Braxin named Nelk," Holian told him before Lasha could speak. "It took a lot of looking because she couldn't give us much information, but Lakin managed to find him. That female has so many contacts with various species I'm almost jealous."

"Who's Lakin?" Lasha asked.

"Oh, you've got to meet her," Jinna said. "She's great. Probably one of the most cunning people I've ever met. Almost as good as my Holian."

"Thank you," Holian responded and Tamerin could hear the amusement in his voice. "It's nice to know I'm smarter than a human."

"I didn't say smarter. I said you're more clever," Jinna countered with a teasing smile. "I'm not sure you're smarter, though."

"I hardly see a difference between clever and smart," Holian shot back.

"My point exactly," Jinna retorted, running her fingers over his scent glands. "But it's okay. I'm here to help you."

Tamerin interrupted their banter, desperate to know what had happened to the Braxin who'd saved him. "Is Nelk alive?"

"His full name is Nelk of Gorl and he's alive and well. He lives with his mates and offspring on a colony in the Sapor sector. From all accounts the colony is thriving and will soon be independent from Talin control according to the new treaty he helped negotiate with us."

Relief made Tamerin slouch for a moment. Lasha was quick to put her lips to his earhole. "I'm sorry. I should have told you I asked, but I didn't think Zia would find anything. I didn't want to get your hopes up. I didn't know she was going to send it up the chain for someone else to look into. Please don't be upset."

"No, this is good," Tamerin assured her. "I always wanted to know but was too afraid to look into it. This was an excellent gift."

Holian's Ident pinged, turning everyone's attention to the Commandant. Unclipping it from his belt, he read the message and then sounded a brief buzzing rattle of annoyance. "I'm being summoned by the monarch. I'd hoped to keep my presence on Talarian quiet, but apparently I failed."

"You said you needed to ask for a favor," Tamerin reminded him as they all stood up. Neither he nor Holian set their humans down. Why let the humans stand when they could cuddle them?

"Both Kalor and Sorana colonies are being inspected. I need to shuffle humans around to keep their numbers hidden," Holian explained. "Originally I was going to send everyone to the Barvarian Colony, but they've been attacked a few times, and they're evacuating all the humans."

"Attacked?" Tamerin questioned. "I haven't heard of any attacks to the colony."

"We're keeping it quiet until we get the humans relocated," Holian said. "But between the attacks and the inspections, we're limited to where we can send humans to hide them. I'm hoping to send our officially registered humans here to Talarian until the inspections are over, and this clinic is the perfect cover for it. Because you have the Prime Son's support, no one will be suspicious if I move humans here."

"But they'll still volunteer while they're here," Jinna was quick to say. "Everyone knows they need to help."

"No human needs to come to the clinic," Tamerin assured them. "My family estate is large enough to accommodate hundreds of humans if you need. We don't mind taking on additional staff and guards."

"Hundreds? That's better than I hoped for," Holian said. "Between your family's estate and mine, that will take care of all the humans I need to move until the inspections are over."

"And maybe some of them will stay afterward," Lasha pushed.

"If they want to," Holian agreed.

"I've got you," Jinna assured her. "I'll make sure everyone knows they're welcome to remain on Talarian if they like it here. I know a couple of humans on Kalor who would really like to have a meaningful job. I think they'd fit right in."

Lasha beamed at Jinna. "That would be wonderful. Thank you!"

Holian sounded a rumble of amusement. "Thank you for sorting that out, little humans."

"No problem, big Talin," Jinna responded with a laugh.

Turning to Tamerin, Holian spoke. "Don't worry about security. The humans will have a dedicated Talin escort."

Knowing Holian, Tamerin was sure the escort would be mostly made up of retired soldiers who'd served directly under Holian. He couldn't ask for a more competent or dedicated group to help him safeguard a bunch of vulnerable humans. Even though Talin law required only one Talin escort per human, Holian always doubled that number when they left the safety of the colony. They'd dealt with Talins trying to steal humans several times, and Holian wasn't one to take risks with those under his care.

"Thank you, Commandant. I look forward to finalizing these plans," Tamerin responded.

After hasty goodbyes, Tamerin found himself standing at the entryway of the clinic, stunned at how much had happened in a short time.

"Hundreds!" Lasha crowed happily. "He said hundreds! If even a quarter of them volunteer, we'll have double the humans helping out here. This is great! And I can give them all the stuff I've been sent. That might make them want to stay longer."

"If anyone can convince them to stay, it's you," Tamerin murmured, leaning his head down to rub a scent gland into her hair.

Twisting in his hold, she wrapped her arms around his neck and hugged him tightly. "I have the most amazing life, and it's all because of you! I was dying, and not only did you save me, but you've given me a purpose. A mission! You've made me more than I was, and it feels incredible!"

Tamerin took a deep breath, his purring echoing in the hall around them. "The same thing is true of you, my sweet Songbird. You've given my life purpose and love."

"I guess we both got lucky," she whispered, nuzzling her face against his throat.

"Lucky or blessed by the Ancestors," Tamerin answered. "I don't care which one as long as we have each other."

"Let's say all of the above, yeah?"

"Or I could say I love you," Tamerin said.

Her arms around him tightened. "I love you too."

Scent-bonded and in love with a human—Tamerin mourned for all the Talins who would never know this joy.

"We should get back," Lasha murmured.

"In a moment," Tamerin answered. "I need to hold you for a while first."

"Good plan," she agreed.

"I'm full of good plans and ideas," Tamerin told her even as he schemed how he would sneak her away. There was a perfect secluded spot on his parents' estate with blankets and pillows already waiting. They could make love to her under the stars. "And you're the reason for all of them."

Dear Readers,

Thank you for reading *Craving Captivity*. I hope you enjoyed it enough to leave a review! As an indie writer without the support of a publishing company, I need all the help I can get. Your good reviews keep me writing.

Need more Talins? Great! I've got good news for you. ***Stealing Captivity*** (Human Pets of Talin #6) is available! *Meet retired Admiral Ignatias who agrees to act as an inspector for the Committee for Pet Welfare. But when he shows up on Sorana early, he finds a bunch of humans running around without proper guidance or even collars! Worse yet, he discovers one tiny female performing hard labor. Determined to get back to Talarian and report when he's seen, he grabs the tiny, helpless human female to keep her safe and runs for the port only to find his presence has been discovered and he is being hunted.* I think we all know where this is going!

And because the stories in my head just won't stop, keep an eye out for ***Redeeming Captivity*** (Human Pets of Talin #7). *Sent to a remote Talin outpost under the pretext of an emergency readiness inspection, Tarquin finds the only human there in poor condition. Unlike the images of Lena given to him before setting off, the woman he encounters is unkempt and volatile. Getting her away from an abusive owner turns out to be the easy part. Teaching her to trust him will be the true challenge.* This book will come out in March of 2025.

Have you gotten *Tender Captivity* for free yet? If not, go grab it! (*Tender Captivity* takes place after *Fighting Captivity*, the fourth book in the series. However, you can read any of the Human Pets of Talin books out of order. They are all written to be read as standalone.)

All links for free books, social media accounts, and other fun stuff is on my website

www.rk-munin.com

Have a fruitful rotation,
-Rye
author@rk-munin.com || www.rk-munin.com

Other books by RK Munin

-Science Fiction-

Hissa Warrior Series
Rescuing Halin (Mian and Halin)
Buying Tiran (Mara and Tiran)
Tempting Selon (Lara and Selon)
Defying Kilan (Deena and Kilan)
Healing Mavito (Raleen and Mavito)
Claiming Yopin (Mouse and Yopin)
Teasing Woken (Safena and Woken)
Defending Revin (Kamaril and Revin) – Coming soon

Human Pets of Talin Series
Loving Captivity (Sora and Searin)
Escaping Captivity (Lakin and Dalt)
Negotiating Captivity (Nalia and Derani)
Fighting Captivity (Zia and Palforma)
Tender Captivity (Jinna and Holian - This is a novella you can
get for free by signing up for my newsletter)
Craving Captivity (Lasha and Tamerin)
Stealing Captivity – Coming soon

Origins (A Human Pets of Talin Series)
Creating Captivity (Ari and Bazium)
Gossamer Chains – Coming soon

-Paranormal /Urban Fantasy-

Ours Evermore Series
Two Wolves for Soren (Soren, Kalli, and Quinn)
A Hacker, Vampire, and Chimera Walk into a Bar….(Tobias,
Briar, and Memphis)
When Darkness Meets Dawn (Imani, Lex, and Mac) – Coming
soon

Alpha Series
Alpha Mage (Emma and Kade)

His Alpha Mage (Avery and Jason – Novella)
Alpha King (Cathleen and Lazlo)

New Clan Series
Stray Wolf (Steph and Eli)
Lost Lion (Maeve and Cyrus)
Reluctant Cervid (Tavi and Donovan)
Broken Thorn (Sabina and Theodosius)

-Contemporary Romance – Her Fighting Chance